Don Taylor was educated at grammar school and naval college. He has worked at a wide variety of jobs: ships Officer, postman, sales manager, the wool trade, water bailiff, gardener, taxi driver, art gallery owner, barman, charity worker, social worker. He currently lives and works on the banks of a river in Co. Durham. He is a naturalist, fisherman and painter.

DIRTY LAUNDRY

Don Taylor

Library of Congress Catalog Card Number: 97–81171

A catalogue record for this book is available from the
British Library on request

The right of Don Taylor to be identified as the author of
this work has been asserted by him in accordance with the
Copyright, Designs and Patents Act 1988

First published in 1998 by Serpent's Tail,
4 Blackstock Mews, London N4
Website: www.serpentstail.com

Set in 10pt ITC Century by
Intype London Ltd

Printed in Great Britain by
Mackays of Chatham plc, Chatham, Kent

For nobody

"The world advances, how it strides! ... But the one mystery we shall never solve is the mystery of human identity. What am I? What are you? ... What of the spells that are woven after birth, the subtle processes working from day to day in the darkness of a young head, as it grows from childhood to adolescence and so reaches maturity?"

From BEYOND BELIEF: A Chronicle of Murder and its Detection by Emlyn Williams (Hamish Hamilton, 1967) copyright © 1967 by Emlyn Williams. Reproduced by permission of Penguin Books Limited.

CHAPTER 1

Maxine is back on the pill, a device solely aimed in her case, she insists, to quell period pains.

Well undoubtedly so.

Sunday morning. Thank God I don't work weekends. Lying in limbo before the day sweeps in to claim me . . . seedling thoughts cruise without roots, a pale wintry sunshine lightens the curtains' colours and every so often I nudge Bernard to change his phlegmy rattle but with his built-in obstinacy he keeps rolling back to snore on, a sound like no other, the snore of the great white stranded whale, just one more irritant to add to a list that includes his bigoted mind, his sanctimonious prattle, his cleverer-than-thou attitudes, and so on and so forth. Distaste for the man impoverishes my composure, my mind fluttering within its shell, my eyes following a crack that starts as a hair-line above the door before meandering to skirt the overlooked husk of a last year's spider.

Bernard is so *scared* of spiders. In every room an empty jam jar stands ready for their capture, at which he either rushes for boiling water or hair-sprays the poor creatures to a permanent standstill.

No matter. What's one spider less?

I have had a bad night. Hot sweats and belly pains. There was a time when I could digest anything. Now with my fingers I can identify the upper bowel and move what I guess must be bubbles of gas. Check it out, this hard lump. What odds, too, death by poison?

I've a hell of a hard on.

"Hello-hello, ground control, this is 14a Welbeck Parade, Lambton Spa!"

My mind sings that out because living here I feel marooned like him sometimes. Major Tom, that is, not David Bowie.

Lambton Spa is the name of this village – Lambton Spa, smack-bang in the middle of fuck-the-fox country (the local hunt is well known); say two thousand souls, a sprawling hotchpotch of mainly Georgian and pre-Georgian properties attached to the edge of town by a five-mile belt of green. Lady Muck survives up the road. The Duke of Somebody once gathered his ten thousand men hereabouts before marching north to beat holy shit from the marauding Scottish hordes. Our church is picturesque Norman. Our river scurries seawards over rock, gravel and through idyllic surroundings of woods and fields. Migratory fish run its length in such numbers that people pay large sums to fish the crack beats. Of the spa itself there is no sign beyond a deep pond of clear bluish water that is known as Hell's Kettle.

The familiarity of these surroundings brings . . .? Well, the best I can hope for is a certain sense of *belonging*, I suppose, and I make that claim because apart from my treatment in hospital and the occasions of being on the road, sleeping rough and all that (so fucking romantic it sounds), the village has been my home for the past fourteen years, the first seven with wife-Linda and stepdaughter-Daisy, the last five with Bernard, whom I persuaded to buy the ground floor of this largish property which is split to *up* and *down*. A village of happier days. At least I have recollections of such times till Linda sold up and departed south along the motorway. She took Daisy with her, last seen in Lincoln, I heard. Not that they'd want to know. Not that I could ever approach with a rueful smile and say, "Hello, remember me, do you?"

Ah, such self-indulgence in self-pity! Death where is thy sting, as-it-were? I lie hands folded effigy-like on chest, eyes closed – a couple of pennies to blank off my eyelids would ready me nicely for the long wooden box with the lacquered brass handles.

Thoughts spring unchecked from amnesia-proof brain-mud: a constant bombardment.

I remember . . . once as a sailor: Jamaica, strange and exotic, after midnight, the road dark, with raised wooden sidewalks and shacks either side, the air infused with the smell of diluted dung, and crickets were whistling, and women on the porches in cheap print dresses saying, "Come on in, Johnny, I've something to show you." The floor was mud, there was dancing, women and kids and grandmothers, calypsos on a wind-up gramophone . . . and in a cubicle, on an old army blanket thrown on the bedsprings, she was teenage, giggling with big square white teeth, her dress pulled high up, a rag in her hand to wipe herself off.

(And here perhaps I should mention I possess an established aversion to dark-haired women, which as far as I can tell is a hang-up connected with an image I carry of black pubic hair and knickers left lying around soiled with menstrual blood. But whose blood, hair and knickers, I haven't an inkling.)

Splat! A cockroach fell off the roof. She slapped it flat on her leg. Yuk, distasteful. But I was younger then. Now I am older – old enough to be affected by such off-putting moments – old enough, also, to recognize that to analyse relationships is a big waste of time and that I should know better. HAPPY BIRTHDAY, WALRUS! and carefully lettered inside, *May all your dreams come true, love Maxine, xxxx*. At work on Friday she gave me a card; not posted but handed to me along with the laughter for which she is famous, it stops restaurants dead, so infectious, so bubbling, her smile so contagious, her eyes flash and sparkle, behind them the taunting enigma that fuels this incessant itch.

The woman is driving me crazy. I know she is. Or at least her disinclination towards anything physical between us is becoming ridiculous. Although, of course, to her face I cling to pretence and tell her, "Maxine, sex isn't an issue between us, believe me" – and this perhaps she sees as the stupidity of the extent of my ambition, that I should be continually shooting myself in the foot, except to be fair on myself I'm not exactly sure what my ambitions are. Moreover, I don't like to speculate too long on a subject that throws up such pictures; namely the possibility of her spread out and grunting at each inward thrust . . . *from somebody else.*

Strange: I wake thinking of Maxine, yet in dreams I dream Linda and Daisy. They stay young in my mind; they will never grow old.

The immediate task now I'm up is to Germolene the cat.

Jesus, I tell you I love this cat: found him, in fact, or he came upon me, as a stray on the river: a smart little bastard who by name is called Zero. He rules the large garden, which is strictly our province, high-walled, the brickwork laced back and forth by established wisteria. Upstairs lives Trevor with his very own entrance via fire-escape stairs but our paths rarely cross.

Forget Trevor.

I make tea. "Maidens' water", Bernard says of my brew. He arrives in the kitchen: baggy jockeys, string-vest, a bald head for Sundays, Zero rubbing his ankles. As he strokes him, he says, "What an excellent cat, what a beautiful cat, who's my best and most favourite boy?"

I can feel my back arching. "Jesus Christ, Bernard," I reply, "he's been fighting, he almost needs stitches!"

He curls a contemptuous eye. "All toms fight. Fighting's part of their nature and any fool knows it."

I am seriously irked. Bernard, where my worth is concerned, dismisses all possibility of equality and always talks down to me – which is one of his ways of making sure I realize there is no misunderstanding. In fact "A miscreant immature slob" is a more direct description he likes to lay on me. However, people in glasshouses, I reckon, shouldn't throw stones, and his vanity, to my way of thinking, is surely as big a failing as any I have. Because here is a man who is known to indulge in shaving his armpits; plus he has a big thing about plucking his eyebrows.

To separate us further, encompassing the gulf that divides us, he is older. We are not the same star sign. He earns far more than me.

Today is my birthday. I expect "happy returns" but know I could wait forever. So I don't hang about but go down to the basement.

I'm security conscious, to keep Bernard out. The key I wear on a string round my neck unlocks its padlocked door. Ten by ten, cramped, an old coal-hole really, its contents all in apparent disarray, but my private sanctuary nonetheless.

Here live roaches, silverfish after dark . . . *and a great place for spiders*. Porky Pig is here, too. Porky is the big outline poster I got free from the market, all the butchery joints clearly marked, its rectangle sellotaped above my desk, while pinned up beside it, though he'd never recognize it as himself, is a large silhouette drawing of Bernard *unclothed* that I've done, size 42 waist, a big joint of meat, the dotted lines for the cuts still in pencil and needing more thought before inking in.

"You there, are you?" comes his voice.

These intercoms, items that fell off a shelf where I work, are wired one to a room through the flat. The electronics is only a hobby, of course – a circuit-diagram to me is like a good read – but once in a while I get recommended. The colour TV and VCR I have fitted up down here are junked ones I fixed for my own private use; nothing flash but they work.

"Yes, what is it?" I ask.

"We'll be eating at one. Don't forget that I'm going to Robert and Tina's."

"Ten-four," I reply, "over-and-out."

Robert and Tina, I guess, are the only people we have in common these days, although frankly poor Tina in her confined circumstances hasn't much choice about who befriends her. It just rubs me sore they were *my* friends to start with until he took them over.

It's only five minutes later. "You still there, are you?"

"Yes, still here," I drawl.

"I see you've done it again. You've used the last of the toilet-roll and forgotten to replace it."

"Did I do that?"

"Would I complain if you hadn't? *Would I*?" He sighs emphatically before clicking off – like he's fit to die, like it's the end of the world.

Never mind. There's things of more interest to keep me occupied. For instance, always close to hand is my miniature seashell which, if put to my ear still sounds of the sea off Vancouver – it's for luck.

Cop the rest. Like here, my well-thumbed *World's Famous Paintings* that offers such deep emotions expressed in full-colour; and here, a very fine magnifying-glass with stainless-steel guard and ebony handle which suede buffs up nicely; and here, my Walkman, my rods and nets, a jar of cheap hand-cream, my camera, old biros, some sticky-ended from stirring my coffee, my video tapes, my mother's pearl-handled tweezers, my tall mirror so I can see myself either standing, sitting, posing or whatever, and here a few packets of fish-hooks, notes and poems jotted over the years that would make me cry if I read them, and here, and a joy to handle, though a fear of it deepens my breathing, my .38 Smith & Wesson, World-War-Two, millions made. I own two shiny bullets. *If it comes to the crunch, no one's taking me anywhere.*

A saved magazine cutting makes me smile:

ATTRACTIVE widow 42, with daughter 19, seeks executive gent for drinks/friendship/relationship at their secluded dales farmhouse. Wonderful scenery. Must have good sense of humour and enjoy music. Genuine replies only. Photograph if possible. Absolute discretion guaranteed. All letters answered. No fees, just good fun. Reply Box No. 2654.

Aladdin's cave! The point is I like having around me my bits and pieces: the touching, the reminiscing, the thought *they're all mine*. All is safe within these four walls; though perhaps if Bernard were less arachnophobic nothing would be.

Open Sesame! Behold, my little freezer-bags, each carefully sealed, each containing its own perfumed hanky: Eternity, Obsession, Chanel Number 5, L'Air Du Temps, Fendi, Samsara, Giorgio, Femme... I know them all.

In my mind the rascals wear them. Thin girls, fat girls, blonde, brunette, shaved and hairy. When magnified through the glass, the printed dots separate and spoil the effect. There, back a page, look at her doing that, and she's not very old. A one-time ambitious runaway. Such as her fall prey to pimps who lurk at main line London stations. *Dear Mum, I am managing quite nicely and have a job in a laundry...*

A point, too, to notice, they all have nice teeth. Models do. Maxine does.

I'll go further. In the enlarged snapshot above my desk Maxine is posed in a summer dress in her garden, while beside her, pinned up, is a centrefold spread of a tall naked, willowy girl. I especially chose one with small breasts, fair pubic hair, legs erotically parted. Thus it works as a teaser that I glance first at Maxine, firmly implanting her face on my retina before I cut swiftly to girl number two.

I'll say more. All these hankies within their sealed bags and bearing their own perfumed smell. I unwind the freezer-twist, clamp my nose to the gap, a deep sniff —

"Down there?"

I need a second to adjust myself and my breathing. "Yes, what?"

"Do you want a few nuts with your salad or egg?"

I think what I'd like is some meat. Red meat. Not day after day of this rabbit-food shit. "Nuts will do fine."

"You don't eat nuts!"

"All right, make that eggs, then."

"There's no need to shout. Lunch at one."

Very clever. Note, he's told me that once. Repetition confirms that I rank as a moron who needs telling twice.

Well, he who laughs last... I get up, check my watch, then set the little short-wave transceiver how I want it, a nice little gadget, all automatic. God, I'm hungry, my teeth shriek to murder a steak, a happening that I know won't come to pass — which I curse Robert for, because I sure as hell blame him for introducing Bernard to the vegetarian way of life. And I enjoyed a smoke, too, till he exposed its perils.

*

In the kitchen, Bernard's already eating. I stare down at half a lettuce, one hard-boiled egg, two whole tomatoes, three large sprigs of green stuff, and a handful of nuts. There's nothing creative or appetizing about this at all: it's just plonked on my plate like it's still awaiting preparation.

"Is some of this out of the garden?"

"It's fresh if that's what you mean."

I have to be careful. Even in winter there's days he serves nettles, dandelion leaves, flower-petals even.

He says, "No birthday cards? Is that what's upset you?"

"Not especially." Idly I glance at my watch.

"In a hurry?"

"Not really."

"In that case you might think about doing some hoovering. I'm just so sick of housework."

"I know the feeling."

"You should worry," he says. "As far as I can see you're the last person to complain. You never do a job properly as far as I can see."

I stare coldly. I feel like saying, "Bernard, I want to tell you this now before it's too late. Though I know people who went out of their way to tell me differently, there was a time when I imagined that your being disagreeable and malevolent was *not* done on purpose. Now I have learned by experience."

Deliberately I peek once more at the time.

"You sure you're not going somewhere?" he says.

And again I don't answer but maintain a vacant expression while following the second-hand's sweep on my watch. The secret is this: I'm the one who knows that moulded to the underside of this kitchen table is eight pounds of Semtex high-explosive, plus high-frequency timer. "Bernard . . ." I say, and I give him a wry farewell smile, "Bernard . . . *any moment now.*"

CHAPTER 2

Of course I've not blown up Bernard; it's just make-believe. All the same, I guess I'd admit there are times when I worry that what with my fantasizing, my drinking and all, I may still be a confused person. Never mind. Self-respect has been passing me by for what seems a long time now.

Picture this.

Six years ago, Christmas week, I'd been out of hospital some months and was kicking my heels in a bus-shelter up near the barracks and wondering if that was where I should kip or if I should go down the kilns – I'd be hungry as well, that's for sure – when this young bloke slid in. "Chilly night!"

I forget the guy's name now. Naturally he was fooling nobody, while on my part was a kind of relief that even if I was squatting like having a crap in the corner, carry-bags and all, I wasn't feeling as scabby as normal since down at the Salvation Army they'd had no beds going spare but I'd done okay for gear, plus a shower.

"Skint?" he goes – blah-blah-blah! – and then passed me a drag, during which, thrown half a chance, he goes for a feel of my balls and the squeeze he gets back must do something for him because he asks do I fancy a party he is catching the bus to?

Jesus, free food and heat? I should kiss his arse . . . except five minutes inside the door and made to feel welcome and, "Piss off!" I told him. And here's where I first met and got snared by Bernard. *Come here, big boy!*

I could see that delight in his eyes. *A real deadbeat to practise on!*

Drinks, some flirtatious chat – I think we might even have had a dance or two – after which he took me home, a bath, supper at his flat. Then beyond that, I guess I'd prefer to profess a discreet drunken blank but suppose I most likely struggled to accord him some honours. A half-teaspoon of weak-looking sperm was for me a big deal at that time. Something to do with the miserable diet: I was touching ten stone when I should've weighed twelve.

Nothing penetrative, either. That was never my bag.

Anyhow, that was a fair while ago, and right now comes Monday morning. Off to work. Another day, another dollar. Even when we first moved in here the place needed lots of attention. The corrugated-iron garage was my idea. It was me planted the ivy and look at it now.

"Hi, Rosie, babe!"

Rosemary, aged three, her feet in borrowed high-heels, grins familiarly from the other side of next-door's low front wall and I wave to her mum who is polishing front windows. Although we've never spoken, she is always ready with a smile: single-parent, buck-toothed, wide-hipped, not my sort at all, except presumably someone must have fancied her madly.

"Okay, Rosie, which pocket the sweeties?" I say. "This one? Or that one?"

Rosemary points.

"Oh no!" I gasp. "Rosie wins again!"

I love kids.

While Bernard's middle-management job rates a decent car, I need to conserve what's left of mine and am stuck with a ten-minute bus ride to get off in town by the shopping arcade. In winter, when living rough like I was, we often sneaked in here when we could to take advantage of the hot-air blowers, and I've known Sol from then, the poor scrag-arsed bastard's few belongings plus his bottle of shine in his carrier bags at his feet, above which his legs lagged with papers to protect collapsed veins, polythene keeping damp off his shoulders, his good eye one-eying my progress towards where he's paused in searching the litter bin attached to the wall outside the shop doorway.

I haul change from my pocket and thrust it at him. "Bog off, Sol," I say; then, as I let myself in, the air rushes out, carrying the warm unclean smell of perished rubberware and last week's spilled shelf of barbecue sauces. Walls are hung with vulgar declarations on bright orange cards. *FROM FACE-CLOTHS TO FLOOR TILES, BARGAINS GALORE... KNOCKDOWN PRICES YOU CAN'T AFFORD TO MISS... SALE ITEMS AT GENUINE REDUCTIONS.*

I shake my head, recognizing it's a depressing fact that anyone who shops at this or any other Thrifty Miss Betsy emporium can't be too fucking fussy.

33, 23, 33: I disarm the alarm. Maxine's measurements near enough.

Here is how I came to have a job at Thrifty Miss Betsy.

Bernard speaking: "Even accepting that blood doesn't come from a stone, I suppose I have lived in the infinitesimal hope that you might one day buck your ideas up. I am absolutely sick and tired of keeping you. You laze around. You do nothing. You spill crumbs. You don't clean up. Your clothes smell. You move in here, you leech off me. You make no contribution whatsoever."

I'd been bunking for two or three months at the flat he had before Welbeck Parade. Long enough to have determined that acrimony and malevolent tongue-lashings were more his preference to living in harmony. Only this night, at Welbeck Parade, brought extra, the ULTIMATUM, which was cleverly timed. It was snowing outside and he'd come round to realizing I was frightened of snow.

He said, "Get a job."

I said, "Christ, who'd employ me? I've nothing to offer. I've no clothes, no references. They'd laugh. They'd want medical records."

Mentally and physically, in bow-tie and dinner-jacket and fresh from some Lodge affair, he was ideally geared to pooh-pooh such misgivings. He said, "Rubbish. I've been chatting tonight to a friend of mine ... *Denzil*."

Denzil – not someone I'd heard of before. (It was only later that I came to remember there were nights soon after I'd moved in when I'd noticed a man watching the flat. The happening became so regular that at 3 a.m. one morning Bernard jumped out of bed and rushed outside for a head-to-head, at which point the man, when his car wouldn't start, ran away round the corner. I've thought many times since that it could've been Denzil, a free-mason also, his lumbering frame. I know he and Bernard were "jolly" together for some length of time.)

Whatever – it seemed Denzil had recently come to the end of an Army career. I think Bernard actually said, "Denzil had a *commission*," stressing rank as though the distinction and experience placed Denzil in the higher echelons of intelligence, good taste and decision-making.

Denzil, as officers do, Bernard said, had also emerged with a sizeable sum, and the plan that he had up his sleeve was to launch a discount retail chain. "Of course, he can't pay much at first, but it's work and you'd be there at the head of the queue as he grows. Work would mean self-respect."

Bernard, secure in his own little niche, could spout shit like that.

*

So that's how Thrifty Miss Betsy came into being. And now five years have gone by and my worst fears are realized. I still earn the same size of crust. I've not bettered myself one iota. The job's still as menial.

"Bernard, be fair. Denzil's paying less than the minimum wage."

"Well, he would, the man's mean," he's replied more than once – they are no longer friends. But to that he then adds, "Don't you *dare* lose that job if you want to stay here."

And *I do*.

But it rankles. My place in the scheme of things is not exactly a conspiracy but it constantly features as part of the tightrope I walk. And here it should be understood that within our domestic set-up Bernard is *satisfied* with receiving half the meagre wage he knows I draw, while as far as sexual favours are concerned – there are none. In short, I am currently undergoing the trauma of sleeping with him only because we've no greenhouse.

(That will sound odd and needs explanation.

The fact is the man is a gardening freak. Plants *everywhere*! On every flat indoor surface. Plants extraordinarily stretched by light, plants stunted, plants dead, plants left to shrivel in desert-dry pots, plants savagely pruned, plants being taught their lessons for not responding to discipline like they should. And affecting me directly in this regard he has requisitioned my tiny room, so that on my bed, on the floor, on wooden staging he's knocked together to reach to the ceiling, he's got trays and containers of seedlings and cuttings avoiding the frost. The result being that, really, only Zero could find space for kipping in there, though he too is currently banned because given the chance he quite naturally scratches out furrows to shit in, which when back-filled like cats do you can never locate till it's too stinking late.)

Even so, staying here has much in its favour. I prefer to be in the country and close to the river. Moreover, I haven't the fibre for making fresh starts. So, with food, warmth and shelter made available and all at small outlay, I should be grateful, you'd think? Perhaps. Except you need to read between the lines. Or as Robert succinctly put it before he himself got the glad-eye from Bernard: "Errol, know the truth? That bastard's turned you into a houseplant."

Or to phrase that another way. The price that I pay and why I'm worth what I cost is that who'd Bernard be to himself without someone like *me* to look down on?

A word about Maxine.

Maxine works the full week, including Saturdays; she gets Wednesday off. I do two or three days as required, plus occasional deliveries which I skip if I can – the shop's diesel van upsets my stomach on short stop-and-starts and the last thing I want in my life is more barium-meal pumped up my bum and x-rays that go with it.

But shopwork itself. Perhaps nothing would grate so much if I thought I was going to live forever. Serving, stocking shelves, tidying up. I never thought I would come to this. The world's biggest drag.

On the other hand, Maxine and I still enjoy a few laughs, and lunchtimes are especially good, when from the town centre's Marks & Spencer's I buy the kind of prawn sandwiches she likes and picnicking in the back we talk, idle chat covering her circle of friends, which is wide. I know all their names, what they do, the states of their marriages and who's screwing who, when and where.

I suppose it might be said that I live her life for her.

Anyhow – it was a year ago that Denzil took her on. I walked in – into every dark corner a little sunbeam will eventually fall – and there she was: boyishly-chested, cracking long legs, a sparkling ring-of-confidence smile, divorced.

I was straight to the chemist's for new toothbrush, comb, expensive cologne and some violent green mouthwash. Did I have what it took to be some kind of hero?

That was the question as I dived headfirst into my role of adolescent loon cum dog-on-alert at the heat she was giving off; though oddly, as it eventually turns out, she is celibate: a popular claim in these dangerous days, and one I found hard to accept early on because here is a woman who really attracts. Yet "I just can't be bothered" is what she says, although somewhat inexplicably and in direct opposition to such professed disinterest she can on occasions be atrociously forward. A young handsome kid comes into the shop and is doing his best to earn a crust through selling some brand of cleaner. He says, "It removes ink, grease, blood, fruit juice, you name it." Maxine, eyes diamond-bright above one of her smiles, asks him, "Does it do sperm?" The poor kid dies on the spot.

So it came to a time when my bravery took over. "Maxine," I said off-handedly, "we must have a drink one of these nights?" and she laughed, like she'd seen it was coming.

All the same, she accepted. I chose McCoy's which as restaurants go is pretty extravagant: a deliberate choice – *one*, to make up for being out of circulation for so long; and *two*, to sweep her off her feet . . . except at the time I'm taken aback to discover it's only the previous evening she's been there with somebody else. Then, thereafter, what the fuck did it matter? In nervously talking non-stop I literally frightened her sick, so that at her front door she bolted from the car and then next day announced she never again wanted to meet me outside of work. "I've said the same to my mother," she said: *"you're a really weird person!"*

Weeks passed. I couldn't even bear to look at her. Then it worked out all right since, despite all her charms, she's abysmally poor, the whole of her divorce settlement having gone down the tubes through some stupid investment in a failed beauty-salon. Her twenty-fifth birthday arrived. "Maxine, truthfully," I told her, "believe me, you deserve better than the status quo of everyday crap."

Thus we made up. And in the face of being handed a new Gucci watch, what choice did she have?

So Maxine's my friend, and the rest here are workmates.

With today being Monday, the shop is busier. Hustlebustle – the Monday market behind the town hall makes a big draw. High-sided trucks full of scared stamping beasts rumble in for the auctions up by the abattoir.

Farmers'-glory.

Shit-and-cruelty.

We get to mid-morning. Minding the counter, I doodle, make paper-clip sculptures, shoot rubber bands. To keep track of the folk who venture inside we have those crazy mirrors that provide views along aisles. I see Terri come down needing cash; she loves scouring the market's open-air stalls for what *she* thinks are *bargains.* Aged forty-nine, divorced, ten years Denzil's senior, and in her eighteen months in the upstairs' office she has made rapid progress from what began with her and Denzil working late to Denzil leaving his wife so they could shack up together. Frankly, as Maxine and I agree, you need only to watch her antics to see she's committed to regarding Denzil as the best meal-ticket she's now likely to manage and that a band of gold and an early retirement to the Costa del Sol is what she has in mind. Already her newly acquired Toyota sports car is parked round the back.

Locating sixty quid in the petty cash, she calls to me, "Put this down as petrol and postage." But then *no*, she decides, it's still not enough, and before leaving she raids and empties the BLIND DOGS' net stocking.

An hour drags by. From my spot behind the partition where I am sticking prices on to a load of cheap hand cream, I can see the vee of Karen's knickers as she swings her legs. She is perched on the ledge by the till; her job upstairs is word processing and other paperwork; early-thirties, divorced with kids, big unfettered tits. She says, "Maxine, listen. So that's his name – Ollie. So what d'you reckon? He likes funny condoms. I think they're awful."

"Karen, your contraception is absolutely nothing to do with me," Maxine says, which sends Karen on her way, miffed, her high heels clattering on the interior stairs, leaving Maxine to wait until the noise is beyond the halfway point before pulling a face as she calls to me, "What a tart, she was known as the school bicycle. On, off, ring my bell!"

Which perhaps is unkind.

Never mind.

We get past lunchtime. Trade had faltered to zilch. For something to do, I head upstairs to have words with Sanjay.

Sanjaturk Associates reads the plaque on his door. He rents the smaller of the two first-floor offices from where, as a one-man outfit, he arranges the buying and selling of impressive quantities of assorted sundries, plus having a sticky interest in a number of back-street shops and various other adventures. Whereas I personally rate him no mean achiever, Denzil, jealous of the big cars and so on, is less generous. Bloody kaffirs, he says of visiting cousins and uncles, of which there are many.

The door is locked, so I turn into Miss Betsy's larger open-plan office where Karen of the contraceptive-predicament ignores me.

Paula smiles. She does accounts, nineteen years old, a nice girl, single-parent with a young son named Andrew, aged three, conceived via *coitus interruptus* coming seconds too late in the back of a car, so she says.

"Maxine's minding the shop," I announce in case they care and grab a chair and swing my feet on to the window-sill, thus gaining a leisurely view of the shop's backyard and adjacent square of town park. Railings, tired rhododendrons, a public convenience that's been heavily barbed-wired. A spindle-legged dog skulks in one border searching for smells. It goes into the privy. It doesn't come out. Why . . .?

Often I regard long bouts of contemplation as the scourge of my life.

Two or three weeks after giving Maxine the watch for her birthday she said she wanted me to know she had one other *special friend* besides myself. A man, she meant, and offered the details.

"That's amazing!" I said, and was *truly* amazed, wondering if she was actually meaning who I thought she was meaning. (I think it best in this instance that I shouldn't name names.)

She said, "I'm telling you because it shows I trust you implicitly. He sometimes rings me here at the shop. We met when he was being interviewed in the next studio when I went for my you-know-what show." (She meant the time she was once a *Blind Date* contestant, an event in her life she hardly likes to lay claim to.) She said, "No one else knows and you should be flattered I've told you."

And I was ... *flattered*. He's famous. That's how big the secret is.

"So you're sleeping with him?" Naturally the question cropped up fairly early.

"Oh good Lord, no!" she said. "It's only once in an age. We just meet for a drink and all totally harmless."

I sit thinking about it, and it all makes me wonder.

Then from my feet-on-window-sill pose I see Denzil parking his Jag in the yard.

After another five minutes, the stairs have him blowing, his today's swagger-stick is a rolled-up *Financial Times*, and he has with him a pair of *prospective* franchisees – I know from past experience he will have brought them up the inside way so he could point out that above the counter of every TMB shop is a large red-and-white plastic board that reads *This is a Thrifty Miss Betsy Shop operated as a franchise under a licence granted by DENZIL K. MURRAY.*

By which time I am industriously on my feet. He says, "Let me introduce you to Errol Oldfield. Errol's been with me ever since I began with the one shop down there. He painted it out for me all on his own, didn't you, Errol?"

He's made me sound like some kind of trained chimpanzee.

"Mr and Mrs Clarkson are thinking of opening a Miss Betsy shop in Brighton," he says. Then as if I count for something, he continues, "How much would you say trade's built up since we started, Errol? Three hundred per cent? Four hundred? Maybe more?"

I frown like maybe it's a hard question to be answering off the cuff. At which he gets tired of waiting. He tells the Clarksons that things are moving ahead so quickly that another two years should see at least sixty outlets in operation.

Somehow, spectacularly, he skips mentioning the four shops that have failed within the last three months, plus the others that've gone down the drain since franchising was started.

"Right, come this way," he says, and he's easing the Clarksons towards his office. Only wait, he's torn, because in his absence there's been a delivery and overflowing from the waste-bin are rumpled sheets of brown paper, string and used polythene bags that he'd love to be rescuing and straightening out. Except he *can't*. He remembers: *he's an important man.* "Yes, there's more to tell," he says, and by then the three of them are at his door where a dropped rubber band on the floor stops him dead. He can't force himself by. He brings it all the way back for the stationery tin.

"You might need that," he says.

Pathetic really.

Five-thirty approaching. I'm not working tomorrow, thank Christ. Maxine says, "Right this cross-checks," and places the till's takings into a cash bag that Paula will collect for the safe. She has her outdoor coat on. "If I shoot I can give my mother a lift as she finishes," she says. Her mother works on assembly at Foster & Washbrook.

"A drink later?" I suggest.

"Can't," she says. "I really must tidy my bedroom tonight."

"No, that's Wednesdays."

She turns impish. "Yes, you're right," she says.

I watch her depart: tall and sleek. I lock up and put CLOSED on the door. Paula comes clattering down the inside way. She grabs the bag. "Thanks, I must rush," she says.

I bolt the interior door and then at the counter remove the till drawer. The dark recess behind looks uninviting to the hand. I rake out rumpled banknotes, letting them fall to the floor, a small precaution that allows me to retrieve them without being seen from the window.

Denzil figures he's so fucking smart.

He should grow up, I growl to myself. He's an arsehole.

Fight fire with fire is what I say.

Jesus, some weeks I make so much I don't know what to do with it all.

CHAPTER 3

Big question. If I had use of a chest of drawers instead of living out of cardboard boxes and carrier-bags would the quality of my life be improved? Fuck knows. As I upend an old refuse-bag, an assortment of unwashed socks – always odd and never a pair – rains out along with unwashed jockey pants, silt, old bus tickets, the odd coin, a musty smell, and a forgotten snapshot of my mother and father strolling a promenade somewhere. Probably Scarborough, I guess, because that would be the furthest their travel extended.

And, God, I tell myself, I hate such touchstones. In fact I have a rule of restricting talk and memories of family history to a minimum, especially in respect of my father where the story I most tell concerns the childhood shiver of disgust I experienced daily at sight of his worn nicotine-stained teeth in their mug of salt-water on the bathroom window-ledge; though to that, if pressed, I might add that he never once bought me a present for birthday or Christmas. "And honestly," I'll say, "I don't ever recall him taking me anywhere – outings, that is. As far as I know, I was probably conceived out of bitter-beer lust. End of story."

But Mother was different, and *sad-sad* to see her pictured so young and ebullient when I know how arid and hollow her life turned out to be. Olivia by name, a big movie buff. Always on her bedside chair was a pile of well-thumbed cinema magazines; although to what extent such tinselled thinking affected her judgements, I can't be sure. All I know is she used in her final years to write me fond letters, as if even at that late stage she still worried she might not have done the right thing by me.

And there, of course, she would be thinking of my relationship with Uncle Lewis and Aunt Milly, of whom I own an abundance of recollections, with the earliest floating vaguely around that it was usually Sundays when they'd drive over. The car's horn would sound in the street. In would waltz Milly, glad-ragged to the nines, to lift me up for a kiss and cuddle, pressing me against her softness, enveloping me in her perfume. Sunday visits that I came to recognize as bountiful times of their car's boot being filled with groceries, and always included was the treat of an ice-cream cake that had to be eaten straightaway because we had no fridge.

But markedly none for my father, I recall. Puddings and toffees and all that sweet muck, ice-cream included, was for girls and nancy-boys, a view that was all part of his natural inclination to be a hypocrite, I came to realize. On the sly, he ate toffees and chocolate by the barrowload. Moreover, with Aunt Milly being his doting only sister, and therefore a soft touch, he made sure he got his sugary bonbons of a few quid shoved his way whenever he saw her.

But exactly where my sister Grace featured in all of this, I'm not sure. At eight years my senior, she must have received her share of whatever goodies were available, I imagine, though later she would come to blame me for being ignored in other directions. Still, at that time I was only as perceptive as my years would allow, and groceries and ice-cream was all I could see. Then came a live hamster, a bicycle, a train-set (sold in The Lord Raglan pub by my father) . . . and eventually trips to the zoo, the speedway, the panto, a flight in a plane, the periods away extending pro rata with age until I was ten or there-abouts, at which time Uncle Lewis and Aunt Milly turned up one Sunday and my mother unbeknown to me had my suitcase packed and there was an amount of talk like I wasn't there, and at one point my father took me aside and said something about me doing all right for myself if I played my cards right.

So we didn't go to the seaside that day. Instead we went straight to Uncle Lewis's house where I'd mysteriously acquired a room of my own and a wardrobe of clothes.

And there I found I settled straight in to having ice-cream on tap, and I was also by then accustomed to my aunt being crazy, I guess. Not crazy enough to be sectionable, perhaps, but her hands-and-knees searches for microphones and alien rays were everyday, she had a Howard Hughes' fear of germs that included a habit of aerosolling people who coughed or sneezed, and her fits of jealousy knew no bounds. By day she threw things. Her screams shredded nights. No hysterical outburst was too much trouble for her.

Poor Uncle Lewis. He gained his escape via his bottle a day, and if he occasionally staggered it was always with style. Besides, he adored her. Halfway up the stairs hung an antique print of a gorgeous creature with long flowing hair, its lettered title reading *Beware Beware She Is So Fair*, and he would swear to God it was really Aunt Milly.

So whatever she wanted she got.

He gave her *me*.

Nowadays, what grudge I should bear him for that, if any, I'm not sure. Instead I feel more inclined to retain a memory of the remains of the poor man, aged fifty-three, sitting upright in bed shovelling peanuts into his mouth in the hope their nutritional value would stop the rot in his liver. Scenting the vultures, he had already by that time set up a trust-fund to look after Aunt Milly. "Milly, get me the most expensive doctor you can find." They were the last words I heard him say. But, of course, money can't buy you everything, and by then it was too late, anyway.

After the funeral, my father drove off in the car to get petrol, then forgot to return it. He also took a few paintings, including a Lowry and two Russell Flints. "You never know, these old frames might be worth a few quid . . . and I'll have these gold cuff-links and that, shall I, Milly?"

Odd socks, I decide, will do nicely. I pull on the army-surplus Long Johns that I wear for deep wading; then watching myself in the mirror while swallowing my medication, I can see that in the suave-and-debonair department I perhaps haven't too much in common with my namesake, the late Errol Flynn. Mother's heart-throb, of course.

Still, I suppose all things considered I'm not ageing too badly. A six foot wiry body tending to stoop, muscles perhaps not so firm any more, but I still grow lots of hair and have no need of glasses. A penis of seven-and-a-bit, the last time I measured. That's erect. Trouble is, stare too deeply at the eyes and there's so often no spark – which seems proof of a kind that I mostly look backwards.

I recall being sixteen years old . . .

Okay, so these once-upon-a-time stories are guaranteed to lose you friends. Nevertheless, a stormy night, winter-north-Atlantic, "ALL HANDS ON DECK!" Needless to say, only in Errol Flynn movies do they yell such puerile commands but it helps set the scene of a ship cavorting in heavy weather, everything loose on the move, and really an *inauspicious* event as far as wind and seas go because I was to see far worse. But young and immortal I gawp at a purple-grey sky that seems partially obscured by mountainous white-crested waves. Then *I fall*, the wooden deck is a slope of increasing incline down which I'm sliding with nothing to cling to, the spray whipping my screams; I shoot under the railings and slide over the side and I'm DEAD – dead, except the sleeve of my oilskin has snagged round a cleat, a miraculous happening that has left me hanging bat-like overside, and it takes a while to heave me back and I've shit myself.

Not a fictional tale, and perhaps *auspicious* after all because much much later I am to recount its details to a psychiatrist who seems to think it important. Yes, my adventure, true or invented, he says, has similarities with people indulging in free-fall parachuting, and/or climbing impossible mountains and/or driving cars at suicidal speeds. Rejoice, he tells me, you have experienced the walk on the precipitous wafer-thin line between *being* and *not-being* that crystallizes the true joys of living. Get out there and live, he instructs. *Be yourself.*

He also made notes of two of my recurring dreams.

In the first I am of unknown age: I cough heavily and something snake-like comes out of my mouth. I grab with both hands and pull, only to discover I am pulling myself inside-out because the opposite end is attached to the lining of my stomach. (There is a possibility here, the shrink said, that I may have suffered an enormous tapeworm as a child.)

In the second I am older, the scenario is weird and hazy, and the body is . . . *human, animal or what*? I don't know. Neither does its state of freshness or decomposition emerge, but the burial place is always damp and what disturbs most is the fear of exhumation, and the subsequent terrible punishment of incarceration. I dread this dream. It is the most disturbing among the many by which I am pursued and from which I wake sweating, heart racing, often disorientated to the point of not knowing where I am.

Later, this same shrink, a man named Zissler, would get the two of us into a terrible tangle because he seemed never able to make his mind up about anything. "Paraphilia," he said – paraphilia, he had to explain, is a dramatic impairment in the ability to love, and a long standing erotic preoccupation and a pressure to act upon the erotic fantasy. "Paraphilia," he said, "which might easily apply in your case, often stems from poor family connections in childhood and can have all manner of spin-offs."

"In layman's language, such as what?" I asked of him.

He chuckled; he'd a weird sense of humour. He said, "I don't know. Like you could easily have grown up as a serial killer."

An hour passes. I have moved to the river.

Sex and good fishing! Two of life's more pleasurable pursuits. Anticipation comes big in both. Many times, looking from higher ground and into the crystal-clear water, I have marvelled at how effortlessly the salmon sway Zeppelin-like in the currents. Zip-zip, such maximum control with merely a flick of the tail, and often thereafter, seeking to take one, I have unsuccessfully tried every fly, every lure until, for no apparent reason – bingo! you've got one.

Maybe with Maxine that's how it will happen.

Here on this fine March morning, white puff-ball clouds mask the sun, just a child's breath of wind on my cheek. Conditions: *perfect*. I am on the gravel at the Maidens' Pool, named thus by the Romans, stuff of legends, I guess, and I've to smile at the mental gymnastics that have brought Maxine to mind: MAXINE – ubiquitous in the sense that she is everywhere I go. Adrenalin pumping, psyching myself, knees bend, flex the shoulders, a cough and a spit, nervously rubbing my palms hard together, on and off testing the fly for sharpness against my thumb.

The salmon Denzil needs for his house-warming party is best taken legally. He is certain to blab that I caught it for him.

I wade in and up to my waist. My studded soles grate on the rocky bottom as I lean back to balance against the river's thrust. Waves and vibrations can't be helped and a few reddened kelts are triggered to leaping. The depth where the fish lie is beneath the opposite bank's trailing sycamore's branches. It's only twenty-eight miles to the sea and I'm looking for something fresh-run that has lately arrived. I cast again and again. As the sunken fly on its long length of line swings round on the current, I have the spare loop lightly held . . .

The loop tweaks free. I feel the slow heavy pull that puts a fine creaking arc to the sixteen-foot rod.

The job takes only minutes. I beach the fish on the gravel, an unmarked cock of seventeen pounds, a bar of silver, the sea-lice still on his flanks. I give him a flick on the head and he's dead.

That's how easy it is to kill. I could walk up behind Bernard, with a hammer or something, and whack! I could do it. Although, let it be said I'm not serious; it's not like I'm on to a dare or a promise. Nonetheless, in the garden are plants that can kill. Some in minutes, some in hours, or those that take time.

Undetectably so; so he says.

I get home. And I've that thought to ponder again because, in the kitchen, Bernard is at the chopping-board.

For further provocation, the big wide-bladed knife is razor-sharp and, not pausing in glancing my way, he works so swiftly, and he is not HIV or even promiscuous as far as I know, but Jesus, who can be sure, and the thought he may one day nick a finger and unknowingly feed me some blood is a worry.

He says, "I'm doing lots for the freezer for while I'm away."

Which casts some fear aside and rouses within me the elation of remembering he is travelling to London for six days tomorrow. "Ratatouille?" I ask querulously.

"Something wrong with that? Not good enough for you? I don't suppose you caught anything, either?" he says.

I wag my head. "Never saw a thing." I enjoy rewarding his sarcasm with a lie. Eating fresh salmon, and/or trout, mackerel or herrings (oily fish) is his one departure from the vegetarian way.

All the same, I tense as in shucking off my long tarpaulin coat I see its front is plastered with the tiny sequins of salmon scales which catch the light as they fall. The ungutted salmon out in the boot of the car will keep for up to three days in the present cold weather.

"God, will you look at the state of that coat?" Bernard says in rebuke. "Can't you keep it outside? Are there worms in the pockets? What's that smell you've brought in? Don't leave those waders there, *please*! Odd socks as usual, I see. Will you wipe up those footprints or d'you intend they should stay there?"

"Jesus Christ," I snort back, "I'll drop dead for you soon."

"Good. Make it quick ... and don't forget a signed cheque because I'm not paying for you."

I get the floor-cloth from the space under the sink. Wood-lice and other insects lie dead on their backs on a slime you could write your name in, killed by the chemicals spilled from packets jammed in between pots and pans and split from damp; disturbing really.

"And *there*," Bernard says, and uses the toe of his shoe to nudge my hand to a mud-speck I've missed.

Jesus, I say to myself, I swear one of these days I'll swing for the bastard.

CHAPTER 4

Tomorrow comes. Bernard's departure means six days of freedom and the bed to myself!

But first things first, I decide, and after melting one of the bags of ratatouille I force some of its browny-green mush through a sieve. The tiny traces of white that get trapped on the mesh could be garlic or ... *what*? Better safe than sorry, I decide, and dump all five bags in the bin.

After that, I wait a while before I dial Robert's number. More than once, because she's confined to her wheelchair, I've suggested that Robert should get Tina a cordless but he hasn't, so it's important to let the phone ring. "How're you feeling there, Tina?" I ask, and she says she's okay and is glad of a chat – she doesn't get to talk to many people – but I don't mention Bernard until well into the conversation, at which point comes a satisfying indifference at hearing that Robert, too, set off at lunchtime for six days in London.

Bathtime next. Privations endured, rewards gained. Luxury after all stems from comparisons.

Mud-pack on, lying flat on my back, reaching out to work the hot tap with my toes, not switching off till the heat grabs my balls. The pinnacle of now? I work up a lather round my crutch, locked on to the pressure of erotic fantasy, and we are of course back with Maxine again. *I could choke her with this.*

Which reminds me of Linda. Which is largely because anything sexual reminds me of *her*.

*

"Linda, good evening, this is Errol, he's recently given up the sea and is visiting us here."

I got introduced to Linda in that fashion one hot August night at a Friends Of The Hospital's barbecue, all proceeds in aid of a scanner appeal. Her husband had been dead just six weeks, having succumbed to some kind of renal failure, plus complications, none of which she wanted to talk about, except to say that they lived at the end of a narrow country lane and that the ambulance had got stuck behind a combine-harvester going the same way.

Five minutes sooner might have saved him. Instead, she'd been left with a five-year-old daughter named Daisy and a hamper of bills. She came over as *special*. At twenty-four she looked sixteen, impossibly beautiful, everybody's darling – which explained the high bids – but at the barbecue's slave-auction she finally got knocked down to me for twenty-five quid.

Then when not long after that, the raffle got drawn, she won a screw-top bottle of wine and we sat drinking it in the back of her car in the hospital car-park. I was ten years older than her and felt *travelled*. She said, "If the nautical chit-chat's supposed to impress, you score high. My knees are like jelly. If you want, you can have me."

I guess, looking back, she probably made me feel chosen.

My parents travelled up for the wedding. My sister Grace declined to come but really missed nothing more entertaining than Aunt Milly stealing the show in hoisting her skirt to make a pool in the gutter outside the registry office. I laughed off the embarrassment. Uppermost in my mind was that I'd long back arrived at seeing Aunt Milly as my secure financial future even though there was no way of immediately taking advantage of her wealth. The trust fund's executors were settling her bills. She couldn't even sign cheques.

Not that my *immediate* lack of access to her money caused concern. Even as newly-weds, we had Linda's house in the village, the job I'd landed selling insurance paid reasonably well, plus we had spare cash coming in from the four or five hours' market research Linda was doing every week. So in effect what I'd done was to step effortlessly into the slot left by Linda's departed and it took me a while to accept I'd struck that lucky.

Good times. At the local school they turned to thinking of me as Daisy's dad. Linda's friends became my friends – Robert and Tina, Oscar and Jenny.

Oscar looms large in my memory. Physically big, a sociology lecturer with psychotic ways. His wife, Jenny, in contrast was a mouse hardly seeming to have strength for housework but who found time to watercolour exquisite Kandinsky-style abstracts.

"Linda," I said – we were talking of Oscar – "you're a person who's attracted by extremes."

"Am I?" she said. "Yes, perhaps so. He reminds me of Rasputin. God, those armpits of his."

We were making love at this point. She had a big appetite and was good at it. So perhaps the best thing about the job I had was that in coming home from a day away down the motorway I near enough grew wings through thinking of the hot time we'd have.

Only on this particular night I had Oscar's wrist-watch staring at me from the bedside table. "Yes, it's his," she said – and really hadn't much option since, with its distinctive feature of many dials, it was hardly one I could have failed to recognize.

"He called in for coffee this morning," she said. "The

light bulb up here blew. So I asked him to change it. You know how I'm scared with electric."

We left it at that. I'd been away for over half a day and couldn't get enough of her. Then sweated-up and ostensibly to make a drink for us both, I went downstairs and while there looked at the kitchen trash and among the used tea-bags and plate-scrapings was the old blackened bulb alongside the cardboard holder from a fresh one. So that was all right.

Yet I couldn't leave well alone. "Linda, I still don't get it," I said. "Why should Oscar leave his watch behind?"

Turning her head towards me on her pillow, she smiled playfully, presumably regarding any light suspicions on my part as some kind of compliment. "I wasn't up here, how should I know?" she said. "Shall I ring him and ask?"

"Don't be silly."

"It's not *me* being silly."

"Which chair did he stand on?"

"Errol, for God's sake . . . you're awful!"

"I'm just curious."

"No, you're not . . . Come on, put the light off."

After which, as we lay in the dark I could sense that as well as both of us struggling to keep our breathing at normal she was thinking more about how things might seem. "I don't know, but I suppose he perhaps might have wanted to wash his hands," she said after a while, like it had just come to her. "Yes, now I remember. He was in the bathroom."

"Right. That's the answer, then."

"Lampshades get filthy."

"That's true. The heat attracts dust. Shall I give it back?"

"No, I'll do it," she said.

Then that might have been the end of the matter, except that what was to etch the happening on to my memory was that Robert called in next day on his way from visiting Tina in hospital. Tina by then was pretty sick. On the morning of their fifth wedding anniversary a few weeks back, she had literally fallen out of bed, having been struck down by some form of paralysis. She'd been an active, handsome woman, and now the latest prognosis, he was telling us, was that she might never walk again. "I'm distraught. Legs are so important," he said.

That struck hollow, I thought later. It was ladies' final day at Wimbledon, our TV was bust, and he hadn't been so distressed that he hadn't wanted to hurry home to watch the match.

As it was, quite coincidentally, the importance of legs seemed forcibly rammed home within the hour when Daisy holding her crayoning book and pencil-box fell down the stairs.

She had grown to be six. She lay spread-eagled among her scattered pencils, some broken. Her right leg was swelling and turning blue and sickeningly I realized the entire length of one unbroken pencil had knifed in and run up alongside the bone.

"Don't cry, Daisy," I said.

"I'm not," she said, and I gathered her up. "Oops, no knickers," she said, and flapped her hands in trying to keep down her skirt.

I put the car's headlights on full and kept sounding the horn to declare we were involved in an emergency dash, which we probably weren't but it felt like that. We reached the hospital within ten minutes, anyhow. A slight incision, a few stitches, an anti-tetanus jab, and she was going to be okay.

She lay on a trolley between us. Linda had her fingertips pressed to her nose in an attitude of prayer. She said,

"We've been here a few times. Remember the day that rabbit bit her finger? All that blood."

Tears appeared in her eyes.

"Don't," I said. "She's going to be fine."

"Remember she tried riding that two-wheeler and gashed her knee? It's all my fault. She's always having accidents. She pays for my sins."

"Linda, she doesn't."

"Yes, she *does*."

"No, she doesn't."

Her tears spilled over. "I feel awful," she said. "I spoil everything. I think I'm going to be sick. Punishing me through her is God's way."

Which was crazy and upset me a lot.

She didn't even believe in God.

Watch out!

Evening has arrived. Maxine lives with her widowed mother in a small broken-down terrace at the top of a hill, and here she comes down the path to take my breath away. She slides into the car. She is wearing the amber necklace I got her and Oscar De La Renta, yet another of those ingratiating little offerings I am always trying to surprise her with. I want to reach over and squeeze her hand or maybe plant a kiss on her cheek. Instead I say, "You smell fabulous." You have no idea how immature this makes me feel but that's what I say.

We head out of town. I drive a twelve-year-old nondescript Ford and thus pass *unnoticed*. I couldn't, anyhow, on the pittance I get from Miss Betsy explain affording anything better. However, the engine's tuned up and I've spent a few quid on an Hitachi stereo.

Lou Reed playing all the way.

At the little place we've got to know we have seafood pancakes for starters, then afterwards some kind of chicken kiev that, when I shove in my fork, spouts garlic butter so the ensuing stain looks like I've come down the front of my trousers. Maxine laughs her famous laugh. Chic and leggy, she attracts the kind of admiration that makes me jealous. My stomach is killing me. I wash down another analgesic with a mouthful of Perrier while she's sipping her wine. Nets and lobster-pots on dimly lit walls, a congenial backdrop to all the one-liners I've the urge to be whispering.

She has already commented on how *handsome* Petro looks tonight. I catch her eye as we watch him arrange her dessert so that an accompanying finger-biscuit is erect between two scoops of some kind of fudge-cake, a collage that becomes all the more audacious as he ladles whipped-cream across the plate's landscape. "Don't you dare say a word," she hisses, as he moves away, then takes the biscuit between her forefinger and thumb and delicately feeds it point-first into the O of her mouth.

God, my tongue up her front is what I want. How is it she eats so amply and yet stays so slim? Why with a 33 bust does she tell me she wears a size 32 bra? The shape of her breasts? The size of her nipples? How and to what they respond? These are unanswered questions.

Healthily she never smokes more than half a cigarette. As she takes a fresh king-size from her purse I spot a little hanky on view. I say, "May I?" and pinch it.

"Another one?" she says. "What do you do with all these hankies? Are you making a quilt?"

"Just keepsakes," I say.

She smiles to herself, like she knows that I'm hooked, and I don't mind about that – I like her to know I think about her all the time.

In the rear of the shop on a day that has come to stand out I was eating my share of the corned-beef pasties I'd been out to buy as a change from prawn sandwiches; she was reading one of my poems and seeming *unimpressed* by the blood of my struggling to write it. The telephone rang. She answered, and I could immediately tell who it was. Because now – *she's impressed*.

She perhaps spoke for five minutes, her voice and manner flirtatious while she was using her lips and eyes as signal-flags to keep me there. Finally, "Right, bye-ee!" she said. "Lots of luck for tonight. It's been lovely to hear from you."

She hung up, beaming. "They're away. Sheffield. A cuptie. They'll win tonight."

"So they bloody well should. They could get a new team for what they paid out just for him."

She looked close to hugging herself. "I just had a feeling he'd ring me. He can't play without."

"Without?" I said dumbly.

"His *luck*!" She pointed a warning finger. "Don't you ever dare repeat what I tell you . . . the goalie they've got, he always snips his wife's hair and wears a piece round his – well, you know! He does really! The whole team's the same. Superstitious! *He* always rings *me*."

"Every game?"

"Every game. From all over."

So there we have it: she is some kind of rabbit's foot!

And, okay, I tell myself, this guy she has is a mite too far over the hill to continue making the England squad, but City were lucky to sign him, and here in a soccer mad area we're talking every local kid's hero: like down at the airport on the day he arrived they put out a banner that read WELCOME THE SAVIOUR. Millionaire, ex-model wife, kids, big house, name in headlines, his face smiling from adverts.

So what's she got that he needs . . .?

Petro's lingering smile towards her as he hands me the bill offers one choice of answer.

We leave. In a cobblestoned alley as we walk to the car we are under a Van Gogh brand of sky and I'm caught again by her perfume. Maxine, tell me the moon is green. Tell me I'm tall. Say I look great in a jacket for once.

How tired is she? The cats' eyes swing lazily away round the bend, then drum noisily under the wheels as I take the wrong line. We talk about . . . *very little* . . . and here, I realize, is a hurdle between us. Which is sad, because even with people with whom I have nothing in common, my preoccupation with the river often provides a topic of conversation, but not with her. "No, thanks, it's got bones in," she's said to my offers of salmon. Likewise, she hasn't an interest in nature and such. I've perhaps put her off. It's all shit-and-cruelty, I've told her so often.

"Watch out for sheep," she says.

The road has no walls or fencing.

She says, "Don't get annoyed, but that camera you bought me – it's so complicated."

"Really? Cameras are like people. They work if you know how to press the right buttons."

She makes no reply. The inference evades her, I guess. "Bring it in and I'll show you."

"Ah," she says, "good. How's Bernard?"

"Away, but don't ask." She knows how things stand between Bernard and me, or at least what I've chosen to tell her.

"Sharing's awful," she says. "A place on my own, that's what I'd like, wouldn't you?"

"I'd be camped at your door with my tongue hanging out."

"Just your tongue?"

The crack's hardly subtle. Still, innuendo's a game that we play, so I laugh nonetheless.

She says, "I'd love a nice house. My mother never tidies! Honestly, she really gets on my nerves. Mind you, if I was in the Royal Family I don't think I'd worry so much."

"Another couple of years, you'll be married."

"Once bitten . . ."

"Will it be like that?"

"Will what be like what?"

"Will the day come when you won't want to know me?"

Her cigarette glows afresh in the dark as she sucks hard for thought. "The Royals," she says. "Getting waited on hand and foot; it must be easy for them, getting everything free. If you were in the Royal Family would you worry so much?"

Sometimes in her company I see myself as a man without fingers attempting to extract a marble from a bag of oil. Either she's as dumb as a brick or particularly clever at evading what I mostly want to discuss.

When I reach over and gentle her cheek with the back of my hand, the effect is immediate and startling. She elbows me clear. "Just get off!"

"There, see!" I say weakly.

"See what? Can't I be tired now?"

I ease on the speed. "Let's talk about this," I say, with some desperation. "Can we talk? Haven't I earned the right to touch you?"

"You've done *what*?"

"I meant through *time*."

"I should hope so. You know I'm not like that."

"Like *what*? I had a dream about you last night. You were in this big feather bed. I was putting a pillow under your hips."

She emits a nervous laugh. "Why, what for?"

"What?" Real or feigned, her obtuseness is baffling. "We were naked," I tell her. "Look, listen to what I'm saying, this is my head on the line here. Sometimes I try to imagine you without any clothes on. I imagine *all sorts*."

She stays quiet. I've perhaps overstepped.

"It's mind over matter," she says finally. "Most people don't think like you do."

"Yes, they do. For instance, let's say it was somebody else who'd invited you out ... *Mr Superstar?*"

"Ah ..." she takes her time answering but seems pleased he's cropped up, "well, all right, he'd take me to bed like a shot if I'd let him."

"But not *me?*"

"It's just not crossed my mind!"

Well, I tell myself, it should have! In fact it probably *has* and she's fobbing me off. And that hurts because somewhere in the depths of my head is an instinct that says I should park, summon up a big burst of testosterone and physically launch myself at her, full-frontal. Most blokes would, and she'll know that. Only with me, with my past holding me back, there's the snag that taking control rarely feels like an option.

I drive straight home once I've dropped her off. The phone is ringing, and it's Bernard calling to say he is thinking of coming back Thursday or Friday, the hotel is comfortable, the Royal Horticultural Show at Vincent Square was sheer delight, such exquisite blooms, he's fixed to see something truly wonderful by Andrew Lloyd Webber ... but London *on your lonesome* can be a drag.

"Lies," I drone aloud to myself once he's hung up. "Nothing but lies."

Not that what he and Robert get up to bothers me overmuch. I think I prefer animals to people, anyway. Certainly Zero's health and safety feature high on my list. I can't settle till I know where he is. I whistle from the back door and he comes bounding in from the dark of the garden and is the only cat I've ever known to respond in that manner. Otherwise he's a contrary bastard, first rejecting the sardines I offer, then hawking up what looks like a mouse. I give it a prod with a fork. He suffers badly with fur balls and that's what it is, and there it can lie till tomorrow.

I head for the basement. I guess, thanks to Maxine, I feel pretty frustrated. Along with needing a drink, I've a hanky to bag, and the girlies are down there.

CHAPTER 5

Next morning, despite the weather remaining at refrigerator temperatures, I decide I'd better not leave Denzil's salmon in the boot any longer, and I drive to town.

Hobson & Wildsmith, established 1886, bakers, confectioners, chocolatiers, tea-blenders, coffee-roasters, the shop's front window resplendently antique with mahogany shelving, polished brasswork, stone jars of herbs and pickles. Even when combined with self-service, nostalgia sells. The backyard, however, has that unkempt look that most round-the-backs have – grubby, cobwebby, paintwork peeling, a skip overflowing with cartons and rubbish. There's a strong smell of wood smoke.

Mainly it's late-autumn when I have cause to come. Most salmon caught at that time, colloquially known as "back-end", are deemed low in quality, so I generally bring them here to be smoked. For a small surcharge, they also slice and turn out one-pound vacuum-packs that I unload to a guy with a stall on the market, who in turn flogs the stuff to grateful housewives who can't believe that smoked salmon is available so cheaply. Frankly, a high percentage is so beyond its best that I wouldn't even feed it to the cat, but there we go.

Spring fish, conversely – like the prime one I've got for Denzil – are much prized, high in oil content, with a white curd between flakes when cooked. Too good for smoking.

Anyhow, I've said I'll get Denzil's poached whole, and I've been waiting alongside the back door for a couple of minutes when an old Vauxhall van rolls into the yard and two men get out. They're in stained outdoor gear and look useful. Add to this, to put me further on edge, when they open up the van's rear, I can see what I know are net-marks on their pile of at least twenty salmon.

That does it. Hurriedly I occupy myself by inspecting the brickwork and staring at clouds. Only avoiding these guys isn't easy since they're needing the door where I am.

"Let's come by," says the first one. And with short-back-and-sides of yellow-dyed hair, the words "cut here" and a blue dotted line tattooed round his neck, and studs piercing his nose and his ears, he for sure is no Isaak Walton disciple of piscatorial disciplines. He has a fish by the wrist of its tail in each hand, stretching his arms. "What ya gawpin' at, man? Let's have room."

His appearance, and open belligerence if that's what it is, has me stunned for a second. "I've just brought in a salmon," I tell him, smiling in friendly fashion, not wanting him thinking I'm deliberately blocking his way. "They're having it weighed, then I'll get a receipt."

His eyes have shown recognition. "I know ya. I've seen ya afore. Ya fish fly with the big rod an' that."

"That's right. I do sometimes."

"Hold still then," he says, and for Christ's sake, I'm thinking, it's nothing I want my skull caving in for, but in pressing me back against the wall he is making space for his mate to slide by. His pig-bin breath on my face makes me gag. "You can see," he says straightening, "we've a canny few," and he allows me a moment to look appreciative. "You ghillie an' all for the Big House, am I right?"

I nod. "But only if asked. That's why the Right Hon lets me fish free. It's a perk." I can see what he's thinking. "It's only once in a blue moon. I've no truck with the keeper. He can't fucking stand me. He's got eyes like an eagle."

The other guy's stopped to catch what I'm saying. "That keeper's a wizened-eyed arsehole, is that one," he says. Despite the grey day, he's wearing shades that reflect. "And yourself . . . just divvent be taking no car-numbers here either, ya know."

"Not me. I don't care what you catch. Would you sooner I go?"

They exchange knowing looks, then bob their heads. "Aye, that's hit. Why don't you slip roon' the corner an' stay out the way, man?"

No problem, I answer with facial gestures, and make like it's all the same to me – though, of course, sauntering back to my car I'm humiliated. But that's okay, I console myself. Cowards live longer than heroes. The fact is that the bulk of the population simply don't realize that on the river most nights in the dark there's a war going on. These guys when opposed take no prisoners.

Evening comes, by which time the morning's incident has paled to insignificance against how tall I'm walking – and I'm looking good, I reckon. Black woollen jacket, black pants, desert-boots, maroon sweater – although an everyday shabbiness is what people expect of my status, I like to believe I can achieve fair results when I need. Mix-'n'-match. I come in stock-sizes.

For Sanjay, though, it's different. His choices are limited since, while money's no object, it has to be said he is fat. So fat he has trouble in tying his shoelaces – so fat, jokes Maxine, that his sexual activities cannot amount to more than large bowls of popcorn fed to his face before hard-core videos.

Actually, she's wrong on that score; not that I've enlightened her. For me, anyhow, it's enough that he's

bright and perceptive, and the free evenings-out he provides are not to be sneezed at. I'm genuinely pleased
we're teamed up; and, okay, I'll admit to a smidgen of
hypocrisy there because up until Maxine's arrival to whet
his appetite and bring us together he was no more than
the brown-skinned guy I passed on the Miss Betsy's
stairs, and on nodding terms only.

I grab hold of his mobile. "I'll give Maxine a try." I
know that's what he wants; he fancies her madly.

Her mood when she answers is *prickly*. She's doing her
ironing, she says, when I ask if she's busy. "This is the
new Mercedes we're in, not the Peugeot," I tell her. "We
can be outside your door in five minutes."

"Don't you understand English?" she says.

"Be a sport."

"Not tonight. I'm not interested!"

"Do it for *me*."

"For nobody!"

Jesus Christ . . . I hang up. "She's not coming."

"She's perhaps got a date," Sanjay says.

Great! Yet while I feel he should know better than to
upset me with such suggestions, at least I've the consolation of knowing one person she *can't* be seeing. We
are travelling down Tubwell Lane, football country, shop
windows boarded-up, police and no-parking signs
stationed along the road's edge, the night sky above the
ground blazingly illuminated by the City's massive floodlights.

I'm not sure who they're playing but I think Aston
Villa.

Rockcliffe Court's where we land, a converted ivy-walled
manor-house out in the country, elegantly casual, noise,
bustle, expensive smells, a fly-trap for all the best posers,
the bistro's most popular. We order off the blackboard.

Sanjay, permanently dieting, shovels down two kinds of salad, hot rolls and a cartload of garlic bread.

Sure, he's a fatty all right, but a Hindu fatty; for which, come midnight, riding the bullet, feeling the acceleration in the back of my neck, I thank Christ. Abstinence from alcohol is a virtue I rate highly in someone who enjoys showing off to inside-lane traffic like he does.

Arriving safely is a big relief – we glide in along the Wharfside. Haloes around street-lamps suggest frost but there's no shortage of activity – girls in groups, youths in shirt-sleeves, police in pairs or threesomes, with police vans parked handy. I call across to ask who won the match and one copper gives me the thumbs-down.

"Let's not be too late, Sanjay," I say. I don't jog or anything, I've been mixing my drinks and the navarin-of-lamb is repeating on me. "And no gambling again, either. You want to toss money away, then just pass it over."

"I give you my word solemnly, no funny business."

He speaks with forked-tongue. The stupid bastard has become even more hot-brained since his family arranged and announced his engagement and he straightoff picks Annabel's, a raving madhouse that's jammed to the doors, everyone drinking from bottles and cans, tabs of all kinds on sale, the girls displaying, the young guys up on their toes; there's a frightening tension to the atmosphere. As we cruise the three bars, Sanjay flashing his Rolex and offering drinks to any spare birds he recognizes, I don't even like to think that not so long back someone got stabbed to death in the neck right here minding their business.

Darlene!

Through the car windows, the view from the multi-storey is of lights winking distantly beyond the black void of the river like a town seen at night from the sea. Darlene is overweight and wears glasses. I earlier glimpsed the true age of her only by strobe-lighting, and I'm hoping concealment of age via such rapid oscillations is a two-way thing.

The Eagles are playing. Why Sanjay loves music so dated, I don't know. The Merc has a six-speaker system. *Hotel California* playing loudly isn't enough to drown his grunting and panting as up in the front he struggles to wrap his gross weight round Patsy.

Patsy and Darlene! Not my scene: like befriending stray dogs. The big flash car, I suppose, is imparting new proportions to whatever feelings of well-being they have: a tale to tell while sticking on labels, punching holes, soldering circuits, doffing bobbins or whatever it is they do for their bread. My legs ache, the bags beneath my eyes have swollen to where I can squeeze thick folds of them between my fingertips; somewhere in the dim recesses of my head the black DJ is still rapping along with the music he was playing. Darlene works down my zip.

"Look . . ." With fingertips under her chin I ease up her head; she could lollipop for ever and nothing would happen. "I wouldn't."

"You don't want me to?"

"Social diseases. I don't carry rubbers."

"What?" she gasps, handing me off.

"Aw, Gawd . . . my dress!" I hear Patsy complain.

I groan. Up front, Sanjay is signalling premature ejaculation with sounds remindful of the worst of Bernard's snoring – Christ, I sit telling myself, I should have more fucking sense.

I get dropped off at some time after one-thirty. "Hello,

cheeky, you hungry?" I say to the cat on the step and waiting to be let in.

I fill his bowl, but he then needs his back scratching first, though why such attention should coax him into feeding mode remains a mystery. I'm in an even more pensive mood over myself. The night's spilled milk weighs heavy – too much rich food, too much booze, those two stupid tarts. I perhaps should have got laid, but I didn't.

The thought takes me down to my basement. Maxine smiles from the wall.

"Come on, baby, reward me."

At my desk, I flip pages. Alas, not a hope of escape as wife-Linda invades my brain. The insurance job I occupied for some years had occasional treats. At one, "Promotional Hospitality" served as a sanitized description for a company party staged as a carnival around the swimming-pool of a London hotel. All the decorous razzmatazz that modern marketing entails. Lobster. Champagne. Even the ice-cubes had logos inside them. And from a box of mixed face-masks Linda had chosen to be a cute piglet.

"Honk-honk, snort-snort!"

My watch showed past two-thirty. She and a number of others quit dancing, stripped to their underwear and jumped in for a romp. Cigarette-packets and general litter was floating on the floodlit pool, a brilliant blue. Her bra came off. I used a chair-leg to hook it away from some bloke who was wanting to wear it as a hat but she refused to put it back on and instead ran around like a kid at the seaside.

Time didn't change Linda.

Once, returning from a week's absence on a course, I found her sunbathing in the garden, topless, naked but for a skimpy G-string. "It's been such gorgeous weather!" she said. "I've just lazed and lazed." None of which I minded, except she seemed oblivious to lying there with fresh teeth-marks on each of her breasts.

When Linda got crazy for love she got crazy.

Which, God knows, on the home front was an enthusiasm that suited me fine. Oscar and Jenny went for a month in Marbella. She agreed to look after their Labrador dog. Oscar left her some quality grass. She got high, made the dog randy, smeared her crutch with honey, arched herself backwards across a low leather stool to accommodate his rear-end machine-gunning like he did when he phantom-fucked strangers' legs. Not that she managed, though God knows she tried. "Is he anywhere close?" she kept gasping.

I get horny remembering.

Though in those days I didn't; at least not so often. The extent of our inventiveness in trying to satisfy her began leaving me scared. Down in the blackness between us, soft sticky collisions. The absence of urgency, a disinterest in foreplay, an exaggerated muscular tiredness, a lack of sensation, the erection that died while in use.

I suppose I always hoped for sympathy and that she'd get to see the funny side. Only *no fucking joke*. Her tits swinging. All those guys round the pool whistling and clapping, and their wives scowling furiously. You could see all she'd got. Confidence undermined. One's personality under pressure like that.

CHAPTER 6

Stand Alone farm, isolated like the name implies, two centuries of history behind it, the house and outbuildings foreboding, a sort of stockade designed to safeguard livestock and people against the elements. I can't say at what height above sea-level I am, but I can see to the road and its vertical red-and-white poles, the tops of which are to indicate the route in deep snow. The terrain lies on the slant. A few sheep roam free. Four heifers huddle in the only enclosure that has walls still intact. The rusted skeletons of ancient abandoned vehicles and machinery clutter the yard. Hens scatter before me, some with magnificently speckled plumage. Cats, slinking away, glance mistrustfully backwards. On earlier visits I have tried but failed to count the dogs, mostly mongrel-type collies, perhaps ten, barking, dancing frighteningly at the ends of their chains.

There have been offers to buy, Carol's said, but she is hanging on.

Entering the kitchen – "Just this," I say, holding up the dead rabbit by its back legs before draping it across the draining-board.

"One fucking bunny!" scoffs Joey.

"I don't like killing things."

" 'Course you don't," Carol says. "A nice breath of fresh air to give you an appetite, though."

"Look, Mum," says Angela. "Errol's all rosy-cheeked."

"Yes, caught the wind, he has."

"Caught the wind," repeats Angela, and slaps the tablecloth. "There!" she says. "Smack the wind to make him better."

"Two hours for one bloody rabbit!" At twenty-one, it is Joey's way to scoff, plus he has that hard practical side to his nature that is common to many who have contact with the land.

"Take no notice of him," Carol says. "Are your feet cold, Errol, love? Make room for him, Joey, son."

"It'll turn frosty later," I tell her.

"True," she says. "There was a ring last night around the moon."

"Ring round the moon," says Angela, giggling, and does a skip. "Jack Frost coming! Jack Frost coming!"

"That's it, sweetheart. 'The cold wind doth blow and we shall have – ?'"

"'SNOW!'"

"'And what will poor Robin do then – ?'"

"'POOR THING!'"

As Carol laughs and applauds, Joey relieves me of the gun and unused shells. Legally I've no right to be handling a firearm. Moreover, by law, he should be stowing both gun and shells in a lockable place instead of shoving them under the settee.

Miles from nowhere . . . does it matter?

I swill my hands. We sit up. Joey angles sideways so he can keep straight his bad leg. I love this old kitchen where a little muck never hurts and dust and stains have their place. On a massive sideboard of blackened patina, so collectable, an assortment of old pottery and china stands beside what could be Clarice Cliff, while mice of patchwork colours endlessly cavort behind the glass front of an ornate doll's house. Joey's pets. Cat-food when they get too many.

Cold, tinned tongue, baked beans, ketchup, white pre-sliced bread, margarine straight from the tub. I have my tea black. The goat's name is Sally. Her milk is too thick and strong for me. The lights are on because the nights are still closing in early.

It is a grand bit of luxury having the electricity, Carol has told me. In the beams remain hooks where oil-lamps once hung, and perhaps for hams too.

With eating done, Joey is already shaved; they make him smarten himself if they know I am due. When he pulls on his tan dealer-boots and shapeless Harris Tweed jacket, he has only to wet his comb and slick down his hair to be ready for the off.

A little blood has dribbled from the rabbit's nostrils to dot the floor tiles. "Old Ben Allsop don't mind 'em," he says. "So long as he can see its head first and know it's not myxied."

Picking up the rabbit, he is palming the folded twenty-pound note I've laid beside it. "Have a nice time," Carol says, as he leaves, and straightway comes the barking and yelping of dogs. He must've tossed them the rabbit.

Four miles down the track the village has more pubs than shops. We hear the car splutter to life. An old Ford Cortina.

"Will we all have a drink?" Carol says.

We will.

Carol pours. Her piles of old records, acquired mostly from car-boot sales for which she's a passion, add to a house already bursting. She lifts the lid of the radiogram, a veneered monstrosity, not stereo, and its front grille and dials light up green. A collage of Elvis cut-outs is stuck to the lid's underside.

"'Love Me Tender', the tune takes me back," she says, and it is the way of her that more of her brogue is evident now she is openly drinking, and she begins a slow shimmy, her eyes closed, a cigarette lazily dangling from her lower lip. She has stacked her selections on the auto-play.

She says, "Did you know what I wanted before I came over? To be a singer. I used to be all in demand for the Country and Western but I missed my chance. The men, of course, are after one thing only and will tell you anything."

"You're a fine looking woman."

"Sure, I belong cutting peat."

We sway, her head on my shoulder. After a while, as has happened before, the scratches on the records cease to irritate. The fire is stoked high and, with only the corner-light switched on, we have around us on the walls the dappled light and shadows from the flames leaping up the chimney-back. Carol, owning a grip gained from hard work, can be ruthlessly firm when she wants. "A present from your mammy," she says, guiding my hand. She is without bra or vest and has nipples like medals. "I'll let this down too" – releasing the tresses of her thick natural-red hair, then wrestling with her skirt. "Angela, dance with him, darling, this zip is a bugger."

Angela shyly comes forward. "You smell nice," I say.

Shuffling within the circle of my arms, she has no natural rhythm. "I have the last of it on," she says.

"I've got what you asked for in the car," I tell her.

"Is it more seeds?" she asks. Out in the yard old faded seed-packets fixed to the tops of garden canes flutter in the wind: promises not delivered. A small handmade cross marks the grave of some lamb she once nursed.

"No . . . jelly-babies," I tell her.

Carol rejoins us. Sometimes I kiss one, then the other. No regrets as I sway in a haze where everything is seem-ingly reaching me a second too late. "Hey there, you with the stars in your eyes . . .'" Carol croons, then breaking off, "Darling," she says, "check your water," and Angela moves away, tipsily stumbling but steadying herself against the sink as she tests at the tap. "Ow, shit," she says, "with that blaze it's red hot."

"Right, wait while I nip for a wee-wee," says Carol.

Coming with lapses in concentration, caused by the drink, Carol's one false front-tooth slips down a fraction to expose a gap at the gum. She says, "Living out here as we are, you're a tonic. Wonderful rich. Never one to be mean with a girl. Such a lovely motor."

She means *my* Peugeot . . . borrowed as usual from Sanjay, his second car.

"I've Joey," she says; "he's a good lad at heart but gets under my feet and is too big to smack." She keeps me silent with an outstretched hand. "Would you do that for me?"

"Do what?"

"Sure. Someone like you. You could find him a job."

"What in town?"

"He's no cripple."

"It's a forty mile drive."

"We've the car that runs."

She's perhaps taking advantage, I guess. She'll know that I owe her. I live in her debt. She restoreth me. Not just her nakedness, nor the lewdness of her; not just the stimulus of her attentions nor the sensation of being possessed through the sheer weight of her pinning me to the settee, but I have at the back of all that the promise of a short white linen nightdress with bows at the neck, and even better is the feeling of being neither in the present nor the past but pleasurably, drunkenly, floating at a point in anticipation where memories of damp perfumed skin, moistened lips, and moaning submissions skip through my mind.

Comes the bang on the ceiling.

"Did you hear?"

I don't move. "What, the wind?"

"No, that's her out of her water. She's just knocked."

"Am I under your power?"

"Yes, you are."

"Your poor slave?"

"That you are."

Sometimes, having heard Joey return, I wonder if one of these nights I'll come downstairs and he'll destroy me with some cutting remark. But no . . . the fire has burned to embers, he has the television turned to some horror epic, the empty trays of a takeaway are lying by his armchair.

"I hear you're looking for a job?" My words hang as he stares vacantly. Once, very young and on a farm visit with Uncle Lewis, I was persuaded to let a small hungry calf suck my thumb and was amazed by the power of it. Joey, the day I came on him in one of the sheds, merely grinned lewdly, keeping hold of the calf's-head . . . a bovine blowjob, so-to-speak. The recollection doesn't fill me with enthusiasm for having anything extra to do with him.

" . . . a job?" I repeat.

"There are none," he says.

"I can't promise."

"Doing what?" he says.

"Probably just lifting and that. I know someone who might have an opening."

"How much?" he says.

"You'd need to travel."

"I could do it," he says.

"Leave it with me."

I am as far as the door.

"Know anybody who wants to buy a goat?" he says.

"Not offhand," I say.

Outside is a ring round the moon. I look back from closing the tubular-framed gate and the buildings are silhouettes against the skyline, the kitchen window lit up like a yellow eye. No lies, Carol said at my first visit and had a saved *Northern Gazette* to show me, the farm pictured, the report detailing that her husband, locked in the barn and with tourniquet of baling-wire applied, had castrated himself with the old type of sheep-shears, then jumped from a beam with his head in a noose. She said, "The other who answered the advert you saw, he never came back once I told him. A poor widow-man like yourself. But then sure he was never romantic like you. Just an old baldie fella."

I start down the track on full beam. I have an hour's drive ahead. It wouldn't do to get stuck up here. The two bags of jelly-babies I brought with me for Angela remain on the fascia. Peckish and opening one up, I try not to dwell on noticing myself in the window.

We are what we are. I try to be honest.

I was not here as Heathcliff.

But then, anyone, I would submit, is an acquired taste at best. In my early teens, when summoned to have words on my progress and future, Uncle Lewis's secretary would ring the house with my interview time. I'd catch a bus to the factory, then be kept waiting until a moment was found to slip me in.

"Errol, that hair-cut of yours . . .? That jacket . . .? I thought your Aunt Milly bought you a blazer and tie?"

Mostly when he complained about me, I would stay silent and remember he suffered with piles and had to wipe his arse with cottonwool. Such knowledge, I found, could offset his remarks.

He said, "I know that in growing up you believe everything comes on a plate. But it doesn't. The world doesn't spin – it's assisted."

He had a mannerism when talking of tapping his lips with the ends of his fingers, thus giving the impression of words being chosen with care, the sifting of knowledge of years. Reality was that he smoked too many fags and was concealing poor breathing.

"Why do you think we succeed here? Why do you think people look up to me?"

Wages, I thought. Any fool could have told him.

He continued, "Believe me, fate's no sportsman. Little fish don't get thrown back to swim another day. People, one way or another, are educated to fit into the scheme of things."

I thought possibly he was right. I could even appreciate he set great store by our little chats, this ritual of passing on the façade that had been indelibly painted on him at an early age. Only I wasn't much interested in the scheme of things, or what was good for me. At school, it was enough to satisfy my immediate ambitions that I was on the football team.

"Have you done as I asked?"

"What? Yes. Almost."

"You've had the brochure a fortnight. Don't you read ever?"

"I read lots."

"Yes, I've seen. Don't you dare let your Aunt Milly see ... The shops shouldn't sell them. Magazines like that in my day were retouched."

He'd been snooping again. Apart from fitting a lock, there was no way of keeping him out. I said, "This place in the brochure looks a long way away."

"Not at all. I'd been boarding for years at your age." His brow furrowed. "You do follow all this, don't you? A bold step in a new direction?" He was alluding, of course, to my family background, the cross that he'd indirectly acquired through marrying Aunt Milly. He said, "All that fuss and commotion last night. Your aunt doesn't mean half she says when she's shouting at me like she does."

My laugh was as phoney as his.

"Off you go, then," he said. "I've this business to run. Love at home. Tell Aunt Milly I'm here holding the fort if she asks."

Needing a drink, he was starting to tremble; hence my hurried dismissal.

I got up to go. I recall I thought things looked bad.

CHAPTER 7

Bernard lands back late Friday. My usual treat is that he brings me an *Evening Standard*. He knows I believe it's the tenor of London life that dictates what happens up here in the North. But this time he says he forgot, then complains I've no bread in. After six days of having the bed to myself, I don't get much sleep.

Then next morning, bold as brass, Robert comes sailing round. Long time no see, he warbles, meaning the two of us, at which Bernard says, "How lovely to see you. Stay for lunch. I've brought back some new seed catalogues you might like to look at."

Of course the whole charade is pure bullshit. So if there's any irritation at all in my pig-in-the-middle role, it's that I know they must realize I'm aware of what's going on. At no time has Bernard made any secret of his homosexuality. In fact, at the time when I first introduced Robert to him he had as a regular friend a student named Tony, sapling slim, shoulder length hair, and with the longest of legs he somehow fed into the tightest of jeans. So the oddest part in the whole can of worms, perhaps, is that in all the years of knowing Robert, and with him being married to Tina, I never once got the idea that he might nurture a fancy for blokes, though even there I'm somewhat jumping the gun, because exactly what his and Bernard's relationship is I'm not wholly clear. I mean, they're obviously closer than close, but I haven't a clue about who might do what to whom, if at all.

*

Fussily handing Robert a six-pack of Carlsbergs he's had stashed away, Bernard says, "Since you're staying for lunch, leave me be, let me cook!"

We obey, heading away to the living-room.

Nowadays, to some extent, I'm reluctant to get stuck with Robert. Still, as we talk he keeps nestling his beer between his feet like a penguin nursing its egg, and the fact he can do stuff like that around me without feeling self-conscious is indicative that a kind of ease between us still persists – an ease, I suppose, that comes from knowing each other's histories over such a long time.

"How's Tina?" I ask. "Any better?"

"Up and down," he says bravely. "She's a fighter, God bless her."

I take a quick swig of beer; there's a bite to its coldness. Tina, let's face it, is *doomed*.

Robert says, "You and me, we've had a few good benders in our time . . . all that home-brew we used to sup, eh? Lunatic's broth! Linda made those hot vegetable curries, remember?"

"Yeah . . . with mango."

"Sure. Yeah, those are the days that won't ever come back. We could do with some rain."

"For the river?"

He smiles. "For the garden."

Our eyes come together, drift apart, come together, drift apart. We sip our drinks. The cottage in Devon that we all shared for an August fortnight, the seven of us – what year was that? he says, and we bite our lips and crease our foreheads over trying to remember. Tina's legs had become too weak for swimming by then, he reminds me. "Linda had that wee red bikini," he says. "Christ, she had some super figure. Jesus, remember her performance of putting her face on every morning?" His eyes glaze in thought. "Shit, was that the time you had that fist-fight with Oscar?"

"I should've murdered the cock-happy bastard."

"Funny bloke. I often wonder . . . you'd have thought me and Tina would have heard from her."

"From Linda? A bit late for postcards."

"I meant Christmases. Still, a clean break . . . Would we know her . . . young Daisy as well? Christ, what would she be now?"

"Nineteen coming up?"

"Nineteen!" He shakes his head at the impact of it. "You turn round and where does it go? Time flies. You ever see the police again about that?"

I'm taken unawares; shocked, even. "You mean *recent*?"

He twists his face at the unimportance of it, shrugs, then swigs the last of his beer in one go and helps himself to another can.

The salad-and-surprise concocted by Bernard reveals itself as a quiche chock-full of nuts, broccoli, raisins, and other health-giving nutrients. "Compliments to the chef," Robert says. "Nicely crunchy but textured, Errol, don't you think?"

I don't answer. He's dismayed me enough for one day.

Eating done, they decide they'll wash up. They decline my offer of help. Suits me fine. I escape to the basement.

"Oh, I say, look at her!"

She's a good looking girl. I've poured and swallowed a generous nip. But just for a second I find myself stuck with examining my own predilections. Except should I care? Up in the kitchen *touchee-touchee* is probably on the agenda, and that's *carte blanche* of a sort. Anyway, I know from a lifetime of getting tense that jacking-off blows the mind. Only right now I *can't* . . . I *can't* because I am seeing Maxine at Denzil's tonight and I've a rule that applies: *stay-on-heat-be-prepared* – which should make me laugh. If my and Maxine's genitals touched, pigs would fly and shit gold dust!

Yet I'm not sure that's funny. Times like now, having knocked back a couple, I have difficulty in reconciling the ache I feel for her with the common-sense knowledge that people seldom tell the truth about what they get up to. I mean, I don't. Not that I have grounds to disbelieve her celibacy claim but the likelihood is I'm a fool to myself.

I sit sharpening my gaff.

It's a movement that hones my mind, taking me back to the night before last. I was at Baydale ford. A thaw in the Dales had brought a slight rise in level but I was okay in wellies. I had on the long coat. Palm-and-needle stitched by me, its concealed inside-pockets provide ample room for gaff and lamp, both items weighted to sink without trace should emergencies warrant. Round my neck was the dog-lead. If a posse of fishery-bailiffs should show, I'm a pitiful man. "Have you seen my lost dog?" It might save my skin; who can say?

Midnight: I count the church clock's chimes carrying on a south-west wind. No bailiffs here unless lying low with their night-vision glasses, but I err towards caution and wait a further ten minutes before scaling the gate at its hinge – nothing rattles. Then from there it's a fifteen-yard paddle to get to the sluice. My turbulent hot-spot. The lamp isn't needed. Every so often at my feet is that extra swirl of iridescence caused by big fish moving through. I have the hook of the gaff razor-sharp. Crouch, wait, shine, hoike what's lit up. No greed. No wholesale slaughter. Three or four springers dropped off for hard cash at some needy hotel.

Fat chance. A light winks on the left bank below. Just black silhouettes: I could see three or four figures, plus one wading across in the process of stretching a sweep bank-to-bank, and too late by then for evasive retreat. The only route back was the way I'd come out.

"Howway, hinnie! We guessed it was you."

Their second net was a waiting mound on the concrete apron. No lights were used. Like twin fucking terrorists. Combat-jackets and full-face balaclavas with slits for the nose, mouth and eyes.

But ignore the disguises: these were the pair I'd had words with at Hobson & Wildsmith's.

The podgy one circled around me. "He has nowt," he said.

"I've not even started. There's lots of fish running through."

This, my companionable offering to share, earned me a thump on the shoulder. "We're not fucking blind," said the tall one. "Maybies you're crackers. Maybies I've even a good mind to clash yor fuckin' jaw an' all." He then grabbed my lamp, which was fifty quids' worth. "Haad yer gob, divvent argue. I warned you before but you think yorsell clever? No messing . . . just divvent come back or I'll hammer youse nex' time. This is wor spot, all right?"

Wrong, bird-brain.

Sitting here, whisky talks, I know that. Yet trekking back up the lane I could make out their van clear as day. Fucking toe-rags. I'm telling you straight they are asking for trouble, not bothering to hide it.

Shit!

I now can't help but curse. I've suddenly realized I should've switched on and been listening in. These intercoms are what first put me wise to Bernard and Robert. So Christ knows but over the past half an hour I've probably missed out on hearing all sorts being said behind my back – which highlights the trouble with alcohol. You drink to forget and you forget too much. Worse, in disengaging the mind's ratchet one risks the confusion of subjects cross-fusing, one thought disgorging another.

For instance, death is well on its way for poor Tina; and, as sure as petals must fall, with her gone – "We would like you to leave" – I will get shown the door.

"Jesus, Maxine," I whisper, "if that happens, what will I do?"

And silly, really, I suppose, since there's no one down here but me, that I should feel the need to keep my voice lowered. Except that a man of my age who talks to a photograph is an embarrassment even to himself. Plus it pays to be careful.

"Jesus, Maxine, here's the absolute truth – I would sooner be dead than go back on the road."

The evening arrives, and with it Denzil's housewarming party.

Pseudo-pseudo, gilt-edged invitations, RSVP, seven-thirty onwards, fairy-lights in the bushes when we arrived, repro' coach-lamps illuminating a front knocker resembling the one gracing Durham cathedral. If it costs, it must be good taste, that's Denzil's yardstick, Terri like-wise. They've been here a month: overlooking the river, 4 Tyne View Meadows is their new "four-bedroomed luxury residential executive-style dwelling" – which, roughly translated, classifies it as neo-Georgian with a dash of American Colonial thrown in. Some architect's dream or nightmare.

The tour's obligatory. Sanjay and I come down from where we've counted seven types of artificial houseplants in the upstairs loo. The toilet-roll lives in its own knitted holder.

Thank God, meat!

I try the beef, slightly rare, with a salty wetness to it; especially good when you don't get it often. Sanjay declines my suggestion that he should try the salmon. Its length is displayed on a metre-long salver, its laid-back skin exposing the succulence of browny-pink flesh enhanced by slices of cucumber, tomato, kiwi fruit and sliced roasted almonds. Hobson & Wildsmith know their business; at a price, that is.

Both main downstairs rooms are in use, upwards of forty people mingling as they do at such shindigs and I'm not one bit surprised that a sameness of mould applies to so many – the Small Businesses Club, the Chamber of Commerce, the Free Enterprise wolf-pack, and so on. Denzil across by the fireplace has one such group cor-ralled, his hands semaphoring the shit he'll be talking.

"In the land of the blind, the one-eyed man is king," says Sanjay.

"Where else does credibility matter?" I answer.

We grin at how smart we are. I'm on scotch. He's on orange.

I switch topics. The guy heavy-breathing on Maxine at the far side of the room is starting to get on my nerves. He's got curls at his neck and a bad-boy-look face and is here only because he works for the landscape gardening outfit that supplied the shrubs and fancy pink patios of the Tyne View housing development. We're in jackets and ties; he's in tee-shirt and jeans. "How old do you think he is?"

"Twenty-five," says Sanjay. "No, make that twenty-three."

I shake my head in dismay. "Seen the bull-neck on him? He must do weight-training. Jesus, he's nearly as brown as you are. He's even got a bloody earring."

"He goes to Lonnigan's quite often," Sanjay answers. "I've seen him. He's an excellent dancer, you know."

Great! He'll be telling me next the guy's hung like a horse.

"How's Joey doing?" He looks blank and I have to remind him. "Joey. He's the lad from the farm where I shoot rabbits sometimes."

He nods, remembering. "Yusef owed me a favour. I left it to him."

Yusef, known to me only by name, owns a discount-furniture warehouse on the new industrial estate. Joey's been there a week, sweeping-up, general labouring, being paid cash-in-hand to avoid insurance and tax. Carol was impressed I could fix something like that.

It's not one of those parties with music and there's nobody standing idle who looks worth mingling with. So I'm stuck with waiting for Maxine to be left on her own and straightaway head to her side when it happens. "We've hardly spoken. He looked like he wanted to eat you."

"Who did?" she says. "You mean Kelvin? Can't I talk to people now, is that it?"

Her little black number has a round-necked singlet top, and a skirt slightly flared, its hem midway up her thighs. Add black stockings, flat chest, small-bud nipples, long legs that have knobbly knees, and the effect is teenage, athletic, incredibly sensual.

"This man is an air-raid warden," I intone. "Please lie down and do exactly as he tells you."

"God . . ." she groans, "do you have to?"

"Sorry," I tell her. "I see you're wearing the earrings." I use a finger to set one swaying.

"They're fantastic! I was going to say thank you later."

"They were meant for tonight. You will have a drink with Sanjay and me, won't you? Don't leave it too late. Sanjay's not staying long."

Her gaze is a minnow darting all over. "Maxine?" I wave a hand in her face to regain her attention. "I was meaning when Sanjay's gone, *I'll be stuck*. You could give me a lift."

"Oh, could I?"

I don't labour the point. I can see Kelvin coming back with two plates piled with salmon. I pat her arm as I leave so he'll see my mark's on her. I don't think she likes it. He, for sure, doesn't notice.

Back with Sanjay, I find he's been joined by Karen and Paula, and that Terri is hovering. "Me and Paula tried your salmon," Karen says, as I come up to them. "It goes lovely with salad."

"Waldorf, with nuts in," Terri corrects, closing the gap. She's shoe-horned into what I guess is a size ten when she must be a fourteen. To me she says, "I was asking Denzil how much we owed you. He said not to worry."

I can afford to smile, knowing that without providing the fish I wouldn't have been invited and that I've already looted the shop-till to cover above what I got charged by Hobson & W.

"Listen, tubby . . ." I give Paula a prod, "you're the last person to be packing the calories away."

"Oh, I know. I'm a wreck."

Some wreck. "Are you still doing time on the sun-bed?" I ask.

That's her cue. First comes the dimpling of cheeks and the hovering-bird eyelashes before she draws up her top while edging her waistband six inches downwards, exposing the contrast that confirms she is tanned. Sometimes she goes so far as to show pubic curls but lately she's mentioned having a bikini-line done along with getting her legs waxed, and she's baby-smooth. That's except for her stretch-marks, and why these faint concertina-like ripples should excite me so much, I don't know, but they do. I wouldn't mind testing them out with my lips.

Terri meantime, wanting to be the centre of attention, has been soliciting praise for the house. "A very handsome property," Sanjay says, and I don't hold it against him that he's so *outwardly* chummy with both her and Denzil – that's *business* – and, anyway, he's privately got her true number. For example, to quote how unsavoury she can sometimes be: "If I had my way all blacks would be made to swim back where they came from carrying Asians like him on their shoulders." When she shows her true racist nature like that, she can really back-stab with the best of them.

"We skipped the main bedroom," I tell her.

"The chains and the mirrors, eh?" Her hands are raised and fluttering, sending a half-hundredweight of market-stall gold sliding up and down her arm. "Fuck me!" – she's addressing us all and is alcoholically beyond the point of forgetting she's *not* got a Liverpool accent. "Fuck me, last night Denzil said, 'Get dolled up, our kid, let's christen this place.' You should've seen, I was in the black basque, all the gear and everything. Wham-bam! I nearly had to call this do off. God, we had a right good session."

Amusement is what she expects. Envy, too.

"He was out of the shower. I was towelling him dry. Kneeling down, you know, like, *I was doing the business*. I went, 'Go ahead, come all over my face.' He said, 'Sweet, are you sure, I've been gone over three days.' I said, 'Great, let it shoot!'"

Listening to and watching her, I find it easy to assume that in the cold light of late-at-night she must often get the screaming horrors realizing that in relating such crap she's no spring-chicken any more. Her age and looks simply no longer go with her stories. For sickeners there's one tale she tells that I can't take at all – what she calls "Golden Rain". I mean, who'd want to be pissed on by Denzil?

"That woman!" Sanjay says – it's just a while later and Terri and the others have drifted. "She gives no refunds. That clock-radio she sold me from the shop. I paid cash, no VAT. It won't work. The little red light won't come on."

I sympathize. I shouldn't really. Where else does a lot of the Miss Betsy junk come from but via his sources? Ralph Lauren belts! Benetton sweatshirts! Reebok trainers! Chanel perfumes! All identical to genuine in most ways except knockdown prices.

Ten o'clock. The party's swollen to a crush bigger than any number of friends and acquaintances I'd have imagined Denzil might have. Sanjay is booked on an early flight to Lisbon and is leaving early to get a night's sleep. He tells me that as part of a round-trip he is arranging to see Mustapha in Istanbul and Fakrou in Hamburg, these being two guys he does business with and who I know through sitting in on free meals and such when they're here in the UK.

So he leaves, and alone to do as I like I make a quick search for Maxine, who appears to be missing.

There's some noise from the conservatory; I look in there and the source of entertainment seems to be that Denzil, despite the cold night but aided by being three-quarters drunk, has started a barbecue on the outside concrete. "Built this little beauty with my own two hands," he says, seeing me. He pours on more fuel. There's lots of smoke but not much glow.

"Almost got it that time, Jumbo-bobs!" Terri's act comes over like she's breast-feeding him in public, as if she's his surrogate mother. To me, she mutters, "Let him be . . . give him a chance for his fun."

That's asking too much. "You've got the design wrong, Denzil," I call out. "You forgot the updraught."

She glares.

"Now what are you on about?" he says, and he's putting on his blase accent. Sausages and burgers are piled ready for cooking. "He never misses a chance to run me down, this man," he announces to all those who are waiting. "Corporal Errol. Not one of the chaps, not one of the chaps! Should've been in my platoon. I'd have shown him a thing or two. Left-right, left-right."

"It's all right, never mind, precious lamb," Terri soothes.

Moving away, I take a look in the kitchen, but no sign of Maxine there, either. As I use the back door, a couple of snobby-faced women eye me disdainfully as though offended I'm shooting outside for an *al fresco* piss. Well, fuck you, ladies.

I start along the line of cars. Maxine's little Fiat is gone, as is the builder's pick-up truck. Paula emerges while I'm staring up the road. She doesn't ask what's going on. "Lift?" she offers.

We walk along to where she's left her mother's car. I climb in beside her. "The last supper, that was," she says. "Strictly duty."

I grunt in agreement. Even though dropping me off at Lambton Spa isn't going to take her out of her way, I feel obliged to make like I'm grateful. The car warms up. She's not saying much and we've travelled as far as the ring-road where the sodium lamps are lighting up the car's interior before I begin to appreciate how aware of her I am. Her extreme youthfulness keeps washing over me, though annoyingly I can't name her perfume. It could be her hair-spray. "Paula, this body-beautiful chit-chat we indulge in," I tell her, "don't go imagining I think you need to lose weight."

"Yes, I do."

"No, you don't."

"Well, I do."

"No, you don't. You're not fat."

She says, "Who's talking fat?"

I suck at the hint. She's helping me on with a nod and a grimace. Often at work she'll present like she's regarding me as an elder brother or her father: some wise old owl. "Jesus, Paula, you're kidding? Christ, how?"

"How?" She starts a laugh that falls flat. "How'd you think? Anyhow, no question about it, me and my friend, Louise, have done loads of tests from the chemist's."

Being a chatterbox at any time, she has no trouble in unburdening herself. It's her boyfriend who's to blame for not taking precautions, she says, only he's one slob she has no intention of marrying since as well as being unemployed he can't stand little Andy, her toddler. She is particularly not looking forward to breaking the news to her parents, this being her second time round, so to speak, and what's so unfair is she knows from before what her doctor will say. "He's a member of *Life*. That's the rumour. He's so *unsympathetic*."

"Jesus, this boyfriend . . . you've been to bed with him once?"

"Twice actually." She has big doe-like eyes that do her great service. "I forgot to tell you about the other time," she says.

"Christ, there's people who try for years. Stick a tongue in your ear and you click straight off. You upset?"

"Just a bit really," she says, and slants a glance. "Not like you, though. Did you have something planned?"

"You mean Maxine? She's hopeless. What time did she leave?"

"No idea."

We take a sharp bend; she nervously misses a gear, and perhaps I've been misled by what I've read as her coquettishness in peeping from under half-lowered eyelids; but, no matter, I'm placing my hand on her knee, although naturally, if needs be, I'm poised to claim the happening as a backfired joke; except she turns her head from the road – again those big almond eyes – holding the pose for a moment before, still steering, she leans sideways to coincide with my doing the same so our lips brush together.

"Make up for tonight with me if you like," she says quietly.

I'm not sure whether to laugh or what. I rub at the windscreen.

"Don't, you'll make it all smudgy," she says, and reaches knowledgeably to a switch on the dash and a fan starts to hum. "Little Andy's round at my mum's. I'm all on my own till I take the car back. You know, *Friday night* . . . I don't mind a kiss and a cuddle. In fact, to be honest, right at this minute I feel really deprived."

CHAPTER 8

Monday comes. I'm working. There's no sign of Sol awaiting a handout as I get to the shop. That's a worry. No sense, though, in fretting. Whatever his poison he'll be sleeping it off, either down the Black Hole, cardboard city, the Five Arches, or somewhere similarly gruesome.

I open up. Footsteps at intervals break the silence of the arcade. Eventually, thank God, comes the familiar clack-clack of Maxine's approach. She comes in and it's the silk scarf round her neck that grabs me right off. "Nice scarf!"

Bright as a button, she quips back, "You should know since you chose it."

Shit! I've bought her so much I've lost track.

Upset that I've let myself down, I start pricing tee-shirts – £2.99 each, they will bleed in the wash but so what?

She pours herself coffee, settles at her desk, carefully crossing long legs, and holding a cigarette at the tips of slender fingers with nails shaped and varnished red casually exhales smoke while cocking her head on one side to regard how I'm watching from the corner of my eye. "Are you in one of your huffs?"

"The word *huff*," I respond with some vigour, "is not in my vocabulary."

"It means you're *sulking*."

"You enjoy Friday night?"

"So-so. I left early."

"You were giving me a lift."

"Was I?"

"I looked *everywhere*."

The insinuation is heavy but she replies with no hesitation, "That Kelvin something-or-other, I went home with him."

Clever, dumb, or honest? She's given me a three-way choice.

She says, "Can you believe it? He's got a flat on Woodlands Road. I went to meet his tarantula!" She raises her eyebrows at my uncertain glance. "God's honour!" she says. "He spent all night talking about nothing else. What a drag! A pet in a cage, it's his favourite person! All furry with legs! He let it walk up his arm. It sat there and spat till he soothed it. They've got lousy tempers. I was in bed by ten. I watched the end of a film on TV with my mother."

While she's giving me a moment to picture how it was, I consider how nonplussed I am. Jesus, it's always the same when I've steeled myself for catching her out – I've spent all weekend part-suffering, part-enjoying conjuring up images of her being fucked on a rug. One of these days my head will explode.

She shrugs. "All right, think what you like," she says, and moves to allocate the float's different coins to their slots in the till. I reach out as she passes and tweak her scarf lower. "God, really," she drones, "was that necessary?"

I've time to notice her neck is unmarked; not a bite nor a blemish. "Football," I say quickly, looking to jolt her elsewhere. "How's our superstar friend? They lost again, eh?"

"He scored twice though."

I detect something extra. "You've seen him?"

"Why else should my legs ache?"

I was a fool to ask.

"Yesterday, we were up at Arkengarthdale. Walking."

"Sunday? Jesus, it drizzled all day."

"We had coats. All those stone walls and sheep. It was brilliant." She's keen to share the experience. "You've no idea what it's like for him to get free of people. We went into a cafe for tea and two young boys recognized him for his autograph. It was ever so funny."

"His wife and kids . . ." I'm being heavily sarcastic, "you took them with you?"

"Malta. They're there, sunning. It was a really nice day. We just talked and walked."

I turn away to conceal my face. A fresh delivery of biscuits needs splitting. Bankruptcy stock that Denzil's bought for a song. Surprise-surprise, the sell-by dates have expired! Mister Superstar drives an expensive flash Audi which she says he gets free. I slash at a carton. You could easily take someone's head off with one of these blades. Arkengarthdale is deserted, wild, rugged country. Arkengarthdale with *her* in a big warm cosy car on a drizzly, freezing-cold afternoon . . .?

Jesus, I don't know what to think, I really don't.

Being Monday, we're busier than normal. Market-day come round again is the time when the dalesfolk hit town, most of them easy to spot, the women long-striding and capable-faced, like they have the ability to milk cows, deliver overdue lambs and make splendid jam; and for *him* the common uniform of cord trousers, soiled waxed-jacket, brogues, work-engrained hands.

At least I've the consolation that a fortuitous spin-off from finding Joey a job is that since he needs their old banger for getting to work I've no longer the worry that Carol and Angela might show. They are safely marooned in the back-of-beyond, though in earlier times I had to live with the fear that should they ever have walked through the door to espy me in my true colours I would have had little option but to lock myself in the lavatory and cut my throat.

I serve one or two people. Some sales I ring in, some I don't – I make a few quid. The day drags.

Except *surprise*! I get home at six and find Bernard's skipped his afternoon at work and used the time to shift his plants from my bedroom and out to the greenhouse and cold-frames. "Hardening off," he grunts.

So what else should I feel but overwhelmed? No more his snoring, no more his bad breath if he rolls to face me, no more his hand in his sleep on my leg.

So appreciatively I first offer to make cheese-on-toast, I then add, "Black clouds outside: your garden might get some much-needed rain later."

"Oh, yes, really?" he drawls. "And I suppose you get your weather forecasts off the back of the cornflakes, do you? No toast for me, either."

In returning outside, he slams the door, the windows shake. Jesus, I should butcher the bastard while he sleeps . . . and yet again I dwell on this thought as I take my cheese-on-toast to my room, where Zero, never slow on the uptake, has already found his old spot by the radiator. "Cheeky boy!"

With a sigh, I flop out. It feels good to be back. There's a dampness to the mattress which will pass, plus a scattering of compost which I'll hoover a bit when I'm more in the mood, though I probably won't. Last year's rat is under the bed when I roll to feel for it. Supermarket bought, and nothing more substantial than fur stuffed with dried cat-nip, but Zero, catching the scent, is up and beside me in a couple of pounces, then purrs contentedly, lying on his back, rat's head nipped in his mouth, his rear legs working hard at its body, claws out, disembowelling. "Cheeky boy!" He loves his rat.

"Good grief, you might at least have taken your shoes off!"

I'm caught red-handed with Bernard unblinkingly considering the audacity of my misdemeanour from the doorway. He deliberately waits till I've swung my legs clear of the bed. He says, "That was Robert on the phone. They've admitted poor Tina. She was watching some programme and just went unconscious."

"Christ, that's awful."

"I'd better pop round to see him."

"Yes, you go."

"Yes, I will. Shall I say you're *concerned*?"

Such nastiness is unnecessary, I wish Tina no harm – far from it – but I hold my tongue, wanting him gone. Then when he has, I remain fearful that the bastard might sneak back to catch me. It means I need to wait for the sounds of his car moving away before I return to being comfortable, only am again immediately forced upright as Zero starts to cough, head well forward to extend his neck, hawking up more of his fur-balls and swallowing them back. He might even be on the point of being sick. Perhaps roundworms: a pile of vomit that writhes like Medusa's head is not a pretty sight on a duvet.

Life's a bitch. I lie there thinking it over. What if Tina has come to her end? How secure should I feel, if at all?

CHAPTER 9

Next day as I head out through the town centre to buy lunch, shoppers thronging the High Street are lightly clad for the time of year. More like mid-spring than February. An elderly man wearing massive boots is playing the Northumbrian pipes in Mothercare's doorway. Outside House of Fraser, two young men are touching up pastels pre-drawn on large squares of paper which they've sellotaped to the pavement. Not *real art*: strictly romanticized subjects for suckers to ogle: nothing like the values and emotions expressed in my copy of *World's Famous Paintings*. Their begging-bowl, nonetheless, is doing good business. I'm reminded I stopped at the bank moments back. I use my hand to check that the withdrawal I made remains safe in my pocket.

Enclosed by iron railings, the Dene lies further on. At its front, the big stone with metal ring attached, according to a plaque, is where some local Quaker bigwig used to tie up in his horse before the motor-car came.

Once inside, I choose the first bench I come to. There's not much to look at beyond an assortment of trees and some grass where the crocuses are spearing through, though the open space brings recognition of a sky of watery blue and air sufficiently cold to condense my breath. I can hear the buses rumbling by. Women avoid here at nights. By the litter bin an elderly man is feeding bread to an assortment of shabby pigeons. Some have rings on their legs to identify them as racers-gone-wild.

The used puffed-up crisp packets blowing free are from sniffing.

After which, possibly it's my imagination but on seeing Paula coming I could swear she is already walking with feet splayed outwards. She sits down, laying on me a sad schoolgirl-smile as she apologizes for getting delayed. I make an unconcerned gesture and stare at my shoes. She's so close I can feel the warmth coming off her. "Firstly," I mumble, "I just want to repeat I'm sorry about the other night."

"Don't be," she says. "I told you . . . what for? I'm not."

The pigeon-man crumples his empty paper-bag and gives us a call: "Not so cold today!"

I offer him a cordial wave as he potters towards the exit. "Why are English people so obsessed with the weather? Why are the English so utterly fucking boring about it?"

Paula's lost for an answer, she's got more pressing problems.

"You said *Leeds*, right?" I say, getting down to business.

"Just an initial examination," she answers. "An interview really."

"Right. And in here?" I tap the side of my head. "You're at ease? No regrets, no fears? You don't feel you're losing something important, a part of yourself?"

"Me? No, nothing."

I think I'm satisfied but first look left and right to be sure no one's watching before I slide my hand into my inside pocket: we could be spies passing secrets. She's a bit embarrassed over taking the envelope. "You don't have to do this, you know, but I'm ever so grateful. Don't think I'll ever forget this," she says.

We talk some more but without saying much, then agree I'll leave first. And why we feel we should take such precautions, I don't know, but in thinking about it as I depart I decide it could be that in opting for sharing in the histrionics of her life I am perhaps seeking distraction from my own daily grind. In which case, coming as extra diversion, I've covered only two blocks when ten yards in front of me on Bishop's Walk this young guy goes down heavy. Whack! – his head hits the curb. No one stops.

Further along is a jeweller's, small and exclusive.

"Good morning, sir. How very nice to see you again."

Does a cow smile when milked? I wouldn't think so, but after leaving the shop, and abetted by what feels a similar impulse, I bypass the usual prawn sandwiches and buy a large seafood pizza from the Pizza Hut. A bottle of Liebfraumilch completes the load.

"Oh, my God, you've done it again!" Maxine says ... and in fastening the locket round her neck I'm an inch from licking the downy hairs on the nape of her neck.

"This design is called 'foxtail'," I tell her, and remain at her back while she views herself in the mirror, and it's all I can do not to bring up my hands to locate her breasts.

She says, "At this rate I shall soon need an armed guard. Why do you buy me these things?"

Good question. One I prefer not to answer.

We sit at her desk. Since we're involved in eating, I don't mention the guy falling down, nor that his blood got smeared on my hands, nor the ambulance coming.

"Just so long as you don't think I'm a mercenary person," she says. "Don't go thinking I expect you to keep buying me presents."

"I don't," I reply. "You're not that sort of girl. You've not got it in you."

"Exactly ..." her eyes flash and sparkle. "I've not got it in me ... *not ever.*"

With such *double entendres* she spoils herself sometimes.

We clink mugs of wine. Cheerfully I offer a toast:

"Absence doesn't make the heart grow fonder, it just brings more frequent erections."

"You're awful. You just made that up."

That's true, and I regard it as one of my better efforts.

"If we eat all this pizza," she says, "I think we're going to be sick."

Lying alone in the pitch-black darkness of my room, I tell myself that the cause of the hot and cold flushes could be the afternoon's pizza and wine. My stomach throbs. Sometimes I'm big and sometimes I'm little. Surely here in my own bed I should have an idea of which way I'm lying and where the door is? I seem hopelessly disorientated. Nor can I wriggle free of reliving the lunchtime event of the bloke falling down on the pavement.

No one stopped. Only *me*.

I sit cradling his head in my lap – no more than twenty years old in his shitty worn clothes and soiled trainers, the state of him and the length of his fingernails showing his problems perhaps extend to beyond taking fits. A woman appears at the dry-cleaner's doorway. She calls out she's dialled 999 and to come in and wash up when I'm done and I wave that I will. "Lie still, lie still, there's a good lad," I keep saying, firming my grip so he won't bang himself, and at least now I've hooked out his tongue he's not quite so blue. All the same, I'm alarmed by the way he's convulsing: his heels drum the concrete, there's blood in the foam on his lips . . . And, Jesus, it's all so familiar that sometimes it seems to me that within the inner kernel of my mind there are doubts and worries that it is better not to investigate or even recall at all. I mean, who can you talk to?

I move a leg. The weight on my thigh confirms the presence of Zero outside the covers and that's a comfort; then comes the throaty whine of a car passing along the street outside and a beam of light partially penetrates the curtains of my little room, breaking the spell and bringing the relief of "Thank God, there's the door; it was there all the time!"

All the same, I feel forced to wonder: perhaps I'm regressing? I taste fear. With increasing frequency, the past continues to return in what seem flashes of brilliant clarity –

The trip home from head office brought silver rails racing below the carriage windows, the darkness periodically split by the starbursts of well-lit stations. Knowing I'd acted impetuously, I was frightened to death of what Linda would say.

Instead, I got in and there was no sign of her.

At almost midnight, watching from behind the curtains, I saw her get dropped off at the corner.

She attempted to bluff. She said, "I had work to do. I had my quota to fill, didn't I?"

Lies. We both knew that by clinging to working at market-research she was armed with an excuse to get out when she liked. "Is it fair to leave Daisy?" I said.

"Oh, here we go, here we go," she sing-songed. "I might've guessed you'd take her side. She's twelve – twelve's old enough to be left. Can't I go out for ten minutes now? All this fuss. What d'you think I've been doing?"

That's what hurt the most: that she either wrote me off as totally gullible and stupid or simply didn't concern herself with any sensitivity I might have.

"Linda, I know bloody well what you've been doing," I said.

"Oh, yes, do you?" She'd a very crude mouth with a few drinks inside her. She lifted her skirt. "You think you should look? You want to come and make sure?"

"Okay, okay – "

"You're not even due till tomorrow for God's sake."

True, I thought, and that's how she'd been caught out, through not expecting me. Then in the circumstances of seeing her placed in the wrong, I abruptly shed any concerns I'd had of how she'd react to my news. "And I'm early because I chucked in the job, that's why. I *quit*. Okay? Pleased? Happy now?"

"You did WHAT?"

"I QUIT. Selling insurance – I wasn't brought up for that kowtowing shit."

"Are you out of your mind? While we live on what?"

"Do you care? It was me who was here to get Daisy's supper."

"Oh, yes . . ." her expression was savagely caustic, "I'll bet you did. And did you give her her bath? A gay old time, was it? Playing bubbles perhaps? Oh, you'd both enjoy that, I'll bet."

"For God's sake! It's your daughter you're slanging."

"Just don't think I don't know. She's as bad. I'm not blind. You just wait, one of these days . . ."

"That's enough!"

"The truth hurts?"

"It's you who'll get hurt. Shall I shut your mouth for you?"

We were in the kitchen and should have backed off and not stood in combat. She picked up the filleting knife off the work-top. "One more step," she screamed, "and I'll cut your fucking head off."

I heard Daisy's sob. I turned and the noise had woken and brought her downstairs and she was in the doorway, hearing all, and in the short linen nightie I'd bought her, the one with the bows and the dancing tigers and elephants on.

I remember I bit my lip. I thought how sad it was she should witness such scenes.

CHAPTER 10

The next day dawns and it's as well I'm not due at Miss Betsy's. A bathroom and lavatory combined should be banned. All those in favour say *aye*.

"Aye!"

I can't laugh. The joke's on me. Just a while back the pain was so bad I got desperate to the point of considering a crap and a puke in the garden. But every square inch is planted with something that Bernard would have missed; every plant with its name in Latin in waterproof pen on a white plastic label.

"Wait a minute, a minute!" he's shouted each time I've knocked.

Every morning he claims the bathroom as his own. His excessive steam from spending so long in the tub has turned the walls mouldy. The cabinet and window-ledge are crammed with his gels and deodorants. What he gets up to behind this locked door, and how deliberate the manufacturers of toiletries might be in marketing containers of phallic shape . . .? I think I'd sooner not know.

He emerges finally. I rush in. The seat's warm. I hate that. All the same – momentary *bliss*, passing bursts of what feels like hot mulligatawny. But then soreness starts. A rectum that feels like a raw bleeding wound and I'm sitting in salt.

I suppose that since I attend fairly regularly I should perhaps have noticed before that the word "Surgery", wherever it appears, has been roughly crossed out and replaced by the crudely lettered description HEALTH CENTRE. Now I come to think about it, other changes since the upgrade are perhaps more subtle. Undoubtedly the receptionists talk to you less, and we have gained cheerful framed photographs of the doctors on the walls, plus endless piped woodland bird-song to accompany waiting for the miracle to happen. Whatever – a bug of some sort is rumoured, so it's full-house again. Clutching plastic tag number *19*, I fidget over grubby magazines and identify blackbirds, thrushes, chaffinch and cuckoo through what seem slow-motion leaps of precious time wasted, the buzzer and light signalling NEXT . . . NEXT . . . NEXT . . .

"Sit you down, Mr Oldfield."

This doctor's new, here just twelve months, small, not unattractive, a professional smile of concern glued on. I can read the heading ЈATIΠꙅOH on the typed sheets she's flicking through and have an unhappy feeling about the size of my file; like it might be described as *ominously thick*. She enquires how I am. I tell her, "Perhaps a bit worse. I've had a quite bad stomach earlier this morning as a matter of fact."

Blood, urine, x-rays, barium meals, stool samples – all tests negative, she says, reading them off, and passively awaits my reaction. However, knowing the importance of *not over-reacting*, I take my time.

"Whatever illness I've got," I explain carefully, "it's ruining the quality of my life. My stomach plays war, I have what seems a high fever, my heart thumps like crazy, there are times I'm so tired I can hardly walk, and yet we've been investigating these symptoms for over three years, all these infernal expensive machines, four different consultants, and yet I don't understand why is it that no one so far has taken my temperature once?"

She's listened, lips pursed. "Well," she says, after a moment, "medically speaking I should think that's all right. Possibly no one's bothered with temperature because it probably wouldn't significantly add to your existing symptoms."

Is she serious? What's all this emphasis on *possibly* and *probably*? "I'm not being poisoned, am I?"

She sways back. I've clearly given her something to think about. "Do *you* think you're being poisoned?" she asks, and smiles faintly.

Clever. It's amazing how some of these people try to catch you out. "It's okay . . ." I hiccup what I hope is a disarming laugh. "I'll admit I'm perhaps over-anxious by nature. Perhaps psychosomatic?"

"Well, where that's concerned," she says, "it wouldn't be good practice to be dogmatic without first rejecting everything else, if you see what I mean?"

"Not more bloody tests?"

Her wider smile reveals a discoloured tooth at the front that needs fixing. She says, "An endoscopy, maybe. But understand . . ." she taps at the notes, "at your age with your '*history*' . . ." she enlists her fingers to put it in accentuated quotes like that, "it's really hardly surprising that you should have your *off*-days." She nods wisely at this. "We need patience," she says. "Perhaps someone to talk to if things should get worse . . ."

Walking home, I'm thoughtful. Being treated under the NHS, I feel I've been given little more than the bum's rush. Doctors' prescriptions are the very devil to read: "Two tabs a day." That's half my normal, plus she's cut the bulk number, and I would turn back; except my notes told her . . . *what*?

And, ah, there's the rub, to be having a "past" hanging over you. So I'll leave it for now. I know and can picture from experience how mouthing off buys you trouble. Stretched out, semi-comatose, eyes hard-focused on the lamp's hypnotic glow while some schooled voice probes your head like a long-handled gaff. All those dormant memories, each a painful extraction, its tail firmly hooked to its neighbour, the bowels from some dream-eating serpent draped round your neck ... "Calm yourself, Mr Oldfield, we are merely letting you see yourself for what you are."

Well, I know what I am. So fuck off.

I arrive home to an empty flat. Do I feel more secure in my basement? Ha-ha! I laugh the hysterical laugh of the slightly hysterical.

"Hello, baby, reward me."

Lonely children, sailors, lifers banged up, blokes like me, we all have this knack of bringing animation to photographs stuck to our walls. A questionable practice ... does it heighten sensation? I suppose sometimes *yes*, sometimes *no*, and right now I could scream with demands I feel need to be served. I need to act out, be perverse, let my free spirit soar. Now then if it were Friday ...

Errol, try to be honest.

Yes, I will, on my honour. Friday is games for form four. That means hockey, the ball is dangerously hard, and I have only a sketchy understanding of the rules.

Very well. But, such niceties aside, would you admit to an interest in watching the up-bottoms-all in their short pleated skirts?

No, I wouldn't deny I indulge. And what harm does it do? The girls of today are so self-assured; they enjoy an audience. Instead, what I would say is that I despise the games mistress and her funny looks. Ten to one, she's the sort, anyway, to stand at the door of the showers, talking tactics while eyeing their bodies, a hypocritical hang-'em-high bitch if ever I saw one. Or alternatively my point is that it simply isn't *her* place to dictate where *I* walk. I live in the village – she *doesn't* – the pavement is public, I am just passing by to reach somewhere else . . . Besides, the girls all know me. Last week, the one with blonde hair playing left-wing the first half and right-wing the second. Sticks! she cried, sticks-sticks! treating that school fence like footlights; any tackle thereabouts and down she flops, the dying swan. All school knickers are bottle-green but she has her bit of lace. Over to me, Tracy, she yelps, belting jig-a-jig down the line, and on that day when it rained her nipples showed through her drip-dry like Cadbury's choc-buttons . . .

So a tissue is needed. A slight smattering of guilt is natural and unfortunate, and the ensuing leakage into Y-fronts can produce a joyless chore, but I'm brighter, I think. More composed, anyhow. Sharper minded. My thoughts not so fuzzy.

CHAPTER 11

Travelling with Sanjay, I am used to calls coming in on his car-phone. *Money-money*! – I mightn't understand the language but know talk of a deal taking place when I hear it. Then replacing the handset, he says, "Damn and blast, I am wanted at home by my mother."

Okay – I smile to myself – so you can't win 'em all.

Westgate Park's where he lives. Executive housing. I'd just as soon stay outside when we get there but he clearly wants me to be impressed, parking the Merc in the road and leading the way up the gravel, past the Peugeot, and round to the kitchen. Naturally everything's space-age, ceramic hobs, gleaming equipment, and the layout's open-plan so I can see that the rest of downstairs is similarly lavish, although perhaps a bit too Taj-Mahal-restaurant for me, and I can't place the smell – either joss-sticks or some kind of spice, a bit overpowering. But causing my feet to take root is his mother. More dark-skinned than Sanjay, she is wearing a sari of subtle shades, her arms ringed with bangles of light-coloured gold, her bare feet in flip-flops, and besides giving him stick in whatever tongue they speak she is acting as if I'm not there.

I suppose it might be that to her I'm white trash.

Then a man, perhaps attracted by the noise, comes down the stairs and she just slips away. I don't know where she goes. "My uncle Mohan," says Sanjay.

He's late fifties, expensively suited. I get to shake his hand. As the only brother of Sanjay's late father he occupies the important role of eldest male in the family. Based in London, he globe-trots a lot and has wide business interests.

"And much respect," Sanjay adds while explaining, and by now we are twenty miles further on and have entered the Metro Centre, which was where we were headed before interruption. "Mohan will play a big part at the wedding," he tells me.

I wait. But nothing more is forthcoming. Which is typically Sanjay – close-mouthed, cards to his chest.

Of course, more than once the further thought has crossed my mind that I could tax him about his various unknowns, but then the role I pursue where he is concerned is that of the three wise monkeys combined into one. For instance, if in his office the phones and fax are never idle, if there are racks and shelves of clothing and items he has available for sale, if he owns a lock-up garage on the north side of town that has a door reinforced like Fort Knox – I was there with him once but never went in – it would certainly never be my intention to show curiosity about anything he doesn't freely want to tell me.

Never look a gift horse in the mouth. Why spoil a good thing? Both sayings apply.

Even so, what's amazing, I guess, is that with his wedding only a spit away I still don't know who he's marrying. I figure the likelihood is that he's slightly embarrassed. His knot's being tied by *arrangement*.

Like a lot of fat men he's got small suffering feet. He's wanting shoes for his honeymoon. In Russell & Bromley he tries on four styles, finds them comfortable and takes the lot, plus shoe-trees for each, a purchase that necessitates opening his plastic-laden wallet – which in turn leaves him trapped, because now he has little option but to react to the photo I've spotted on view. His *intended* no less.

Her name is Kamala, he says. He's travelled to see her a few times. Their respective families are involved in exchange visits. She has three unmarried sisters. "A gift of jewellery for each sister is expected and next on our list," he tells me.

We move on. I'm guessing at fifty quid maximum each. Instead, at Northern Goldsmiths, in spending close on five grand, he has one of the female assistants acting like she wants to lick his dick at the counter.

I guess she's not the only one shaken. And there's a worry, because one of these days he's going to try buying Maxine, and I'm not sure she'll have what it takes to resist. Come to that, his way to her is likely to be through bribing *me*, I know it is.

"Sanjay, have you ever tried sleeping with Maxine?" I ask, the question emerging from the line I'm following.

"Good Lord, no!" he reacts. "When we all three have evenings going out together I always tell Mummy I am going with you and a very nice lady and no funny business."

To someone like Doctor Zissler, the *Mummy* gaffe, I guess, might offer special insights into his personality. I'm allowed no time. "Maxine was married, you know," he says, and looks over to gauge my reaction. I wish he wouldn't. The rain's bouncing knee-high off the road, he's got one hand clasped round a veggie-burger and the car's doing ninety. He says, "She's been divorced for how long ... four years? She must have got used to enjoying ... you know, *satisfaction*."

I grunt *affirmative*. Even the long-distance buses are using the inside lane. One wrong move and we're mince-meat for motorway crows.

"Except that man in McDonald's," he says. "Don't forget him, that man in McDonald's."

Shit! I curse under my breath; I can do without him

wanting to play Mister Memory. The guy's name was Stephen. We were sharing his table, he was fresh from some club and half-cut, and we slipped him a mention of Maxine.

"Yeh-yeh, know her," he said. "Nice looking chick, got some style. Always good for a joke, and that laugh, have you heard how she laughs? But I can't work her out, never could, if you know what I mean?"

We both had our tongues hanging out to hear more.

He said, "Her husband was known as a whizz. Board-room level, went right to the top, then he dumped her. Strange really. She could have been the perfect hostess for someone like him. Still, randy sod, he was banging loose crumpet all over."

I think we bought him a jam roly-poly.

"Funny girl! We were at the same school. Always the top two buttons open, always one to give you a flash of her knickers, if you know what I mean, a real prick-teasing type. I've known blokes take her out but no one's ever got near to the best of my knowledge."

Nice one, Stephen.

"Tell a lie!" He'd clicked his fingers. "A mate of mine, Dave, was living with some bird. Maxine gives him a lift home from some pub one night and bang-bang! – he nails her one in the back of her car right outside this girl's house." He grinned lewdly. "I remember him saying he'd had too much to drink, so she blowjobbed him first; you know, *got him going*. Yeh, that sounds about right. Anything for the devilment of it would be just like our Maxine."

Did we laugh? I don't remember. Perhaps not.

"Sanjay, that bloke in McDonald's. He was full of shit."

"Right," he says, glancing over, "you don't have to tell me," and he's doing a hundred-and-ten now.

*

The rain's stopped. I looked out through the Pizza Hut's window and to my eye there's a Jackson Pollock effect to the town centre's wet pavements reflecting the night-time colours. Sanjay noticeably, wherever he is, operates under the rule that since he's paying he can do as he likes. It seems to work. One plate for his vegetable pizza, a second for a range of different salads across which he spills an avalanche of vomit-like sauce, a third for his garlic bread. Between mouthfuls he noisily sucks his shake through a straw.

It's a moment, I guess, that reinforces my slight concern that the alliance between him and me unquestionably has to be seen as odd. He's not bi-sexual or gay, so there's nothing like that going down. He fancies Maxine like crazy; there's that to remember. But what people actually think, I don't know, unless in looking at his car and what his clothes cost, and so on, they suppose I'm his minder and go-for or something. But if so, that's a laugh, because if he ever needs back-up I'm the one who'll be running, and in any case he doesn't operate in that line of country. In fact it's that he doesn't operate in *any* line of country is what's so hard to grasp. A smoothie cum softie. So the most influential factor upon us both, I guess, is that an equation of human dilemma we share is we each know the need to buy friendship, or more or less to insure it. He is *gross* – Mister Wobbly – and that's the monkey on his back. As for me. . .? Well, there are things that I don't put my mind to unless I've no option.

He says, "You met my uncle at my house today. An important man. Denzil heard he was visiting! *Dreadful man!*"

He sounds like that's a taste he's been getting round to spitting out all day. When he puts down his spoon –

knives and forks aren't his style, spoons hold more – it's as if to emphasize how appalled he is.

"Denzil," he continues, "invited my uncle and I out to dinner. *He* invited *us*. Can you believe that when the bill came he said we would split, half each? I tell you, Errol, his lack of hospitality was the greatest insult to my uncle." He adds impact by ramming his erect right thumb into his left fist. "That's the sign we do. You want to know what my uncle calls him? A suck-up pretender!" He leans towards me. "You see, Errol, we are traders by nature. We have a market-place culture he does not belong to. He is not one of us."

"A pillock!"

"A pillock," he agrees. "And he's shitting himself. Last week . . . you know what he asked for?"

I shake my head.

"MONEY!"

He's released the word like he's been sponged on for blood; maybe even a kidney.

"He would let me buy into a large percentage of the Miss Betsy operation tomorrow. The man has solicitors' letters a foot high on his desk. The bank is *demanding*. The auditors are asking him *serious questions*. I told him, 'Denzil, you want to know how to operate? Give me ten thousand, and in three weeks, water to wine, I will give you back ten times ten.' He shut his face fast."

"A suck-up pretender!"

"Exactly!" He licks his spoon clean. "You want ice-cream?"

It's about an hour later when he drops me off outside the Otter and Trout.

Walking up the path to the flat, I'm in reasonable spirits. The size of the puddles foretell of the river coming into flood and a big run of salmon.

"*Miaow*!" – Zero, having the ears to catch my quiet approach, has descended from the greenhouse roof, his favourite vantage point where on warm summer evenings he especially enjoys having an aerial view of low-flying bats.

Mildly drunk, "Shush," I go at him, as he rubs against my legs. "Psycho-killer on the loose."

Only maybe, I decide on second thoughts, that's not so funny. The dark figure, with torch, is Bernard prowling the patio's concrete, killing snails. Like he's walking on cornflakes.

I creep by unnoticed and descend to my basement.

Then it's a combination of things – despair over Bernard, the evening out, a few drinks – but I can feel myself being turned inside-out. Introspective, as happens so often. I can picture my father.

When people ask and I say my father never took me *anywhere*, I know I am not being totally truthful. In actuality there were occasions when I rode long-distance with him on the lorry: rare but hugely formative trips, because as well as tiny-tot remembrances of sitting fretfully on pub walls, clutching lemonade and crisps, and with him too infrequently sauntering outside to check on my welfare, I can conjure hazy memories of the beer and tobacco-fart smell of him, and the girlish giggles from whoever we were giving lifts home to. Different giggles on different occasions.

So sex, I think, must have been as important to him as it is to me. A genetic thing . . . and such a slant to my thinking is kick-started into being because I'm finding it difficult not to dwell on remembering I have fixed with Sanjay to borrow his Peugeot tomorrow. No great skill is needed to bring this about when required. The old folk rate highly in his culture and consequently the vehicle is always on offer whenever I tell him I need to shoot south to check on Aunt Milly's welfare – he's got no way to know she's been dead for years. Also he likes me to remain acclimatized to how the car handles, because occasionally I ferry things for him. Never anything special and it's never too far.

At any rate, a trip to see Carol and Angela is on the cards. The thought turns me hot, I feel stoked – I need a hair of the dog to stay cool.

One for the road.

Two for another road.

I switch on the TV, press the remote and *P* for *play* appears on my VCR, bringing on screen a videoed BBC serial, one I've watched countless times.

Forget words – I don't have the sound on. The actor playing the cabinet minister is part of my past, a long time ago. Hugh is a household name, greatly sought after by chat and quiz shows despite his paunch and bald spot. Almost certainly his success is as big a surprise to him as it is to me, because I don't suppose he ever imagined he might need to earn a living. We were at school together; we weren't to know what the future would bring, and at that time his father was unbelievably rich, a much-lauded business tycoon. Nowadays, of course, after the unusual death that we've all come to wonder about, his father's name is blackened by exposes of bribery, under-age call-girls and missing mega-bucks.

Never mind. What I want are Hugh's hands. There! – as he stealthily slips the vice-squad detective his Downing Street pass – his fingers are offered in colourful close-up.

He would remember me, too. I have no doubts about that. I wrote to him once – which took courage. But the only address I had was care-of the BBC where star personalities and such are protected by departments that read and handle their mail, and the jargon I'd used, the times and places, the name RISEMAN – all of that would've meant nothing to them, I guess. So I got no reply.

Still, the sight of Hugh's face and hands takes me back.

Captains promoted their own, perpetuating their kind, the world's made that way and it's hard to break the circle once the mould's been set.

"School," Uncle Lewis said, "will make a man of you."

Riseman, a year older than us three junior boys, was captain in charge of our four-bunked room: short, wiry, uncoordinated, excessively weasel-featured – all of which somehow always ran second to the clusters of pus-headed spots he grew mushroom-like in the creases alongside his nose.

Although his background was never made clear, his father owned half of Argentina or somewhere else big and flat.

"I am a junior, the lowest of the low, not fit to shovel shit. I will obey the orders of my superiors and betters. I shall always . . . I shall always . . ."

As juniors, we were made to degrade ourselves at every opportunity, and my mind was blank, the creed gone.

"Pronto! Pronto!" Riseman urged me on for a while longer, before "GUILTY!" he shouted. After which, required to touch my toes, I could see him in the mirror, his teeth exposed in a savage grimace each time he wound himself up for a two-handed swing with the four-foot long broom-handle, aiming to catch just the fleshy edge of my backside.

The broom-handle whistled through the air. Blows known as *bacon-slicers*. Two, off-target, brought the pain and noise of wood striking bone.

Then punishment over. "Get wanking the bunk-boards!" Riseman ordered, and his savage kick to my shins brought further flickers of sympathy from Hugh and Giles. We were not allowed to talk. Every week from stores we juniors collected *wank* for polishing table and bunk-boards, *crap* for bumpering the parquet floor. The room had no chairs, no carpets, no pictures, no curtains, no dust, no fingerprints. I was forever writing home to Aunt Milly, "Urgent, please send more yellow dusters."

Lights out. "Are you asleep?" I could discern the silhouettes of Hugh and Giles squatting six feet away from me along the room's cross-beam, the three of us clad in shorts and singlets so as to cram in more spit-and-polish between reveille and the six a.m. run. All windows were open. The cold air owned a bite. Foggy or not, the siren on Drummond Spit buoy boomed its warning once every thirty-two seconds. "Are you asleep?" My whispered question brought no reply, so there was nothing I could do and soon came the gasp of one of them starting awake as he fell and the awesome thud as he landed.

Sobbing quietly, Hugh said he thought he wasn't bleeding. "You can have two hours' fatigue for that, you wet prick," Riseman told him. "Now into your bunks."

Masters were few. Devised by the founder and principal, known as "Shylock", the school revolved around a regime that designated the bulk of control to the boys, or at least to the captains. No scholarships were available. Fees were enormous. The constant threat of the disgrace of expulsion kept us in line. We had Arabs, Greeks, Swiss, a few from the Commonwealth. All *new money*. Giles's father owned a chain of well-known shops. I had surprised myself by how easily I'd found copying his and Hugh's tones and affectations and if anyone asked what my father did I said he owned an ice-cream factory.

"The essential thing," said Uncle Lewis, "is to join in the swing of things and to do as you're told."

We dressed for dinner. Bum-freezers, wing-collars, bow-ties. O hallowed portals: the refectory boasted panelled walls, a gallery of signed photos of illustrious visitors, each room's table and silverware gleaming from its daily polishing. An elitist's fantasia. "Gentlemen!" Shylock at head-table would bang the gavel. "Gentlemen ... *England*!" We would stand, raise our glasses, only water, never drinking. "England!" we'd chorus.

"You three." Riseman would mean Giles, Hugh and me. "Refuse every course except soup. Look at the salt-pot. Don't move a muscle. Not a blink the whole meal. That's an order."

Why did the captains have to be so cruel? Why obey, anyway? We were there to learn what?

I asked this of Hugh when I wrote. I penned page after page, telling him I often looked back to our time together and that I saw no harm in such reminiscing. And yet, I explained, I sometimes wondered if within such reflection I might be unconsciously including lessons learned in later life, perhaps even unintentionally exaggerating some events into appearing larger and uglier than they really had been, perhaps even making them emblematic of what I had come to despise and fear?

Did he feel that way, too? I asked of him. Because I knew for sure he'd decode what I meant, though in case he preferred to pretend otherwise I added the underlined postscript, *Besides, where lies truth? Who's to say? A slight slip here and there would be human.*

And perhaps there was my error and that I hoped for too much, and it upset me for ages that he didn't write back.

CHAPTER 12

Three days go by and I again find myself driving the Peugeot, this time paying off the favour of borrowing it for the trip to see Carol and Angela – which did me good, I enjoyed every minute.

Only, what's going on? "Yes, I'm talking to you," I say aloud, nodding as in glancing again to the rear-view mirror I take note of the big black BMW still on my tail.

I'm unhappy. Some frigging salesman wanting to play chase-me-Charlie all the way to Newcastle is not on my itinerary, and with that in mind I ease across to the outside lane and jump a few inside cars with an accelerated burst before easing back.

Not a lot is achieved. Glued on at thirty yards back, the black BMW is for real. The situation would unnerve me more, I tell myself, if I thought I was carrying something I shouldn't, but all I have in the boot are some innocuous open-topped cartons of stuff that Sanjay needs delivering.

"Paranoia". I know I suffered from that once before and remember I looked up the meaning. "A type of insanity formed by fixed delusions" – which meant I thought people were against me and after me; and at that time with good reason, as it happened. Trouble is, I was hoping I'd put all such problems behind me.

I see a sign: "Motorway Services – 1 mile". Probably it's an over-impulsive move but I decide to check. I turn off, keeping an eye on the mirror.

Then as I park on the forecourt, the BMW slides in astern, and now I can see two guys up front and a pair of miniature football boots hanging mascot-like behind their windscreen. I get out, lock the car, walk into the cafeteria, stand in the queue, buy coffee and carry it across to a table. The two guys follow suit. Both in their late twenties, dressed in jeans and leather blousons, tanned and with pop-star haircuts, neither is smoking and the one wearing dark glasses is chewing gum.

Definitely not salesmen. They've an ambient glow like they work out regularly.

And this, I tell myself, is getting ridiculous, but I can't keep from panicking. What to do? Although bursting for a pee, I've seen too many movies where guys get worked over in public lavatories. Trying to act casually, I skip finishing the coffee and get the Peugeot back on to the motorway. I glance to the mirror. The black BMW is four cars behind me.

I cut my speed back to thirty. Everything is passing. I could almost walk quicker. A car like a BMW isn't made to go slow – they slide by. Now's my chance. A slip-road comes up to my left and, without bothering to signal, I take it.

So I'm free. Free, anyhow, to allow me to wonder if the whole thing has taken place in my head. No matter. Once round the roundabout at the bottom, I find a quiet stretch and stop and empty my bladder behind a tree; after which, staying off the motorway, I've not far to travel to cross the Tyne into Newcastle where I'm quickly into massive self-ridicule at seeing BMW cars all over.

I've done these trips before. Ilkley, Sunderland, Harrogate, Leeds, Bradford. The location this time is Byker, and the place when I get there is on par with the other dumps I got sent to: a small warehouse unit on a shabby industrial estate and stocking a bit of everything by the look of things. When I park up and go inside to see what's what, a young tarty piece guarding the front desk disappears through a door and I see an elderly Asian gent come to the glass partitioning to peer at me.

She comes back. "He says just leave it out here," she says, and I return to the car and over a couple of trips lug in the ten cartons of after-shave – twenty-four to a carton – the big bag of assorted screwdrivers, the gross-box of packeted stereo-headsets, and some bundles of paperwork.

There's nothing to sign for.

And that's it, job completed, and I can take my time on the return leg, during which I play the radio loud to take my mind off myself. But then on returning the keys to Sanjay a while later I return to wondering about letting him share how stupid I can be. Except I don't, because he mightn't see the funny side – even slight mental aberrations can be worrying to people who don't understand them. I don't want to be denying myself further use of the Peugeot.

Strange all the same to think I might be back to imagining I am being persecuted like that.

That night Robert calls in on his way home from the hospital. He has delivered clean nighties for Tina and has her used ones crammed into a cheap carrier-bag. She's had some sort of relapse, he says, then in adding a detailed description of the variety and ingenuity of the machines she's plugged into annoys me a bit with a manner that shows he reckons he now possesses an assured right to sympathy. There's a total question mark hanging over her future, he says.

Mine too, I reckon.

"Now what are you doing?" Bernard snaps at me.

"It's Brazil versus England," I reply, looking back from the set.

"No, we're not having that."

"It's all right," Robert offers. "Don't mind me."

"Sod him," says Bernard. "It's tennis, not football, we want."

He gets up, bumps me aside and puts on *their* channel.

What needles is I'm expecting Robert will throw me an understanding smile but he doesn't.

The match is indoors, abroad somewhere. Three-one, first set, two bronzed overpaid warriors.

"This is shit. I think I'll nip down the river," I say, and watch the announcement cruise right up Bernard's nose.

Parked in the lane close beside Baydale ford I'm in green; never black – black at night shows up densely.

But a wasted trip. Reading the river by its noise, I can hear the level's too high for wading. I nibble a Kit-Kat. A light rain spattering against the windscreen could be spray. When I close my eyes, I can hear the howl in the rigging. The creaking trees hold the sounds of a ship under stress. In the threshing of twigs I hear waves –

If only I wasn't so haunted.

Penetrating a pregnant woman!

I recognize this as "knight's-move thinking", a rapid sideways leap in consciousness and often a danger signal of an increase in stress . . . or so they told us.

And not even a woman for Christ's sake! A kid!

"Paula, you won't say anything to anyone?"

The plain truth is that in her mother's car I might have been mentally masturbating at having someone her age make me an offer, but the probabilities of anything further didn't strike me as possible until I was confronted with the unexpectedness of finding myself in her flat. Fitted carpets, decent furniture, modern kitchen, little Andy's room a menagerie of furry toys. The property belongs to her father; bricks and mortar put by for his future, she said.

What plans did she have for her own?

"About this, you mean?" She patted her front. "My mum's going to kill me. I can just see her face. She's always saying, 'We want no more worrying about you my girl.'"

"Your boyfriend wants what?"

"Oh, he's hopeless." She must have been reading my mind at that point. "He won't turn up here by the way. There's a night match; he'll be stuck with his mates. He's a City supporter."

Another of Superstar's fans; I remember I told myself that. Then as the memory comes to an end, carnal thinking swiftly fills the void. No point in sitting here, anyway, I tell myself, and turn the car short-round in the lane and drive to the call-box not far from the ford.

"Hi Paula!" I say when she answers. "I was just thinking of you. I'm out after salmon but the river's too high."

She giggles, probably assuming I'm making it up. She says, "What a shame. I'm here on my own, do you want to come round?"

She likes vodka. Even including a stop on the way for a bottle, I arrive at her flat inside fifteen minutes and am still reliving the erotica of last time to the extent that when she answers the door I carry her on to the settee with the momentum of a big hug.

She laughs. "God, look at you – you remind me of the SAS dressed up like that!"

She doesn't look too fashion-conscious herself as it happens, but her baggy shorts at least allow ample room to get my whole hand up her leg. She's on fire, leaking juices, speculating while waiting, I guess.

Breathless she jumps up and puts the bolt on the door.

"Don't you ever dare tell Karen or Maxine you come round here," she says, as we undress.

"I wouldn't do such a thing."

There's no foreplay needed. She just wants it straight in.

Only then she complains, "This way hurts my knees."

England in white, Brazil in gold, and I clamp her waist between my hands to keep her kneeling as she is. "Stay like that if you can."

"I can stand it," she says. "Just don't stop."

I wasn't. In pausing I was only taking a moment to consider leaning over her shoulder to get to the volume. God knows what the score is; the sound was turned down when I got here.

Then in looking downward I become savagely engrossed in watching myself going in and out of her. The stretched delicate crease of her backside, its tight little hole like the top of an orange. I screw my eyes shut as I strive for the feel of more depth. Her backside is going like crazy. Then when I glance up again, the pitch and the players have gone, the programme is back in the studio and includes . . . *Mister Superstar* – he possesses enough medals and caps to be one of the regular panel of experts.

I watch his mouth silently opening and closing in expounding his views, and can feel my lips working in silently copying.

"Paula, now? Shall I come?"

"Oh, yes, do! Do it now if you want; it can't hurt since I'm carrying."

CHAPTER 13

As I leave the health centre, I ignore the tar-macadamed walkway and use the foot-stomped path between the rhododendrons so I can turn *right*, not *left*. Left would carry me into the village and towards Blind Lane where I once lived with Linda and Daisy.

I avoid there. Paranoia again, I suppose. I figure the men may forget but the women remember.

As to the rest of the village, I suppose time has dimmed much; at least if there are people who smile to my face but spit at my back, it no longer cuts so deeply that I let the blood show. Mostly, anyhow, they judge by rumour; I see it in their eyes. They don't know the half of it. How can they?

"Hello, Maxine, it's me."

"You don't sound at home. The shop's really busy. Aren't you coming to work?"

"I've just been to the doctor's."

"What for this time?"

"I had a bad night. Ratatouille."

"Again? Then why eat it?"

"Because it saves arguing, that's why."

She sighs, cutting me short, then says she must go, she's got customers in. The line hums. Left feeling unwanted, I slam down the receiver. The call-box's door needs a shove with my shoulder. On the grass outside, a thrush is making use of a stone as an anvil. The bird flies off scared, leaking whitewash. The snail lies wasted, oozing froth. *Shit-and-cruelty.*

If Paula should let slip about me and her, and if Maxine should hear . . .? Except *no*, that can't happen: Paula won't want it broadcast.

Thus my mind vacillates with my stride. Space and deep breathing are a tonic. Soon the pavements become scraggy grass verges. Fields and woods lie beyond budding hedgerows, shades of winter edging spring. All colours darken, deepen and look fresher after rain; everything sprouting too early in this mild weather. We shall pay for it later.

Deja vu.

Where else, anyway, was I headed but here to the bridge? Built 1722, dated by its masons' marks.

I lean on and over the parapet and from there drop a spit-bomb on the river surging brownly through the main arch. Fish fresh from the estuary are running unseen on the flood. I can sense them down there and know just where they'll be – which is a good feeling, to own that kind of level of intimate knowledge. It gels comfortably with having the toll-house fitting unobtrusively beside me into the worn sandstone structure. It's like I feel I belong . . .

And there! Three, four – *five magpies*! Ungainly in flight. Black and white. Put out a small glittery object – they'll come and they'll claim it.

Some memories, they say, never leave you.

When I first took off from the village, blinkered, propelled by despair, hell, I had just experienced how destructive love could be, and so who at such times gives a toss about basics? I never stopped to consider the US-and-THEM syndrome: who'd have what going surplus while I'd have fuck all.

Travel, booze, dope, and by any other means possible

come to that – escape ruled. I saw various places, met a lot of new people: old men, young men, boys even, and so many Irish. Many an intelligence concealed beneath grizzled appearance. I learned lots I'd not known. Rules you could live by, rules you could die by. Plenty of cruelty. No shortage of shit. Becoming charity's cause, I mastered holding my hand out. A ladle of soup and a big hunk of bread; the Holy Ghost, too, if you got unlucky. You'd not to mind all the coughing and spitting and those without teeth who'd be dipping and sucking.

So myself, when I could, I preferred going solo. Bin-diving. Restaurants mainly. You got to know where, though the stakes on your own were high risks. If a dosser gets bashed, who's to care? But a kind of existence was possible once the knack was acquired to spot who'd got what going spare. Fourteen guys fucking one bit of skirt, her legs never closed while she drank a whole bottle and given a case she'd have fucked a whole army. It was Sol saw me right. "Get a wee pup," he said, and I did. Called him Punch. We hung out where the shops were. Punch in arms cradled babe-like. "Can you spare us some change, the dog's starving?"

But word soon spread about. Punch got thieved.

After that, I hung on for a while. But every creature to its own locale, as they say. I think I always knew I was coming back.

Salmon provided good eating, raw or cooked. Partridge, pigeon and pheasant. I could never fool rabbits. Spuds, greens and fruit came pick-your-own-free from unknowing farmers. The mysterious man-with-a-beard who lives by the river and runs when he sees you was no fucking myth.

Until at this same bridge one August morning – I was catching eels – I saw what seemed a sack eddying endlessly round. Yet *not* a sack when I checked, and on the bank the shock of a coat neatly folded and a note that read, "I tried my best for you, Mam."

"God rest the poor drowned man."

The voice behind me made me jump: I knew only through avoiding Mavis that she lived alone at the toll-house. She had the looks of a wizened old bag-lady, spindle-limbed but was strong, so I remember I worried an arm or some water-logged part would come off as we pulled; but no, she insisted, she'd seen many drowned and this one was fresh, by which time I'd cupped hands to my eyes and could make out the rocks he had tied to his feet. "So best left in peace, we'll not bother the police," she said – which suited me fine. It was only later that I came to wonder if we might've shown more respect. Except *dead* is *dead*, a maxim backed up that same day by how Fate sent a twenty-foot spate, and the body was gone the next time we looked.

So the outcome was that I'd found me a roof. No gas, no electric, no taps. Mavis's smoke-blackened pots hung on hooks in the grate. We burned wood, used river-water, ate lots of fish, went outside with a spade when nature called. At delivery of Mavis's week's bit of shopping every Wednesday, I always made myself scarce. "Mavis, dear, you should be in a home," the silly do-gooding cow begged all the time, but Mavis said *no*, and that she valued her *freedom*. A sensitive soul. She wouldn't kill insects or nothing. The place crawled with rats. She would come on a toad or creature and carry it round in her pocket all day and by nightfall would know who the toad had once been and the life that they'd led. "Hallelujah!" she'd laugh, "this wee mouse was a wee bitty man."

As for magpies – Mavis smoked home-rolls. Dried haw-thorn leaves that she mixed with Old Holborn. She saved the gold and silver paper from them, and from other

items, and twisted-up gaudy pellets that the magpies
loved fetching.

The ones I can see flying now will be from her same
family – descendants, anyhow.

So I was never lost. Not until Robert *found me*. In
retrospect, a coincidence beyond belief really that he
should have stumbled upon me while venturing along by
the river – gathering dandelions for wine-making, he told
me later. "Errol?" he said that day, shocked and squinting
to see through the unkempt appearance of me. "Errol, is
that *you*? Where the hell have you been all this time?"

Yet, strictly speaking, he did me no favours. "Post-
traumatic stress". For openers, where they put me, they
hung that round my neck, though a problem, they said,
was how far back did it stretch? When I said I'd quit
wondering and I didn't know, either, Doctor Zissler named
such talk obstructive. My confinement could go on forever,
he warned. He expected much of me, so that later, on
reflection, it seemed to me he missed seeing I had energy
only for staring from the window. I had my *World's
Famous Paintings* to look at by then, and I would sometimes study the prisoners pacing in Van Gogh's *The
Exercise Yard* and the picture seemed to depict exactly
how I regarded the daily round of mealtimes, interviews,
group sessions, endless TV and early to bed. On and
on, week after week . . . until unexpectedly happened the
headline, ELDERLY RECLUSE FOUND DEAD AFTER
ACCIDENTALLY DRINKING THORNAPPLE JUICE.

The short report contained within the *Gazette* gave me
more of a jolt than any recognized therapy.

I couldn't stop crying.

"That's right, Errol, let it all come out," said Doctor
Zissler, and he called it a "breakthrough".

Of course he was wrong. The milestone of my salvation,
if that's what it was, came through knowing there was

no one like Mavis for understanding the wild things, those that killed you for certain. The message she'd sent, or at least the inference I drew, was that life was too short to be staying locked up.

A dog all this time has been barking.

How bizarre the past seems.

A man in a waistcoat has emerged from the toll-house, these days painted, its once wild garden tidied, and I can tell by his stance he is pondering my purpose. Why, he asks of himself, does this idiot regularly come to stand and stare and annoy his poor dog?

The answer is *I don't know.* Perhaps here is a sort of shrine, I suppose. Mavis, her ideas on reincarnation, her compassionate nature, the drowned young man – I guess the whole of that period was suited to what in a sense was my own time of mourning.

I get back to the flat and the phone is ringing. I answer and recognize the Right Hon's river-keeper's growl in my ear. A miserable bastard.

Lots of fish on the move and the level is falling to "fishable", he says, and he needs me to ghillie tomorrow. It will be my pleasure, I tell him. Since I value my access to some legal fishing, I really haven't much option but to dance to his tune.

CHAPTER 14

No compunction, I tell myself. Since the world makes its profit on cheating and little white lies, why the fuck should I be the exception?

"A kingfisher! See, the dippers? A mink! Ah, too late! Look, a heron?"

Only the last-named is true. Grey and stick-legged, he tenses in the shallows on catching sight of our approach, then as if piqued launches upwards, flapping away with sullen slow-motion wing-beat, dismissive of the crows who have ganged to attack, wheel and dive.

Angels and bandit, I describe them to myself – which might equally apply to the three of us.

Captain and Mrs Forbes-Tyson have borrowed the Right Hon's Range-Rover to drive down from staying overnight at the Big House. They have parked at the bridge, and Cotherston is their draw, one of the best of the named beats. Easily walkable, thank God, they say, because being only just back from their skiing holiday they are absolutely exhausted and only sheer bloody will-power has allowed them to fly up specially to take advantage of hearing the flood has brought in a good head of fish. Even then, they can stay but one day. They have the Caribbean to pack for when they get home.

"What pattern of fly then, Errol?"

Aged thirty-something, more plain than good-looking, Mrs Forbes-Tyson speaks in clipped regal no-nonsense tones, and even inelegantly dressed in chest-waders and short wading-jacket radiates a certain exclusive polish.

The first year they came, she said, "Call me Davina". Her husband, pompously, prefers to be addressed as Captain Forbes-Tyson and clings to the feudal idea I should tackle up for them – which is what makes him scowl as I hand her a Thunder & Lightning to knot on for herself.

I can afford not to care. I know he daren't speak his piece because she's got the money. She hails from some brewery family. For toeing *her* line he enjoys full-time at horse-trials.

At Bellforth Corner we watch him wade out up to his nipples and start thrashing about. "Nicky, we'll leave the thermos flask here, darling," she calls to him. "I'll just walk on with Errol to try Lower Biggins."

She knows the way, leading, threading herself and her long rod through Oxenflats wood. We see two jays and a squirrel; then when a jet plane goes over low, on re-heat or whatever they do for the airport, she cries, "Oh, Errol, look!" as five fallow-deer break cover and bound from the blackthorn, their rumps bobbing white. She loves all of nature and sees only the good.

For instance, the last of the crocuses are droplets of colour among vivid green shoots of wild garlic. All a bit Gustav Klimt, I say, and she raptures at that. "Are you still doing this work part-time?" she asks.

"It pays only pennies."

"How *awful*," she says, but is pleased; she likes to regard me as lean, gnarled and starving. "Still, I suppose someone has to do it," she says.

I smile back. How this country has gone all these years without a revolution is beyond me.

In the meantime. Stone-built, no windows, wooden bench – the fishing-shelter would soon get disgusting if Joe Public ever acquired right of way. She removes her mittens and blows on her fingers. In here one day she got out her compact and began doing a line on its mirror and

I had to get awkward; however, I'm not unhappy she's remembered her hip-flask. A couple of swigs and she's soon pulling hair. She says, "God, I just love your pigtail, it's wild!" – which is all part of what we're engaged in, an event possibly tame in comparison with the high-jinks of the London scene that she talks of but, nonetheless, somewhat crazy and unique in that our antics are restricted by knowing that latex chest-waders sweat badly and would need to be talcummed to get them back on if she took them right off.

Lower Biggins lies waiting outside when we're done. By far the best holding-pool on this stretch. I borrow her rod and tie on a purple-dyed shrimp from the tin in my coat. By rights, the shrimp, fished sink-and-draw, is a quick deadly method not allowed on the river.

Ten minutes later. We arrive back at Bellforth Corner where the captain, still chest-deep and fishless, looks unhappy on seeing she is carrying a twelve-pound salmon by the gills. "Oh, well done, that woman!" he calls. "Darling, that looks a beauty!"

"Fresh-run," she calls back. "Still smells of the sea . . . took the fly with a bang."

We break for lunch. I've brought nothing but they have sandwiches and nibbles that I'm allowed to share, though the captain draws the line at offering me a swig from their thermos flask's cup. But then that's his loss. That Bellforth Corner rarely, if *ever*, holds fish at this height of water is something I know and he doesn't. I tell him he's bound to succeed but he's got to keep trying; then I put him back in there.

So by three-thirty he's knackered, bushwhacked by the casting, the wind and the glare off the water, his eyes stare from dark caves. He says we'll call it a day. I agree. "Better luck next time," I tell him sympathetically, as we trek back to the bridge, where at the Right Hon's Range-

Rover he backhands me three tenners and a bottle of Bell's. He says, "I should think we'll return for our week in the summer, and then August again for the grouse. You'll get word via the keeper as usual if we should need your services. But I wouldn't bank on it."

If that's his best shot, I can smile. Neither, I tell myself, have I any objections to drinking his whisky.

And on getting home that's the first thing I do: I knock back a dram in my basement where, while about it, I hook out the hanky Davina squeezed round my penis. White lace, finely drawn. As it dries it will stiffen. I have a bag ready.

Then I switch on my TV to have sight of Hugh. Fight fire with fire. Given a chance, I shit *captains* for breakfast.

At school, Riseman smirks as he shows me Aunt Milly's letter, one I watched him remove from my wardrobe only moments ago. "Oldfield," he says, "this was found with your name on in the *no-paper* dustbin. How many hours of fatigue to work off?"

He knows exactly. "Fifty-six," I tell him.

"Right, book yourself down for three more."

Such is the way we juniors are made slaves of. Most of our misdemeanours are contrived, our punishments unwarranted, so that each of us possesses our personal wedge of fatigue that grows day by day like some sort of tumour we have to drag around with us.

Wednesday and Sunday afternoons, "officially", we are allowed to "walk-out", but we never get to go. The fatigue-bugle blows. We fall in. The last to arrive gets two more hours added.

Names are checked by the captain in charge. Forty or so of us, naked beneath our boiler-suits. We double away from the parade-ground, pounding along eight-hundred snaking yards of ankle-twisting, foot-hardened path through landscaped gardening gone wild. The running warms us. Although youthful, we cough a lot.

"Company . . . *halt!*"

At the end of the Burma Road, we are set to doubling on the spot. Last year's dried rushes rattle in the onshore wind. The chill factor must be very low today. Veneers of ice on scummy puddles reflect the leaden January sky. The *swamp* is acres and acres of salt-water marsh much beloved by sea-birds, its grim expanse separating Shylock's baronial house from the extensive school grounds. Hence a road is *essential* so he may stroll to work instead of wasting time and petrol on the longer route: overall a task that's been under way since he founded the school, which is years, and if at every spring tide the sea seeps in to erode what's been done . . . never mind. "*Exitus acta probat* (the outcome justifies the deed)," he likes to remind us, illustrating his beliefs with a cine-record he likes to show twice a term, known as "film-nights".

The captain splits us into teams.

In we go. The mud has the consistency of double-cream. We doggy-paddle to withstand its suction; it complains by bubbling, exuding a smell I can never get used to. Halfway up our chests is as far as we, the "divers", are allowed to sink. Other teams are manhandling *straw*, which is anything handy that might be tied into bundles. Driving it deep with our feet, we are forming a platform of sorts to support the gravel being constantly humped from the foreshore. "MORE STRAW! MORE GRAVEL!" The "mud-walker" carrying the life-line – a job given only to toadies – wears boards on his feet. "ROPE OVER HERE!" – and someone is duly lassoed and dragged to comparative safety.

Our bodies vainly squirm to avoid contact with iced-wet boiler-suits that cling as second skin. At our turn on wheelbarrows, running with full loads, a half-mile round trip to the foreshore and back, any spillage brings extra punishment. To protect our hands we snatch broad leaves from some variety of evergreen shrub growing alongside the path, wrapping them round the wheelbarrows' handles. The captain keeps us hard at it because sometimes Shylock likes to stroll down, to wave, to shout encouragement, or to shoot a little film.

"School," Uncle Lewis said, "will make a man of you."

All this money being wasted on me. Constantly I worry about where I am going wrong. Most of the others appear to possess some kind of inner vision I don't have. "Just wait till it's our turn as captains," says Hugh – which is an attitude I truly don't understand of him, since he is small and weedy, his father's immense financial clout carries little weight and he is endlessly picked on.

Worse about Hugh – what I know is that Riseman takes him down to private places. There he makes Hugh suck his cock and he comes in Hugh's mouth.

I don't even like to think about it.

"JUNIOR!"

Back at school, we have survived the afternoon, our skinny teenage bodies filthy with mud, our shrivelled genitals. In the outside ablutions, Victorian-built, rough drainage-channels criss-cross a concrete floor, lavatories are square blocks with a hole for your bum, shower-pipes without sprays jut from walls, icicles hang from window-openings without frames or glass. A place fit to milk cows, or torture prisoners.

"JUNIOR!"

We rush to respond to the call from a number of captains enjoying hot water. Riseman among them has growing off him a long yellow penis, its shape not unlike those rubber nozzles that get fixed to taps. I know this without looking because sometimes in our room from under its end of loose skin he scrapes off white cheese with his thumbnail and laughs as he shows us.

"Get rid of this flooding," he bellows. With all showers in use, the place soon floods calf-deep.

"Me, Riseman?" gasps Hugh.

"YOU WERE LAST! GET IT FIXED!"

Gratefully, we scuttle back to our cold-water queue. Hugh left behind, hunched, chilled to shaking and clutching his balls, gingerly uses his toes to divine and follow the channel. He locates the main drain. He stands cringing; it's like he's maybe a hamster or some small cornered animal. He says, "Riseman, I can't . . . the stick's gone."

"ARSEHOLE," yells Riseman, "I GAVE YOU AN ORDER!" – which is the ultimate threat, because the punishment for disobedience is immediate expulsion.

Do we all have a gift for reprise?

I know I do and that thanks to the video of Hugh I can go one stage better.

I watched Hugh squat on his heels; he thrust his hands down the drain.

"HUGH, DON'T DO IT!" my mind silently shouts.

But too late.

I press *freeze-frame*.

It brings a slight snow and some flickering but I can stare at Hugh's hands for the whole of five minutes before the VCR re-engages, during which time I am able to recall Hugh standing screaming, his head in his hands like the famous Munch painting, his wet body streaming with crimson that ran down to his toes.

Riseman *knew* . . . Captains had always made use of that drain for their old razor-blades. We all *knew*.

Riseman swore blind he didn't.

Rumour that night was rife. Hugh had been whisked away for hundreds of stitches and huge blood transfusions. Without his help, Giles and me were hard pushed to be ready for evening inspection. "Please," I had to keep saying, "don't talk to me, Giles."

Everything spotless, everything in its place, sheets folded precisely to one forearm's width and tightly draped between top and bottom bunks. "Tossing-off after lights-out, that's two hours' fatigue," Riseman said, spotting a blemish on one of Giles's sheets.

Ramrod, we stood at attention as he studied our faces from inches away. He was hoping we'd blink. Blinking wasn't allowed.

"Do wise monkeys snitch?"

We shook our heads.

"Are wise monkeys deaf?"

We nodded.

"Can wise monkeys see?"

We dropped our gaze.

"You wet fart, Oldfield." For me he had a special spotty grin, looking back over his shoulder while searching my wardrobe. "I saw your name on today's tuck-board."

Aunt Milly's tuck-parcels, packed and despatched weekly by Fortnum & Mason, were highly regarded. "I didn't have a chance to tell you, Riseman," I said. "I was going to."

"Are these those salted peanuts I like? D'you want these?"

"No, Riseman, you're very welcome."

"You want me to have this two quid as well on this shelf?"

"It's just sparo. I won't need it."

"It's a loan, right?" He shoved his face into mine. "Right, what are you, Oldfield?"

"A nobody, Riseman . . . less than an ant."

"And what do you do?"

"I fool no one, Riseman."

He beamed and swelled. "This place is a crap-house. You, prick-face," he said, turning on Giles, "there's a mark on this table."

"Where, Riseman?"

"There, bollock-brain," he said, his finger making a mark that would take us a week to rub off. "Two hours' fatigue each and that's letting you off bloody lightly."

"Thank you, Riseman," Giles said.

"Thank you, Riseman," I echoed.

Then later – and my God, I could spit – before lights-out came, he took me down to private places.

CHAPTER 15

Saturday morning and Bernard, coming indoors, has a slug neatly skewered on the end of the old Bic biro he favours. "Just look at the size of this one," he says.

Robert's straight there, appreciative. "It must be four or five inches, the biggest yet."

"It's nearly dead," Bernard says.

I back off. I don't care if it's made out of fucking plasticine.

They go into a huddle to enjoy the moment.

How quickly the triangle tightens.

Tina, the doctors have said, isn't totally brain-dead but should she emerge from the coma she'll be worse than before, needing lifting, spoon-feeding and so on, and "God knows how I'll cope," Robert's whined more than once.

I'm not fooled. That he has already made other choices is evident in how he has taken to eating all his meals with us and would also by now, I have reason to assume, be sleeping here full-time if I wasn't. Only last night – distasteful this – I lifted the lid on the grizzly surprise of a knotted used condom, and there's really no way of avoiding proof like that. The cat's out of the bag, so to speak, and who eventually pricked it to sink it . . .? Well, it wasn't me.

"Lunchtime," says Bernard.

My taste-buds are dying. Lentil & Tomato Loaf. Plus potatoes; never peeled but always *nutritiously* boiled in their skins. Secretly I am starting to keep a list of the things they are giving me to eat. I think this is a smart idea.

Lunch over, I head for my sanctuary.

The recent rains have brought a damp that's put a mould like a fuzzy white hair on these whitewashed basement walls. Me, the girlies, a sniff of *parfum*, and a good belt of whisky.

Oy vey! An eventful half-week . . .!

Wednesday. Midnight. Bitterly cold, windless, no moon, dark but not black, every sound magnified, so much unknown through being unseen, and somewhere the occasional heavy splash of an active fish, and at Baydale ford, late, I snatched two good salmon. One I sold on. The other is stacked in the freezer for eating.

Thursday. Midnight. Same spot. The phlegmy cough of a deer, an owl *whooshed* downwind, a few animal screams, but it was one of those times when the salmon weren't moving. I tramped back to the car and . . . *a shock*. The aerial and wipers snapped off. Clay packed up the exhaust. A note on the windscreen that read, "YOUR LAST FUCKING WARNING."

Perhaps another small scotch? I pour myself one and smile up at Maxine. "Hello, baby, reward me! I sent flowers to Tina. That's more work for the nurses, but what else can you do?"

Salut!

Last night was Friday and was spent round at Paula's. "This is Louise, my best friend, come round to meet you, ha-ha!" she said.

Louise, aged nineteen, a lovely girl of exquisite soft skin. She can certainly drink, I'll give her that, but her trick of drumming tunes on her teeth wore me out, plus when in a paddy she sits cracking her knuckles. "Jesus saves, the Lord is King!" Is she serious?

Then of the camcorder by the bed Paula got to say, "On loan from Daddy so I can have little Andy on record for when he grows up" . . . but a few shots of her own present *delicate* condition while it lasts – she is due at the clinic on Monday – now appealed to her also, and would that be a giggle, Louise?

Say no more, I'm your man!

All of which goes to show that the release-oil effects of alcoholic refreshment should not be underestimated.

Louise naked: "Get these in close-up" – wriggling the crucifix crosses tattooed on her fingers, after which for her solo she first did hand-stands, then arched in a back-crab for rapid hip-shakings to some heavy-metal. I think Guns 'N' Roses. She was "rattling out evil", she said. The strain when I tried nearly killed me.

"Whose one is this, Errol? Go on, guess."

"No idea" – my face held captive by soft inner thighs.

"You're not allowed to touch the blindfold."

"Errol, is this a *beaver*?"

"No peeking, that's cheating."

"All right, Errol . . . coca-cola . . . since you're looking – watch this. Bottle shot. Now you see it, now you don't."

Louise, I swear, hosts the devil and is right up my street.

Skol!

I think that makes four. Shades of poor Uncle Lewis. You grow. You mature. You drink a little whisky. You spot the bastards if you're lucky. *C'est la vie!* I lay my head on the desk. My mind sleepily weaves through a maze of old and new dreams. An open-topped car speeds along mile after mile of white sands. Sanjay and me are taking Maxine for an evening's drive. *Hotel California* is playing. I can smell the brine, there are stars so bright they reflect as jewels in an unrippled sea, Maxine laughs her famous laugh, slightly vulgar, and every so often we have to keep stopping to take turns to fuck her.

CHAPTER 16

Next morning, Sunday, brings the chance of a lie in, Zero beside me, purring in sleep. I can hear Robert's voice. Has he come early? Did he stay overnight?

When I finally get up – "Morning, Bernard . . . Robert" – they largely ignore me, murmuring tersely of a plague of vine-weevil larvae while poking spoons at the soil of a dead-looking plant removed from its pot. I get as far as boiling the kettle for a mug of tea, then think *fuck it*, put on the famous long coat and leave.

The famous long coat? My cloak of invisibility, my disguise, my comforter, call it what you will – there are people who will tell you they know me by it; and, true, it has seen better days but its age is part of its charm to my eye, while thanks to a regular oiling it retains most of its weatherproof features which I need in this grey dismal weather for the two-hundred yards' walk to the Otter & Trout.

A pint of beer and a chat – a regular habit of Sunday mornings – and I nod to those I know. The crowd is predominantly male, all acquiring an appetite for the meat-and-two-veg that the little woman is slaving over. Darts and dominoes are in progress in their respective corners.

Appleyard sees me and is quick to close and claim me with an offer of a drink. Middle-aged, middle-manage-ment, he likes at weekends to be seen in his green Hunter wellies, his tweed deerstalker-hat, his waxed Barbour jacket suitably embellished with world wild-life badges, save-the-whale stickers and so on.

"Fallow-deer," I tell him. He craves rustic tales. "There's a tale going round that they've killed one or two, letting running-dogs loose down by Oxenflats woods."

He understands "deer" and "woods" but shakes his head over "running-dogs".

"A cross," I tell him. "Say a greyhound for speed bred with something that's got lots of neck-strength to grab and drag down."

By his pained expression, I can tell that I've inventively tapped in to what will earn me more drink. Stupidly, he's one who continues to regard poaching as part of our heritage, a jolly *one-for-the-pot* rural pursuit. So I tell him of fish-hooks embedded in raisins for pheasants. I describe mist-nets for pigeons and drag-nets for partridge, plus there's lamping at night, shooting rabbits and hares with silenced .22s, whereas a shot-gun sawn short gives a more lethal spread if a deer is required. Bright eyes shining back – BANG-BANG! Bambi's dead with his brains hanging out.

And I can tell it's the Walt Disney mention that does it, breaking through to the anthropomorphic side of him and sparking his immediate leap onto his high horse on behalf of anything endangered. Which is fine: my pint is free and he's having his fun.

Only my satisfaction is ruptured as the pavement door opens and I hurriedly swing to look elsewhere, not wanting to be recognized. Bill & Ben. This by now is how I'm thinking of the duo who've still got my lamp from our clash at the ford. I've not seen them drinking in these parts before.

"Right, over at the counter," I say, interrupting whatever Appleyard was jabbering about. "There's two just walked in who'll take anything living." I keep my eyes downcast because I know I've been spotted; they're staring right through me.

"Don't look," I say. I urge this on Appleyard because Bill & Ben, in mud-smeared army-surplus, are already visibly unhappy about the attention they're attracting. They've got dogs at their feet to kick clear. Jack Russells and Lakelands. Blood-snot-and-snuffling. One Jack's got a lip and a nose torn away and the others are crowding it, wanting a lick.

"That's unusual," I say. "They don't usually waste time on mutts that get injured. A thump on the head with a hammer sees them less of a bother."

What, why, how? Appleyard's questions come as they might from a kid on a bus-trip.

"You've heard me say 'shit-and-cruelty' lots of times," I tell him. "See all the mud? They've been digging. They'll have gear in the van, spades and that . . . after badgers for baiting."

"They've got badgers outside?"

"No, hardly, or they'd not be in here, would they?"

I feel a movement beside me and Sammy slots in at my elbow – I only know him as Sammy. "Saw you there, Errol." Even when there's no need for secrecy Sammy still talks out of the corner of his mouth, his eyes directed skywards.

"So have they been after badgers?" asks Appleyard.

"Sunday morning. They'll have been roaming round, *sporting* – like you when you go after mushrooms. A bit of fresh air."

"Anything doing then, Errol?"

"I dunno, Sammy. Like what?" Sammy works the open markets, York to Newcastle.

"You mean, they actually kill badgers?"

"They'd say *foxes* if spotted. Digging foxes is legal." I glance to Sammy. "You need anything special?"

"Quiet time of the year really. What you got?"

"So are they after badgers or aren't they?"

I raise my eyebrows at Sammy as if appealing for patience. "Just a second, Sammy," I say, then give Appleyard my full attention. "Those guys will know where the setts are. They put a dog underground, then start digging. If they come on a badger, they make sure it's trapped so it fights. They'll break its back with a spade, maybe chop its front paws off, then set the dogs on. They take videos sometimes. It's their idea of fun to be watching 'em later. They do swops with others." I swing back to Sammy. "Now then, Sammy?"

"Mainly just cheap kiddie's stuff I'm after. Anything at the right price really, old son."

I'm denied time to say anything by Appleyard gripping my arm. Although the description of badger baiting I offered to him was really a pale understatement of the gore involved, he looks like he's just been told he's got maggots crawling out of his nose. "Errol," he says, "*nothing* is worth the mistreatment of animals or not treating them decently."

I nod; I couldn't agree with him more. At the same time I'm trying to visualize the shop and what we've got plenty of. "Sammy, I can do you some little pants and vests. Some soft toys. A few socks maybe."

"Nice."

"There's no bloody justice!" Appleyard appears to have run out of patience.

"What's his problem?" says Sammy, as we watch him stalk off.

"Ignore him. He's crazy. Would tomorrow night suit . . . eight o'clock, the same lay-by?"

"Lovely." Sammy lifts his glass. "You having one?"

He gets them in. We stand talking. He knows a million

filthy jokes. This one is about a bored housewife, a parrot and an oversized cucumber.

Until – "Watch it," he says, "here comes your friend back."

Appleyard slides close. "I've been on the mobile outside," he says, his face flushed. "I could tell which their van is. It's got nets in and all sorts. The police said thanks for the tip. I gave them the van's make and number. They've said right, they'll sort it."

I can't think what to say for a moment. He's spoken resolutely and clearly imagines congratulations are in order, and in glaring directly at Bill & Ben he's sending the message they've got their share of pain coming. All of which leaves me gripped by realizing there's no way of pretending he's not with me.

"Christ, look at the time." I start drinking up. "I've my dinner to get to. My wife's going to shoot me."

"Yes, duty calls," Sammy says. He's been gulping his pint since he heard the word *police*.

"Got your pains again, Errol?" Robert asks. "Or aren't you hungry?"

They've prepared Sunday lunch between them. Salmon again. I start catching a few and we eat nothing else.

I finish what I can, then wipe the rest into the bin and add my plate to the mess in the sink. I take it we're not washing-up. Bernard is setting out their brushes and tubes while Robert is laying down old newspapers to protect the carpet. I grab an armchair, clamp on my Walkman, and dismiss the pair of them by moving my lips and silently clicking my fingers to the beat.

The truth is *no batteries*. This style of eavesdropping is nearly as good as leaving the intercoms on.

"All right by you, Robby, if I do one and five? I feel much more at home with these bright jazzy shades."

"Oh, you would! And how about nine and twelve? I think red's more your colour. It's so robustly hot."

After another ten minutes of this bullshit, I am quietly going crazy. Next on the agenda will be their weekly performance of sorting through seeds, though it's not the thought of future sowings that holds their interest from what I can see. The attraction is the packets, the brightly illustrated fronts, like saving stamps.

"I'm off out," I announce.

They nod, smile and don't ask where to. Like I'm nothing.

The drive to town takes ten minutes, where up a side-street a neon sign says BOOKS on a shop's blacked-out window. Most Sunday afternoons I'm usually not the only bored bastard who needs catering to; normally other customers are prowling the shelves, furtive-eyed. This time there's just me and no way of avoiding the elderly geek who minds the counter.

"Haven't seen you in weeks," he says. With long thinning hair, he's always in out of date suits. "Your brother keeping well?"

"Mustn't grumble," I answer.

"Can't be much fun for him in a wheelchair all the time like that," he says. I nod vaguely. Although sealed cling-film wrappers prohibit close inspection, one gets to know the titles one can trust. *No Holes Barred* and *Chateau Perverse* look reasonably imaginative and receive his nod of approval as I lay them on the counter. He says, "No harm in him looking, anyway." He slides the two mags into an anonymous brown paper bag. "Still," he adds, "you'd think the government would do more for its wounded. Half-price refund on these, by the way, if you return them unmarked."

The bag disappears in the long coat's poacher's-pocket.

I stroll the town centre. Tatty, deserted. For days now I haven't seen Sol to dosh him his usual baksheesh and with no rush to be elsewhere I try the doorways and out-of-way corners I know he favours, including the Dene and St Cuthbert's churchyard where the winos hang out. But no sign of him anywhere, and it's starting to rain.

I stop at the next call-box. "Hello, Paula. Me again."

"Errol, is Paula to get nude like this too?"

"If she wants to."

Paula's flat offers pleasing contrasts to the privations I once shared with Sol. Its cosiness warms the cockles, so to speak, and the vodka helps.

Already we're halfway through the bottle I picked up driving over, though since tomorrow is Paula's abortion it's really just me and Louise drink-for-drink, though I'm doubtful if she can be flying so kite-high solely on booze. From flat on my back, a closer look at her eyes isn't easy, and do I want to know, anyway? Let it be enough that she's stopped making noises, fingernailing her teeth like she does, not to mention the verses we've had of her *singing-in-tongues* – which was scary.

"There's thousands owing," Paula says, continuing with her gripe that her wage from Miss Betsy may not be as safe as she's always imagined. "Not just the Inland Revenue, either. I'm sick of telling firms that the cheque's in the post."

"Relax, relax," I tell her. "I know all this crap from Sanjay already."

Louise flicks at my chest. "You're not in bad nick for your age, are you, Errol? God, you're hairy. That key on a string round your neck. What's it for?"

"For my basement."

"Paula, listen . . ." she giggles, "do you know what he keeps in his pocket as well? It's a seashell!"

"Louise, be careful, with me," says Paula.

"Your hook-and-eye's stuck."

"Well, don't force it."

"I won't. There, done! Crikey, Paula, is this a C cup you wear?"

"I've been big from fourteen."

"Here, Paula, look! She's a big girl as well on this page Errol's showing!"

"Errol, that story you told us before . . . those men in that pub with those dogs?"

"What about it?"

"Don't badgers have bones in their pricks?"

"Where'd you get that tale from?"

"I thought you knew all that stuff. Here, Louise, quit with that there and try this. God, I'm dreading tomorrow. I'd sooner be doing this properly."

The room has started to whirl. The phone rings. Paula gets up to answer. I decide no more vodka for me – I still have to drive home.

"Guess what?" Paula comes back to say. "That was Karen crying. She says she's had a phone-call from Denzil to say she's been sacked 'cause she took last Friday off."

Louise's mind is elsewhere. "Errol, why's it gone soft?"

I smile and shrug. I guess it could be the booze, plus that two days on the trot is asking a bit much of me.

"Here, let me," Paula says. "I know how."

CHAPTER 17

Monday morning. A letter by first post is the first I have heard from my sister Grace since the death of my mother and comes as an arrow sent to penetrate my heart and conscience.

Grace writes that at no small expense she has arranged for a headstone: "A personal tribute to a wonderful mother..." It is what a mother has a right to expect of her children, she says, and she would've done it before but she has waited for the mound to settle – which I don't think is true. The marble, the lettering and so on will've cost her a bomb, so I'd say she's more likely been saving up all this time, quietly savouring the moment of dumping her vindictiveness on me.

If so, she scores bull's-eye, and I trust that Maxine smiling from the wall will understand that my inner distress calls for – *skol!* – a little numbing of the senses; although God knows I have to confess I seem oddly vague about how long ago it was that Mother passed on. Years, anyhow; but to take a guess, I'd say her ending was at some point around three months before Linda announced the finish of us, something like that, and it was definitely two years or more after my father got sick and died. He went shortly after Aunt Milly did.

However, one thing I recall for sure: when word arrived that my mother was ill, Linda refused to come with me. She argued that the scenes we caused when together wouldn't be suitable for alongside anyone's sick-bed.

So I travelled down alone. Grace, never marrying, had

remained stuck at home all those years – never been abroad, never had a passport, never had a holiday, couldn't drive, never had a proper boyfriend.

She was greyer and heavier than I remembered and had a lecture rehearsed for my arrival, slanging me for not visiting more often.

She said, "Still, I've told her you'd mentioned you *might* come. I've got out her clean bed-jacket and brushed her hair, so say she looks nice."

I went up. Considering all the years I'd spent pretending to be Aunt Milly's child, it seemed surprising that so little felt strange. "Hello, Mum." I sat uncomfortably on the straight-backed chair carried up from the front room. The light was dim, objects seemed blurred, the pattern stippled on the walls with a sponge had the appearance of frozen amoeba.

"Hello, Errol, my lamb, are you here on a visit?" Her breath was a whisper; the skin tightened around her mouth in a semblance of a smile. Her hair had thinned. It seemed possible to follow each strand down to her scalp. I said, "Linda sends her love. She couldn't come because Daisy's got a school-exam she can't miss. Your hair looks nice and I like your little coat. Pink was always your colour."

The stroke she'd suffered had left her confused. She appeared to think I was still a sailor.

I recall I was desperate to please, perhaps attempting to expunge any guilt I was feeling, I suppose. When she asked for her pearl-handled tweezers, I couldn't refuse.

She said, "You used to as a little lad, but Grace just laughs when I ask."

Her tweezers were in her dressing-table drawer, exactly as I remembered. She had closed her eyes in readiness. Then at first I didn't think I could and had to steady one trembling hand with the other, nipping each hair close to the skin and plucking it out with a sharp turn of the wrist. I counted aloud for her. Four in all. "Is four a record?" she said.

"No, six was the record." I remembered so clearly.

After that she appeared to doze. Now and then she wheezed and sucked on her tongue. Midnight came. I was glad when Grace relieved me. It was agreed I would sleep on the scullery settee and she would wake me at four for my next turn on watch.

I had in my bag a bottle I'd brought with me. I don't know, maybe I was drinking more than I thought in those days. At all events, a nip for courage, not escape, seemed in order; but then when I awoke it was to a fuzziness that suggested I'd perhaps sunk more than a couple of snorts. I could see daylight outside the scullery curtains and Grace was saying, "I was bringing you this."

I took the cup.

"She's gone. Mother's gone."

I couldn't swallow. The tea ran out of my mouth and down my front. The clock on the mantelpiece showed past ten past seven.

"She went just after five. She was holding my hand. She went quietly, no bother."

I said, "She can't have. It was me to be there."

Grace was breathless in triumph. She said, "No, I think those she cared for were present when needed." Then for a moment she seemed ready to hit me. "I saw you'd been plucking her chin. You've not changed one bit; you're obscene. Don't think I've not heard from Linda to tell all about you. There's drink on your breath even now . . . heaven knows what Uncle Lewis imagined you'd make of yourself."

And therein lay the germ of her hate.

Not having been offered the chances I'd had, she'd gone straight from school to a job doing quality-control in a electric-bulb factory. A conveyor-belt system. Probably seeing those duds going by in her dreams she wasn't ever going to forgive me the year upon year and the hour after hour of it.

Upset as I am by Grace's letter, I'm put way behind and so arrive late for opening the shop but find Maxine's already done it. She studies my face. She says, "The day's only just starting, you've been drinking already."

I decide it wouldn't help to start describing my family history.

"Paula's off sick today," she says.

I make like it's news. Of course I know where she is – with her feet in the stirrups or whatever they do.

"And Denzil says he wants words when you've time."

I head up there. Step off the scuffed matting and on to the red-and-black fitted carpet arranged by Sanjay from some failed Chinese restaurant and you're in Denzil's office. King-sized desk, CHAIRMAN AND MANAGING DIRECTOR done in gilt on a dinky oak board, high tech phone, calculator, VDU screen, fax, recording device, electronic organizer, diary and blotter bound in matching red repro leather, walls that blow trumpets via flow-charts and graphs, flagged-pins stuck in maps . . .

Such are the fixtures and fittings of greatness, and what makes Denzil such a tiresome, even dangerous son-of-a-bitch is that they allow him to truly believe about himself whatever he wants to believe.

Listening to him requires maximum effort. He is saying, "In corporate growth the infrastructure and business-plan is paramount, and without statistical input we can hardly hope to stimulate venture capital. So the new system starting this week Monday will cover all movement of goods, daily takings, and et cetera. That way a complete and up-to-date picture will show for each shop on the central computer."

"You going to pay overtime for all this extra?"

"Tough!" he retorts, but avoids my gaze. "Those who prefer to be out of line can always do the other. The streets are loaded with people begging for work. Let lower ranks start dictating and you die in the stampede of being taken advantage of. That's battalion orders."

Denzil, hub of the universe. Truly it never occurs to him that other people have ambitions, emotions, needs, frailties, lives to lead.

So it's Shitsville – which means that heading back down the stairs, I'm still trying to come to terms with how the bottom has abruptly been knocked out of my income. Jesus, when I think of the time and effort I've spent concocting extra receipt books, dummy entries, twin stock-lists, duplicate keys to all doors, not to mention my electronic wizardry with a soldering-iron on the till's *No Sale* button – the masterplan that has served me well since Miss Betsy started is hereby put to waste by his stupid idea.

"Don't ask," I say to Maxine. "He wants you up there to explain it himself."

Then she's been gone but a minute when an old bloke comes in, saying what he needs is a cordless phone for his wife who's got emphysema and can't get out of bed. I take one look at him and he's so ancient he can hardly be a VAT inspector or some other snoop, so I tell him thirty quid off for hard cash. I add, "A real Geordie offer ... spend another five hundred and I'll throw in a biro" – which is a joke he likes so much that he's still laughing while going out through the door with his bargain, a receipt never entering his head.

Thus my mood is improved by £99.95.

Maxine returns. "This new idea of Denzil's is crazy."

"Cheer up!" I tell her. "I won on a horse. How're you fixed for a meal out tonight?"

Greta Hall's where we choose. Ye-olde-coaching-house, classy drinking, three-star bar-meals. The proprietors play to the hilt that they reckon Charles Dickens once stayed here and that Wordsworth penned some rhyme about the local nodding daffodils.

Whatever – more important to the moment is that Vanessa is dishing out toothy welcomes behind the bar. A one-time hostess on a TV quiz show, she and Maxine are old friends, an attachment that gets us a table in a place that's already packed.

So tally-ho, the trappings of hunting adorn the wall. We're snug in an alcove formed by tarted-up cartwheels.

We skip starters: Maxine's on sea bream and house wine.

"Yo! This man is an artist and would love to paint you. Take all your clothes off. Slide over here and sit on this."

The quip's not brand-new and I've time to feel pathetic before she decides to play. She says, "Don't forget, when we come here you always say you're letting me off 'cause the condom machine's never working."

I return her grin. Look, admire, enjoy, fantasize – the game we play provides what I can't put a name to.

"So how's Mr Superstar?"

She laughs. "You want to know, really?"

"Sure."

"Last night. We came here."

Shit! I open my mouth, she shoves her foot in it. I go quiet, toying with my seafood-platter which is virtually inedible because they've used bottled mussels. The vinegar is rubberizing my lips.

"Well, well! What luck! No tables free ... can we share?"

I look up and could puke at seeing we've been discovered by Denzil and Terri. Mentally I'm urging them on, but the best they manage is a big show of reticence before they sit down. "What's good?" they ask.

I recommend the seafood-platter.

The waitress comes and goes; behind her back Denzil refers to her as Greasy Lil. It's one of the snags with this place that it gets heavily frequented by the "upwardly-mobile", so-called. "How's trade?" enquires one who stops to say hello. I recognize his face; he owns a couple of dress-shops. "Fabulous," says Denzil. "It's bloody hard work but I enjoy the challenge. In fact, in confidence, who knows, ha-ha, you may soon be seeing my Miss Betsy franchise on the stock-market list."

Or in the bankruptcy court? Jesus, I'm never quite sure of how stupid he is. For instance, while it's generally recognized that Maxine and I are friendly enough to be seen together, you'd think he'd at least be wondering how on the wages he pays I can afford to eat at joints like this. "Another drink, Denzil . . . Terri?" I offer.

They accept.

At the bar, while Vanessa is pouring: "Your condom machine working tonight?" I ask, hoping she'll assume that I'm getting it regularly off Maxine. Whatever – she must be as thick as a brick 'cause she buys it. "Oh, truly, truly!" she says, trilling it like the catch-phrase from some quiz show she once flashed her legs on.

Landing back at the table with the tray, I'm in time to hear Denzil saying, "Well, I don't know where they've gone but I definitely remember ordering kiddies' cotton knickers and vests."

"Darling, don't fret, forget work till tomorrow," says Terri. She then stretches her lips, like she's fresh from the dentist's. "Is it me," she says to Denzil, "or does yours taste of vinegar?"

"The problem of *missing stock*," he replies, sticking to his grumble, "is exactly why I need a print-out in future, to see what's going on."

"Denzil . . ." I hurriedly seek to divert him, "what the hell did you sack Karen for?" There follows an uncomfortable silence. "You do know it was her grandmother's funeral she took the day off for?"

"Well, I'm sorry." He's rattled. "I'm the last person to be wishing harm on anyone who's dead."

"Karen genuinely thought she was allowed the time. You gave her no reference, either?"

"Oh, really?"

What a prat!

"Errol," he blurts, "I run a multi-million pound show. Shilly-shallying's out, I won't have it. I wanted that typing doing *at once*, and she wasn't there, and where I'm concerned it's front-line action or nothing. I issued *an order*, and as the firm's senior executive officer on duty I was in full command. It was my responsibility, my decision, and I took it, and I'd do it again, sir."

The "sir" leaves Terri not sure where to look. "Darling, darling, don't get carried away." She then shuffles her plate with the tips of her fingers. "I don't think I'll eat this. Can I have Death By Chocolate?"

"Errol . . ." he's ignoring her and now flamboyantly gesturing, "you've a lot to say for someone who works only part-time, don't you think? I built that company. It's *mine*."

"*Ours*, darling," says Terri, a correction that literally throws him off balance and his ungoverned hand by mischance knocks his drink off the table and into her lap.

"For God's sake!" she explodes. "I don't want to spend the evening hearing about some stupid sacked girl and a few missing knickers."

"Don't worry yourself, lovely lamb." He's mopping her

down with a napkin. "If this stain won't shift, then we'll buy you a new skirt tomorrow. That red one you liked showed your legs off a treat."

We sit parked outside Maxine's house, and to my mind it's been a good evening, worth every penny. When the girl brought the bill, I saw Denzil quickly glance elsewhere. "No, have this on me, Denzil!" I said. And the arsehole, he sat back and let me – which I honestly loved. I was paying with his fucking money for Christ's sake!

I lightly touch Maxine's knee. "Okay, my final offer. Three hundred quid to turn back and be fucked in a layby."

"God," she groans, "you get worse."

A frightening thought. Perhaps she is tired of me.

She strokes the dashboard. "You know, not everybody would lend out a nice car like this every time you want to visit your aunt."

"That's Sanjay. Generous to a fault. Can I touch your left breast?"

"No, you can't! By the way, that about Karen going to her grandma's funeral? She's not even got a grandma, has she?"

"God knows. I was just sticking up for her."

"I think you like Paula better. You two seem very friendly."

"She's just a kid. Could we hold hands, then? People hold hands all the time."

"I don't."

I take her hand, anyway, and try stroking her fingers. She stares out of the window. A cat appears on a wall, then jumps down and away. "Look, a pussy," she says.

"Great minds think alike."

"That's not funny." She reclaims her hand. "How's yours keeping? Your cat, I mean."

"Zero? He's fine. Listen, I want to ask ... *seriously* ... would you marry me if I was rich?"

"God, don't start all that!" She hurriedly opens the door. "You know something, you're crazy, you are. One of these days you're going to give me a heart attack."

Later in bed, with a further trip to Stand Alone assured for tomorrow, I know I don't need to worry about letting myself get all fired up.

Chateau Perverse seems good quality printing. I may decide to keep it.

But eventually, tired, I click off the light. The act of butterflying my pillow doesn't blot out that Robert has stayed and he snores, the noise of the two of them zig-zagging down the passage and permeating the walls like I'm being devoured via my ears by great globs of phlegm.

I hope Sanjay's Peugeot will stay safe in the next-street-but-one where I usually park it. Perhaps for my future I should invest more on the lottery every week? The horses are hopeless: a small win won't save me. I hear the wild geese go over. I don't know where they come from or where they go to. The images from *Chateau Perverse* remain fairly clear in my head.

All the same, I wish I had something nice to think about.

I guess the truth is I am really alone here.

Carol parts her hair with her fingers to show me her scalp. "Local anaesthetic," she says, high on relief. "All that fuss and worry and it was just an old fatty cyst."

I am happy for her and pour us a little afternoon pick-me-up. Did she mention the lump in her armpit, I wonder.

I enquire after Angela. "Out following the chuckies who lay all over," she says. "Errol, is my Joey a good worker, is he?"

"Yes, I heard so," I say, though I haven't a clue.

"Your name's not to be bandied, I told him. He says he's been given a go on a fork-lift and can get off-cuts cheap. When he finds it in blue he's getting me some for the bathroom."

Joey's not due till late. City are playing a home night match. These days, earning a wage, he can afford to be one of the rowdy Kop Army. He has a poster of Superstar pasted next to Sylvester Stallone in his bedroom.

The back door opens. "Hello, Errol. I saw your car."

Angela's bucket is half-filled with hen's eggs. I see I was right to think she would suit yellow wellies.

"Chucky-eggs," she says. "Brown, white, sometimes speckled."

"Sure, and you're a good girl but Errol knows all that stuff. Wash all that filth off your hands 'cause he can't be here long now."

Upstairs.

A heady time. I wouldn't wish to debate the morality of it with anyone, especially since afterwards I am usually overtaken by a resolve to stay away – I feel it already, though we've not yet got started. Curtains drawn. I prefer the artificial light. The starker atmosphere enlivens me that touch extra. I am responding, I suspect, to imagining us posed as a photo. Thin slivers of sunshine speckled with dust are slanting in. Angela has on the animal nightie I got her, plain and short, Marks & Sparks. Carol's contours and length of cleavage reveal her as naked beneath her loose housecoat. She takes it off and has exaggerated the sex of herself with lipstick on her nipples. Overdone, I think; for if she has a fault, and though I would never offend her by saying, she sometimes clings to failed ideas.

She gets me going nonetheless. "Big boy. What's this old thing sticking up? Who's a scoundrel today?"

You never know with Carol. Stretched out, I tremble while watching her stand on a chair to get at her box on the top of the wardrobe.

"Don't say what I'm like," I tell her, imploring but hopeful.

"We will say what we will. A horse would blush. What a size. But be still. Don't you dare blink an eye. Not a move, not a muscle."

She wheels up the tall cheval-mirror – which is clever. I am here, yet not here: captive but without being trapped. All the roughness is feigned. I could always pull free.

"Sweetheart, don't just stand yourself idle."

Angela has the tendency to be content with watching or copying unless spoken to sharply.

"That's it," Carol says, now praising her efforts. "Let the dog see the rabbit. How's that, Errol-love? What a throb. We shall get it worked off, don't you fret. Nice and slow. But keep your bum on that towel if you will, else that candlewick spread is a bugger to wash."

Paula rings me that night at the flat. "I just thought you might want to know I came through all right," she says.

Having taken the call in the living-room, I am clamping the receiver hard to my ear, not wanting Bernard to eavesdrop. He is giving me funny looks as it is.

"Good, I'm pleased to hear you're recovered," I say.

"I'm still a bit sore, though," she says; "so I think it's best if I stay on the sick. I'll have this week off."

"Fine. That sounds great."

She giggles. "Leeds is lovely for shopping, as well, did you know?"

All crutch and no sense is what she is. "Lovely . . .

thanks for letting me know," I reply, "and goodbye," and
ring off.

CHAPTER 18

The following evening. Closing-time at the shop. I'm setting the burglar-alarm when Terri surprises me by coming down the inside way. With screwed-up banknotes bulking my pockets – my last raid on the till before the new system starts – I feel caught out, but my worries evaporate on seeing she's tearful.

"Trouble?" I ask, frowning with a sympathy I really don't feel.

"Just give me a minute," she sniffs.

"So what's upset you? Is Denzil upstairs?"

"No, in London." She drags the back of her hand across her wet eyes and nose. "You don't fancy a quick coffee, do you?" she says.

The Continental Cafe lies around the first corner. Close enough to walk. At a corner table, Terri orders tea – a tea-pot, not tea-bags. She drinks tea all day long. Tea helps control her cystitis, she says.

"It's very good of you to cheer me up like this." She shoots a lungful of smoke down her nose in vehement fashion. "I work my butt off, and what's it all for?"

"Money?" I venture, as if I don't know. "Cash-flow problems?"

"Between you and me," she says, "that's why Karen got sacked . . . *to save wages.*"

The tea comes, she pours. "I hear it from Sanjay," I tell her. "Denzil's been bleating to him that the bank is upset. What's outstanding? Five grand? Ten grand?"

"And times five!" She seems astounded that I'm underestimating and understating the seriousness of the position. She says, "Don't breathe a word but he's had mine already – all I had saved from when I got divorced, it's all gone."

"You've risked money?"

"And more. I don't even understand half the things that I've put my name to!"

"Is this why he's rushed down to London?"

"Just don't ask. If he knew I was saying, he'd kill me."

She's brightened; talking's soothed her. She lights up another king-sized. Then it's what I'm expecting of her as she leans forward to see if I've finished my tea. She titters. She says, "You've not had a little go in ages."

I smile to show I'm easy. Always good for a laugh is that she's obsessed with clairvoyance and/or anything occult, even to the extent of having psychic powers of her own, she claims, sometimes telling of her spirit guide, a man, who comes to stand at the foot of her bed in the night. "Yeah, some wanking bastard," is what we generally say.

Now, having claimed my empty cup, she holds it at arms' length in her interlaced fingers while angling her head to gain different views of the tea-leaves. It's a mesmeric warm-up routine that never fails to put a prickle in the hairs on the back of my neck – there's been occasions before when I've got an erection.

"I see Africa," she says, and I grin. "Don't laugh. Definitely, I see Africa." She tilts the cup slightly. "I see Paula as well."

"Rubbish."

She raises her eyes. "Are you kidding? I've been waiting for her to have a few days off for ages. I don't need bloody tea-leaves for that one."

"Well, don't look at me."

She makes a motion to dismiss the subject as *no big*

deal. She'll know all the ins and outs of getting knocked up, I suppose. "Oh, my God!" she says, and inhales deeply through her nose. "My guide's here. He's here now!"

I sit hoping to Christ no one's watching. With eyes closed, she's turning her head back and forth as if it's a direction-scanner. "Smell that wallflower smell? That's *death*. The astral plane. He's here."

I can't smell a thing. Still . . . I grin flippantly. "You'd better watch it – he'll be up your left leg given half a chance."

"No, don't mock!" She needs a long drag. "Two men here . . . *strangers*. A weathercock, too. Some change of direction for you coming up."

"Brilliant!" Then a thought strikes me. "Watch out for two men, you say?"

She's pressing ahead. "Can you take a Barbara?"

"Never heard of her."

"Anyway, just here . . ." In stroking the outside of the cup, her long false nails look misplaced growing out of the fat chubby fingers she's got. "It's someone dancing, an Indian figure . . . *kicking a ball*? Do you know any footballers?"

My face must give me away because she gleefully immediately leans forward to show me the inside of the cup. "I've hit something. I have, haven't I – I've hit something? A figure moving openly like that means big money." She thinks about it. "Sanjay's uncle. It could be."

That sounds like a clue to what she and Denzil might be up to. "So is that why Denzil's in London . . . you're dealing with Uncle Mohan? He's a man of some means."

She's not answering that one. In fact she's seriously concerned she might already have said too much – which is an impression that hardens some minutes later when she gives me a lift. She's gone quiet and her usual rallycross manoeuvres are missing. At the Otter & Trout I'm pleased to get out. She farted not far back.

"You going to be all right tonight with Denzil away?" I ask her.

"A little light masturbation," she says.

"Charming!"

"Well, why not? You should see Denzil's face when he's here. 'God, are you at it again?' he says. It gets him going something awful." She chuckles at the thought. "You're a good listener. Thanks for that."

"No problem." Then since with her I can show a little of the masculinity I daren't chance with Maxine, I reach in and squeeze her shoulder. And it's okay, I don't mind touching her. The actual feel of her doesn't quite reach me through the expensive quilted jacket she's got on, so I don't need to feel repelled or anything. "Drive safely," I tell her.

Next day.

"Jesus!" I look away for a calming breath. "Yes, that's Sol."

The air within the tiled room is cold, perhaps refrigerated. I can hear an electric hum and am deliberately not noticing the sweet sickly smell: maybe wallflowers.

"Sol?"

"Solomon. Solomon Theakston."

"Address?"

"No address."

Scribbling a note on his pad, the attendant moves away and I can see a length of red rubber-tubing and a long syringe of some sort sticking upwards from the side pocket of his long white coat. The uniformed sergeant, who has my elbow snug in his palm, is either keeping me there or supporting my weight. "How come you knew I knew him?" I ask, and he answers by allowing himself a

faint smile, one that besides being loaded shows some
reverence for the place and its purpose.

He then lets go of me so he can peel back the sheet a
bit further. The flesh on view is a dreadful colour, black
in parts. "Did you know he used drugs?"

"I don't know ... maybe ..."

"I have to ask," he says, and offers a quick shake of
his head to show he's not one who possesses some special
immunity to life's inhumanities. "The world is an arsehole," he says. "It shits all over you."

"It tends to depend where you're standing."

"True," he says, then he pulls the sheet back up again.
"You wouldn't want to see the bottom half of him,
anyhow," he says.

"So ... he fell off a motorway bridge?"

"Fell? Jumped? He got hit in the fast lane, I know that
much." He exhales through clenched teeth at the thought
of it. "Any idea of his age?"

"Fifty, fifty-five. From the Midlands somewhere. He
was married, or had been. He carried a snapshot he
showed around sometimes. He got maudlin a lot." I shrug
to indicate I know little more. "He used to wait outside
the shop in the mornings. I gave him a quid now and
then."

"In the King's Arcade?"

I can see he knows – he probably knows *everything*.
"They called him Sol."

The white-coated attendant returns carrying a galvan-
ized bucket and is chewing; a mint or something.

"You want me to sign anything?" I ask.

"No," says the sergeant. "We just had to be certain."

We leave together. A fine drizzle is dampening everything but I decline the offer of a lift. At the wheel of his
vehicle a young attractive policewoman reminds me of
the actress Rosanna Arquette. I fancied her most in her

film about Gary Gilmore. She and Maxine look similar, so that's the type I go for. But I don't like riding in police-cars never mind who's driving.

At The Hole In The Wall, the barman looks anxious. "You feeling all right, chum?"

"A headache. I'm fine, thanks."

But I'm not. To end up like some fucking hedgehog you've got to be desperate. And Sol was – *desperate*, always looking to be free in one way or another. Except aren't we all? Allowing oneself to be lulled by the passing of time it's so easy to forget that your past is a part of some data-bank somewhere, that a press of a switch puts you up on the screen.

"Barman," I call, "better make that a double."

So I've let myself slide. I realize this on waking slumped on a bench in the Dene. The drizzle had increased to a steady rain, and the god-awful despair, the wetness, the spewing up bile in a border, whisks me back to days I would sooner forget.

Next comes panic. I feel a desperate need to get home. Through the town centre to the bus-stop is quickest but offers the greatest chance of bumping into someone who might recognize me. Thus opting for the back way, I hug the lee of the wall along Northgate until I arrive at the bus-shelter. There, forced to queue, I am stuck with ten minutes of myself on closed-circuit TV in an adjacent shop window.

Then it's another half-hour before I get to the flat. A crippled woodmouse, with legs kicking, lies on its back on the doorstep, a tooth-punctured trophy left as a present by Zero. I tread on its head, pick it up by the tail and whirl it away into the jungle of the garden. Although Zero's not to be seen, I know he's there somewhere. He'll be after another.

I feel bad. I'm glad Bernard's not home yet. Seeing myself on TV like that won't go away. I can feel settled on me the old cold desperation, a sensation of acute persecution. Down I go to my basement where I won't feel so threatened.

Here it's quiet. I pour myself a glass of the dew, then switch on my TV and VCR.

When I get hit like this, Hugh on screen sometimes helps. My trigger in time to how I think I once was.

On a hot July afternoon as we walked down the school lane. "Errol," said Linda, grumbling, "you're such a bloody wet-blanket."

"Not true," I said. "You looked ridiculous in that pig mask."

"Well, that's you all over. Your sort never complains till it's happened. Good grief, if you didn't want me to go in the bloody swimming-pool, you should have shouted."

"Linda, no one minded you swimming. It was the running around in the buff I disliked. You could see all you'd got."

"A thrill, was it? God knows, you've talked me into doing much worse enough times."

I said nothing. I didn't want to argue. The lane looked as narrow and leafy as I remembered it; the Drummond Spit fog-buoy was booming every thirty-two seconds despite the bright sunshine. Strangely, I wasn't sure I felt old enough to be looking back over so many years and pointing out landmarks.

"This was Shylock's house." A notice, "Sunnyside Nursing-Home" was fixed to the wide wrought-iron gates we were passing. "When the heather caught fire in his grounds, he doubled the whole school up here so we could piss on it."

"That's disgusting."

"I forget if it worked. As juniors we never got free, but as seniors we did. The village girls used to wait in the bushes all along here."

"Desperate, were they?"

"Out here in the wilds what else was there for them?"

She tossed her hair, then gave me a slanted glance. "Look, why are we bothering with all this?" she said.

Being in London for a promotional event, I'd pressured her into accepting the idea of a flying visit, a sixty-mile drive. She'd argued there'd be little to see, and largely she was right. The school buildings had been levelled. Contractors' hoardings announced the site as a marina development. In the near distance a large flat modern factory of glass and aluminium stood where the swamp and its Burma Road had been filled in and flattened.

"It's a five-hour drive home," she said. "It's not fair on Robert and Tina, leaving them looking after Daisy."

We'd arrived on the dunes and had the view of a deserted beach and flat calm sea. She'd taken her shoes off. I picked up a seashell, hefting its weight in my palm. I said, "Around here, all this brings back some memories."

Veronica.

Hugh and I met Veronica when Hugh's father came over from Cowes' Week to celebrate Hugh's sixteenth birthday by giving Hugh and me lunch at the village hotel. He was an ugly, bejowled, hugely fat man, easily recognizable from the many front-page photographs in Hugh's scrapbook of newspaper cuttings. Veronica, still at school but assisting her mother with serving, asked for his autograph. He obliged on the back of a postcard of his yacht, *The Lady Zenobia*.

After that, I took Veronica to the pictures on one occasion, but it was Hugh who saw most of her. Being a captain he could walk out when he liked. Giles, too, had made captain but wasn't fraternizing with a nonentity such as I'd turned out to be.

Not that the lack of promotion worried me. In fact by our final week, the miracle, I thought, was that I had survived at all. Our futures lay ahead. A number from my year were intent on further education. Most – like Hugh and Giles – were entering family businesses. For myself, while I'd never been on a boat in my life, it was fixed by Uncle Lewis for me to become a midshipman with the Blue Funnel Line.

"Will you miss me?" Veronica asked Hugh and me.

We were on the dunes. "Sure we will," Hugh said, sprinkling sand across her bare legs.

"You will send the autographs, won't you?" she said.

Obtained via his father, Hugh had already come up with Richard Nixon and certain names of that ilk but it was pop-stars she wanted.

"Depend on it," he said. "Still, one good turn deserves another. We want to see your tits before we go, don't we, Errol?"

Did we? I was suddenly breathless. We'd discussed no such thing. On the other hand I wasn't surprised by his outspokenness. He'd always made clear he regarded her as *experimental*.

"Hugh . . ." she turned giggly, "what for? They're just ordinary."

Hugh appeared to have inherited his father's smooth tongue, coaxing and wheedling. I sat spellbound, my knees already beyond my control now I'd sensed what he clearly had in mind for her.

"You boys, you are awful!" Veronica said and she'd weakened. Or at any rate, she sounded like she wanted to be fair about it.

Or alternatively – I don't know – she might simply have realized she was in a spot.

No matter. At Hugh's get-on-with-it glance I began on her buttons which he would never have managed – he'd been excused knots-&-splices for ages because of the scars on his fingers. Beyond that, aware of his hands up her skirt and his mouth clamped to hers, I took for granted he knew what else he was doing since after every school holiday he regaled us with boasts that he'd had umpteen women. Ambitious bimbos who would do anything to get close to his father, he'd tell us. Some as old as thirty.

Apart from seeing Aunt Milly in the nude and that, all my naked girls up till then had been printed-page photos. I looked at Veronica lying with not a stitch on – breasts, nipples, pubic hair – I would have liked to have gone over her inch by inch but we didn't have long before dinner.

By then, Hugh, in only his shirt and lying between the vee of her thighs, was hogging most of her, anyway. "Just a jiff, your turn next," her eyes seemed to say – she was smiling at me over his shoulder – but that was asking too much at that age. I jerked off while she watched.

Then me and Hugh strolling back up the lane and Hugh was bouncing with camaraderie. He said, "Hell's fire, I really slipped her a goldfish. You should've hung on a bit and had her properly." She'd given us bits of paper on which she'd carefully written her address. He'd already chucked his in the hedge. "They use tampons," he said. "Either that or she'd had it before. She was nobody's virgin."

Back in the present, I kissed Linda again.

"Behave!" she said. "Why are you starting all this now?"

We dovetailed nicely, a sort of remembrance of times we'd long stopped sharing. "Because it's romantic. Because this is memory lane. Because it's a chance not to be wasted. Because we're three hundred miles from home."

"God, you're a smooth-talking bastard, *considering*."

"You don't think I can?"

I guided her hand and she let out a gasp. "I see," she said. "So what's brought this on?"

I sank to my knees, pulling her into a hollow surrounded by marram grass. She was glancing around, pretending panic. "God, put it away," she said. "Just look at that thing, you sly sod. Here's me been feeling sorry for you. You've been getting it somewhere."

"You're a fine one to talk."

Her face tightened up. "Do you want me or don't you? Just be nice. And don't ever dare say you don't get your way. I just hope no one's watching."

"I'm pretending there is."

"Yes, you would." She was starting to shake. "All right, say there is. Tell a story."

Then after we'd done it, I had an arm around her waist in walking back to the car – which in itself was unusual, feeling close to her. "Any complaints? How'd I score?"

"I've no tissues left and I've still got no pants on."

Whether she meant that as a joke or not, I wasn't sure but I laughed, a deliberate attempt to keep the mood light because I had one more secret I wanted to tell. I said, "Guess what? Another surprise. I've been keeping this quiet. My last week at this school, I got expelled from the dump!"

Shylock said, "Young man, recorded in your file is an early observation. It reads, 'Like a waterfall . . . useless unless harnessed.' Had you tried to fit in here, you might have succeeded. We opened our arms. You refused to come in."

What that meant exactly, he didn't explain. Nor could

I ask, since I wasn't allowed to speak unless to answer a question. Besides, even given leave to talk, I wouldn't ever have known what line to pursue. I was young. I was shocked, frightened, confused. The plot or the lesson that was available to be learned seemed either too subtle or too complicated for me to take in.

Shylock, at any rate, had his mind made up, concluding the short interview by giving my folder a satisfied pat. "Present yourself at reception. They'll give you the baggage-room key and your train fare. Return home immediately! You can make your own way. Pack and leave!"

That was that. No appeal. Just *fuck off*.

I got back to main school and word had travelled ahead. "Expelled with one day to go," was on everyone's lips, except no one wanted to talk to me. It took so long to find Hugh he must have been moving from spot to spot to stay clear.

"You pig, Hugh," I said. "Shylock had you in first. You must have told lies."

"He said ring my father to see what he thought."

"Yeah, but it wasn't me with Veronica *on my own*. It was all your idea. He point-blank refused to believe you were there."

"Well, I wasn't."

"Yes, you were."

"I was *not*. I've got proof. Shylock watched me dial. He spoke to my father."

"Hugh, you've used your father's influence to worm out of this. I'll tell on you, Hugh. We've got other secrets. I'll tell *all I know*."

"Go ahead. You can tell who you like. Blacken my name and we'll sue. We've got hundreds of lawyers. My father sues everybody. He knows the government, we have them to dinner."

"Hugh, you've ruined my life."

"Talk sense, Oldfield. What life have you got? Your lot counts for nothing. Your sort causes murders."

"Good God," Linda said. "You've talked about this crackpot school for years and years and you missed out *expelled*?"

"Ah . . . but see, you've got to appreciate the irony. I got home and no one even noticed I was one day early. My uncle was constantly pissed. You met Aunt Milly; she was crackers. The school never wrote, rang or anything. All that bullshit I went through was pointless."

"Nonsense. It can't have cost all that money for nothing. You can always tell people who've been to good schools."

"Can you? So all right, you tell me."

"Something must have rubbed off."

"Okay, *what*?"

She was losing her temper. "All right, maybe in your case it didn't. It *couldn't*. It had nothing to cling to."

We'd reached north of London by then. The memory of passion on the beach had a less rosy glow. I could feel the normality of tension creeping back, bringing something close to a sense of relief. She could go to hell, I could tell myself, and knew she was thinking the same. In case I was doubtful, she soon made herself plain. I *liked* Tom Waits, she *didn't*, and at around Newport Pagnell she ejected the cassette, wound down the car window and tossed him out.

CHAPTER 19

I have made a killing.

Stripped to the waist and perspiring. So much blood. White tiles and porcelain spattered red, dribbling, the bathroom being the only place with taps and a receptacle big enough to cope, the tub still requiring that every so often I need to feel underwater to keep clear the plughole. Not exactly whistle-as-you-work, I counsel myself, but then nobody fucks me about and lives to enjoy it. First the big kitchen-scissors to open the belly; the skin parts so crisply. Then I hand-pull the guts, adding an abundance of entrails and gunge to what's already been freed and removed, some floating, the mess worsening considerably as with a thumbnail I scrape out the thick caudal artery which comes off the backbone in clotted black lengths.

Sweet revenge.

Everyone knows that not getting caught in possession is the first rule of poaching. I have bided my time. Then at first light today, a man with a mission, I was out on the prowl along by Baydale ford where Bill & Ben park their van.

The search for their cache took less than ten minutes. A four-foot square hole beneath the hedgerow and concealed with tin-sheeting, grass sods and leaves. Jackpot! – I was looking down on their last night's catch of twelve prime fish of between eighteen and twenty pounds apiece, each one carefully protected with polythene wrapping. Nets, too: monofilament, medium mesh, thirty yards long.

I put their ends on my shoulders and towed their lengths through the briars till they took hold like anchors: a million breaks will need mending.

I ribboned two wet-suits, cut the feet off three pairs of waders, deep-sixed the four walkie-talkies that have kept them ahead of the bailiffs. Best of all, I got back my lamp.

Now, with gutting finished – I always leave on the heads – the considerable weight of left-over innards half-fills a big refuse-bag which I tie off with twine and heave into the car boot for dumping off later.

Cleaning up takes as long. Bleach down the plug-hole is essential, as is a careful scrub with the nail-brush along where the grouting has broken away between tiles. Any skimping at all and the place starts to hum and brings flies in the summer, those big buzzy buggers.

After this, in touting the twelve fish around the usual outlets, I reckon I have to be disappointed that a price of one-eighty a pound is the best I can get. But it's a sign of the times. So long as the chunk on his plate comes coloured pink, your average gourmet couldn't care less if his salmon is wild or farmed. This glut of pellet-fed crap is ruining the market. All the same, I've made three hundred quid.

Robert's in chirpy mood over tea. So is Bernard. As a matter of fact, this illness of Tina's, if anything, is doing them a power of good in giving them a common cause of sanctimonious benevolence. Over these last days, as she's sunk into an even deeper coma, they have begun a routine on their hospital visits of reading to her from her favourite books, of showing her photos she can't see, of playing her favourite old Rolling Stones' tapes. I'm getting fucking pig-sick of *Brown Sugar ... Paint It Black*.

"Errol ..." says Robert, "change your mind. She'd really be ever so grateful if you came to see her."

I ignore him. The man's an imbecile, and how stupid am I supposed to be, anyway? The idea that he should stop off here straight from work every evening, I've been told, is to facilitate his and Bernard's trips; hence his spare clothes in Bernard's room and cabinet-space for his razor and stuff in the medicine cabinet. Okay, fine, but what hasn't been covered is why he sleeps here so often.

"Will you come?" he continues. "There's some terrible cases. He'd enjoy a look round, wouldn't he, Bernard?"

"I can't, Robert. Not tonight." In fact *not ever.*

"Oh, you should," Robert urges. "You'd love it. There's a quaint little pub driving home that does spuds in their jackets with lashings of butter."

A heartbroken husband? He's got a wedge of salmon quiche in one hand and a stick of celery in the other. Sometimes I feel I should take him outside and bang his fucking head against the wall.

"Too busy with your brown-skinned friend again, I suppose?" says Bernard, heavy on the sarcasm.

"Sorry," I say weakly to Robert. "I can't help not liking hospitals."

He raises an eyebrow. "Well, you never know," he says, "at the rate you're going, you may end up in there yourself before long." He nods to indicate I've not eaten much. "Your tummy still playing up?"

"A little."

He mimes *thoughtful*, applying an extended finger to his cheek. "Well ... ever thought you might have a gigantic tape-worm or something?" he says.

That night when Sanjay matter-of-factly tells me Joey's been sacked from the job that was found him, the unexpected naturally brings shock. "Christ, that's fucking shitty," I come out with before I can stop myself, and it's a slip that I should have controlled, because what I should've remembered is that Sanjay is completely insensitive to most things unless he's personally involved.

"The stupid bastard," I say. "What'd he do? I suppose he deserved it."

"He was seen tossing off behind bales. Many girls of good family were weeping and asked to call for the police, but Yusef said *no*, he would deal with the man, and then sent him packing. The man is no good for business. 'Go!' he was told, without references or wages."

I mumble again being sorry and that my last wish was to cause any inconvenience for him and Yusef by recommending someone of such habits. Simultaneously, my mind's doing backflips. Christ, there but for the grace of God goes half the male population. He just got unlucky, et cetera.

However, most important of all, I decide, is that I should drive out and see Joey *tout suite*. I don't want his shit piling up on my doorstep.

However, easy does it, I caution myself and wait until Sanjay's letting me out at the Otter & Trout, at which point I unload the news that Aunt Milly, poor soul, has been involved in a bad fall. It might even be that she's got herself a broken hip and, really, I ought to be zooming down there.

No problem, he says. The Peugeot is free; he'll make sure it has a full tank. Pick it up at Miss Betsy's like always.

Having watched his tail-lights disappear round the corner, I immediately decide I need a drink and head into the public bar. Sammy's at the rail. He says he's shifted the knickers and trainers and what else is going?

"Nothing," I tell him. "The job's knackered. This

fucking computer they've got is watching my every move."
He says he's sorry to hear that; computers are taking
over the world, he says – and at this same moment I see
Appleyard emerging from the Gents and I would like to
avoid him but it's too late for flight.

He comes over. Errol, he says gravely, what would I
think if he was to tell me that overnight in his driveway
he's had his big shiny Land-Cruiser paint-stripped?

I can tell by his tone and expression that he expects
me to be aghast. Only, in recalcitrant mood, I answer him
straight. "A well-known act of retaliation," I say. Then I
have no need to mention Bill & Ben because he beats me
to it, saying who else but them should be first to his
mind?

My immediate thought, and I've a sickening feeling
about it, is to hope to Christ he's not been to the police.

Shit, he *has*.

The law's checked, he says. They have watertight
alibis.

Well, they would have, wouldn't they?

"See, it's what you g-get for upsetting the a-applecart,"
says Wobbly-gob Gordon, who is one eavesdropping at the
rail. Unkempt, never worked in his life, and his countryside wanderings are tolerated. He says, "I heard the Old
B-Bill were busy. F-four houses g-got turned over. One
bloke got done for th-thumping a bobby. I heard they f-
found gin-traps and r-raided a b-barn out at Dalton. It
had a pit used for badgers. There was b-blood up the w-
walls from the d-dog-fights."

I shake my head at Appleyard. "See that? You're lucky
it was only your car. You really *have* upset people, you
have."

"Yeah, b-but Errol," says Wobbly. "Not just him. It's
your n-name's getting mentioned an' all. I'd b-be careful,

I should. There's t-two on the river I h-heard say are g-going to kick your f-fucking head in, they r-reckon."

Wonderful! Great! I laugh devil-may-care and knock back my whisky. Except, hell, if Wobbly means Bill & Ben – which he obviously does – then, for God's sake, it was only this morning that I pinched their twelve salmon and trashed all their gear.

"You all right, Errol?" says Sammy. "Have a quick brandy to settle you down 'fore the bell goes, I should. You look proper peaky."

CHAPTER 20

It's a Constable sky. All across the hillsides the gorse is in bloom, the tiny yellow half-moon flowers inflicting a squeeze to the heart. "When the gorse is in bloom, the kissing season is on" – this stands as a shrewd north-country saying because there is rarely a day when a gorse has no flower.

I come to a drystone wall, breached in places as if by cannon. Grubby sheep, their arses decorated with hanging balls of dung, trot from its lee. A covey of partridge scud away. I don't need to break the gun before clambering through a gap; it's not loaded. All I'm doing is filling in time before I can reasonably depart.

I got here mid-morning, asked after Joey, and Carol said she had made him his sandwiches and he'd gone off first thing. Stone-picking, she told me, casual work for a fortnight but better than nothing, though the bending would make his leg swell. "Sacked from that good job you found him. Lord knows why. He won't tell a word but I gave him an earful for letting you down."

"The recession," I told her. "Don't go blaming Joey. People are getting laid off all over." The envelope I'd set on the table held the three hundred I'd made on the fish. "It's not much," I said. "It'll help tide him over."

"Errol, that's decent. You've been blessed. Sure you've come to this world as my Joey's angel."

That's doubtful, I say to myself. In fact, along with the cash I'm laying out to make sure he stays sweet, I'll be telling him straight that if he's treading deep water I don't want involving.

The track twists and turns. We've had no real rain for days. In leaping the trickle of the beck, I adjust in mid-air to avoid trampling a clump of kingcup; then within the next stride I'm stopped short by the abrupt and fore-boding glimpse of the distinctive blue of the old Ford Cortina parked on the track below.

Now what?

Heart thumping, I take the short cut of slithering down the scree, carrying with me an avalanche of loose shale and stones. No sound, no engine running. Aluminium foil is wrapped around the exhaust to insulate the rubber-tubing that leads to the driver's window. Shock, distress, annoyance, excitement at something out of the ordinary? A precise reaction is difficult at seeing Joey posed upright and staring ahead through the windscreen.

I tap on the glass. Tap-tap – hey, in there, Joey?

Then opening the door, cautiously done, I get a first rush of fumes and know straightaway he can't be alive, not that colour. I reach in and touch him all the same, gently so he doesn't fall over, and his skin's not yet cold; although worse, on his lap lie his sandwiches, unwrapped and part-eaten, a dab of jam on his lip.

So that's me impaled on the barb of imagining him racked and chewing while debating the question of whether he should switch on the engine and was life worth living?

I guess he must have thought *not*. I take some steadying breaths, then decide I've really no choice about what's to be done. I take care in slowly closing the door so as not to disturb the vehicle. I have touched only the window and handle which I wipe with my hanky.

*

"Did you spot those red legs I told you about?" Carol immediately asks as I enter the kitchen.

She is meaning the partridges. "I didn't go by the wall way," I tell her.

"See this toaster?" She is sorting through a quid's worth of junk she got at a boot-sale. "Joey's one for his toast. It needs only a plug." She frowns at me, concerned. "Have you grit in your eye?"

"Just the wind."

"Ah, the wind never stops. Will we have a cup of tea?"

"I don't think I'll stay, not today. I must've picked up a virus or something. I feel really bad."

"We've the aspirins."

"I've a headache as well, and I'm shivery."

"Is Errol not staying, Mum?"

On the settee Angela has looked up from poring over her well-thumbed mail-order catalogue. She enjoys ticking things she might like. Two ticks is *special*. Three ticks means *Christmas*.

"Perhaps not today, pudding-pie. The poor man's not himself. Come and kiss him bye-byes now."

There's not a lot I can do. For the rest of the day, waiting around the flat to express surprise and sadness at the death of someone I already know to be dead proves an unnerving experience. The suspense hangs on through the night and continues up till the following lunchtime when, thankfully, I'm alone when Carol rings to tell me a party of ramblers happened on Joey's car after he was missing all night.

I pretend shock. She's distressed, constantly blowing her nose, but has the clear-sightedness to include she has discreetly waited till everyone's gone before calling me. I mumble the condolences I've been practising and include the suggestion that perhaps I should drive over at once, though know if she takes up the offer I won't.

"That's kind, yet no need. Errol, why would Joey do a sad thing like that? Is it because I shouted at him?"

"Not at all and don't think it."

"There's to be an inquest," she says bravely, and is ahead of me. "But if asked I'll say you're just one who comes for walking the hills now and then and that's the truth of it. We're your good friends here, Errol. The envelope now. I looked inside."

"That's okay. Keep it."

"I will, and thank you. We shall have some expense. You wouldn't believe how it all takes me back."

"Back?"

"With my man, may his soul rest in peace. It is all in the blood and comes out, so they say. Wait, here's someone wanting a word to you now."

"Errol." Angela's voice is a heartbroken whisper. "Did you know what he's done? Our Joey's only gone and gone to Jesus."

Personally I've not that kind of faith. That mid-afternoon, while in town to return the Peugeot, I buy an *Evening Gazette* and see Joey's fame has made the back page, late news, forty-eight words. A lot less than any Warholian prophecy.

I use the back way and take the keys up to Sanjay. I tell him thanks for the loan of the car, adding that my aunt, alas, remains seriously ill and may not live, after which I show him the paper since I figure it's best he should hear the sad news about Joey from me. He says a few words but is not really bothered; his phone never stops ringing.

So remaining in need of sympathy I head down to the shop to see Maxine. She is serving two women inspecting a bread-bin. "It'll rust in a week," I announce, but they smile and buy it, anyway.

"So what's happened now?" She's been studying my face.

"A friend died," I tell her.

"What *another*?"

"It's true, honest."

She appears unconvinced. "Did this one get run over, too? And don't think you're fooling anybody by sucking those peppermints."

"I've had just one small drink. I'm so bloody depressed. Tonight would be good ... *cheer me up*?"

She says no, she can't.

"Oh, c'mon ...?"

"No, I'm not being awkward," she says, "I've got all sorts booked. Still ..." a meaningful pause, "I've a favour to ask. You don't fancy taking me to Tubwell Lane, do you? The night match next Tuesday. I've still never been once."

"Football? You want to stand in the cold to watch football? You're kidding?"

"Yes, why not? They could get relegated. They're praying to win. Besides, it's not *standing up*. I've got two special tickets."

"That still leaves tonight."

"I'm sure you'll find something ..."

Who else can I turn to but Paula? She flutters her lashes. "Well, I thought it was ... well, *a gift*."

"Right ... it *was*. It's just at the moment I've had a lot of expenses."

I'm embarrassed. God knows, I wouldn't have introduced the subject of her returning all or any part of my money if I didn't see my reduced income from Miss Betsy's as a big factor in the major strain I'm weighed down by.

"Well, can I owe you?" She's in front of her living-room's mirror, primping her hair. She's just had it cut and styled so it must have cost plenty. "Mind you . . ." she dimples, "I could always say you've had your money's worth."

I slide alongside her and run my hand up her leg. I'm still getting flashbacks of coming on Joey. The palliative I need is shared erotic diversion. "I could gobble you up."

"Better not," she says, wriggling free. "The bleeding's no different. They said I would for a bit." She rolls her big soulful eyes. "Trouble is, I'm as randy as hell. These tablets I'm on. They warned that's how I'd be."

"You said come at eight."

"That was earlier."

I don't know what this means, except her dressy appearance might be the clue. "Do you want me to nip home and put on something different? Would you like to go out somewhere for a change?"

"With *you*?" she says, frowning. "*Outside*?"

"You did say come round."

"Yes, but that was before . . ." She looks me over: the long tarpaulin coat, the rubbed cord-trousers, the heavy sweater. "Why don't you go and catch me one of these big fish you're always supposed to be after?"

I tinker with a reply, something curt; only at that same moment – rat-a-tat – Louise walks in. "Yo!" she says, covering us both, but with a touch of disquiet to her eyes.

"It's all right," Paula says. "He's just off."

"Ha-hah!" I say.

"Well, we're going out," she says.

I inspect them both. "Two weeks back it was different. Now you don't want to know me."

Louise's scornful expression suggests I'm out of step; like maybe I'm showing my age by reading too much into whatever I'm remembering.

"Ignore him, Louise," Paula says. "All that messing about was just in good fun, wasn't it? He's just being nasty." To me she adds, "If you want to stay here on your own, please yourself."

"You want me to baby-sit?"

"You know very well little Andy's round at my mum's."

"What's planned for tonight, then?"

"Around town," Louise answers. "It's a free night for singles at Lonnigan's later. Paula, we might see that rich coloured fella you fancy from your place again. What's his name?"

"Louise," Paula gasps, "I was joking."

Defeated, unhappy, I look on as she locks her flat, then follow her down to the street. Louise's mini is at the kerb with Louise already behind the wheel and leaning across to open the passenger door.

"Tomorrow night, maybe?"

"Can't. Church with Louise."

"You're not turning holy?"

"It's dead good. Tambourines. Lots of singing."

"This is mean, just leaving me like this."

She squirms beneath my scowl. "Don't be like that," she murmurs, her tone partly apologetic. "If I was older . . . but I'm just far too young for you."

"What about that video we made? It wants destroying."

"It's safe."

"Christ, if anyone should see it . . ."

She smiles archly. "Then you'll just have to behave yourself, won't you?"

"Terrific," I say. "Thanks a lot."

I watch them drive off. I guess there goes my money.

I collect my car from under the street-lamp. Because of its rusted state, I used to favour parking in unlit places but the thought of Bill & Ben leaping out of the shadows has become a very real fear. So much so that I even mentioned the matter to Sanjay: that I'd upset two rough types. "Get their addresses," he said, "and I'll get them sorted; I can reach the right people."

I don't doubt that he can; only starting anything like that would really be asking for trouble. The whole thing will blow over, I'm sure.

Still, safety first, I need to be vigilant at all times, and have taken to carrying my priest in my long coat's hidden pocket.

My priest? That's the short lead-weighted pipe that I use to kill salmon. It would stop an elephant. Any trouble at all, and it's quick-draw, you bastards – take that and that!

Brave talk. It's a worry, because I suspect I can feel my paranoia coming home to roost again.

I head home. Maybe a drink and a thrill in the basement may cheer me up. *No Holes Barred* – I've been saving that one. Except I'm no sooner inside the flat than the phone starts to ring. I answer and the cultured female voice has me stumped for the moment before it declares itself as Davina Forbes-Tyson – she of fishing fame, and not on her hols in Tobago like she planned but calling from London – and her life is in tatters, she says.

She continues, "I'm warning everyone. Nicky's gone gah-gah. Gerald's flat was fire-bombed. Andrew's dog got mysteriously shot by a man on a motor-bike. Then I was in Stringfellow's and two men Nicky had paid came rushing up and punched Teddy's face. It was frightful, and Nicky insists he's got a private detective who's got notes on everyone. He knows about you in that dreadful hut. He says you're on his list as one who needs teaching a lesson."

"Hang about, Davina! Christ, I don't live anywhere near you!"

"I know, and it's all totally silly, but distance no object, he says. He says his good name's at stake." I'm beginning to realize she's slurring her words and that she's obviously drunk. "Actually," she says, "about you in that hut just came out in an argument. It's really all over money. He spends it like water. So if he sends men up there to see you . . ."

She babbles on in the same vein for a while longer and I'm well-sick of listening long before she hangs up. I pour myself a large much-needed scotch. Christ, whoever heard of anything so crazy as someone making long-distance arrangements to have me beaten to pulp over the twice yearly session of groping his wife? No, it seems too far-fetched, I tell myself. However, if her husband really fancies being malicious, then one wrong word from him into the Right Hon's ear would put paid to my buckshee rod-and-line fishing for ever.

What a mess! I lately seem to have acquired this special knack for upsetting people. There's a black thumping haze in my head with what feels like a crack right across it.

Jesus Christ, give me strength. *Skol!*

CHAPTER 21

Daylight outside but the curtains are drawn; the mirrors are covered. Angela is dreadfully withdrawn, Carol's not bothered with hair or make-up, and I can smell the drink on the two of them.

But the situation could be worse. On arriving, I had the fear that Joey in his coffin might be laid across two chairs. He isn't, thank Christ. From Carol I've heard that the preliminary inquest is done and that the Co-op are making the funeral arrangements; so at the moment he remains at the hospital awaiting collection. And did I want to see him? she's asked.

Do I fuck. In fact, as it happens, he's not the only one stuck in the hospital morgue. With Sol, there's been trouble about who should pay, so he's still frozen up.

No, the offer is kind, I tell Carol and Angela, but I won't pop along; I'm more the sort who would sooner remember Joey as cheerful and smiling. Yes, they nod; they agree with that.

Also no disrespect meant, I explain, but it's not like I'm family, or Catholic either, and would they agree it perhaps might be best for me not to come to the funeral or even send flowers?

"Sure, no one could have done more already," says Carol. "You've been awful generous."

Not at all, I respond, and I'm struggling to stick with the role I imagine they expect of me. "He'll be missed," I offer.

Out comes the Kleenex. They dab at their eyes.

Looking at them across the table. I suppose that in having tea of sponge-cake and thinly sliced bread and butter we are, in effect, playing out some minor wake. Noticeably, they have got down the Clarice Cliff instead of the usual crockery, and I can't help but wonder how much each piece must be worth.

On my second cup and words start to fail. But it seems I have been here a decent while. So I decline a third cup, and I would like to stay longer, I tell them, but duty and responsibilities call. They say they understand and I am not to worry. Formally they walk me to the door where comes an awkward moment as I have to explain how I happen to be driving such a wreck.

"God, I know it looks awful," I say. "It belongs to a young Asian bloke who I know. The Peugeot's away being serviced. But I felt I must come, no matter what."

"Errol, you're a lovely man," Carol says, with a hug. "A true man of the people."

I wrap my arms round their waists for brotherly kisses. We shall need time to get back to normal, Carol has said, but I suspect we both know that such a thing is impossible. At all events, the signs of our friendship coming to an end are there in the two of them openly weeping in closing the door behind me – shutting-them-selves-in more than seeing-me-out. I don't look back. Sally, the goat, is walking a wide circle she's nibbled down to bare earth. I take time to peg her out on a fresh patch of green. I fancy the RSPCA will soon get word of animals not being fed. The place smells of trouble. Only how will I be? They were such nurse-maids to me.

"My, you're a strange one, no mistake," Terri says. "Serving behind a shop-counter one minute, a real gypsy-boy the next."

At Tyne View Meadows that night, the bright lights

and soft music make my dismal afternoon at Stand Alone seem longer ago than the six hours that have passed.

I smile weakly and briefly wonder about apologizing for the night-gear I'm in; but why should I? Earlier, with Robert and Bernard out somewhere, and trapped with the stink of myself, I had telephoned Sanjay to say Aunt Milly had died, was he free? Alas, *no*, he was leaving for Hamburg on business, he said. I tried Maxine next but no answer. Then, to escape the flat, I had reached the point of setting out for the river when Terri rang.

Now, with my famous long coat hanging up in her hall, I'm not sure I like how things look. The leather armchair I'm in has an inbuilt hug, and the mistake of heeding her plea to come over is mushrooming inside of me. It could be she's got *plans*.

Settled opposite on the settee, she is within easy reach of the booze and the ash-tray. "Stuck on my own, I was going insane," she murmurs – which doesn't exactly gel with the outfit she's wearing, a sort of loose bolero top and a pair of culottes of some silky material.

I gulp at my whisky. "So where did you say Denzil was?"

"The moon. Timbuktu. Who the fuck cares?"

I smile along. Who's she kidding? Her finger is well up his bum, controlling his brains. Significantly, too, as I see it, she's already made sure to tell me he'll be gone overnight.

She says, "I will let you into one little secret. We consulted the tarot cards before he went. 'An excellent time for financial transactions' was the reading. We wouldn't have chanced it without."

Chanced *what*? I hold off, waiting to be startled by whatever else she is going to reveal. But no joy; I can tell by her face that she's decided she's said enough on the subject. However, the mention of *tarot* has rubbed her two sticks together and turned her mind towards things more mystic.

She drags over an armchair. "We might as well, shall we? That's if you want? On the phone, it was just a suggestion." She waits, expectant. "So what have you brought . . . seeing as how you don't believe any of it, anyway?"

"I forgot. I've got nothing."

"You must have. Have a look in your pockets. Don't be a spoilsport."

I feel around, though without much enthusiasm. "There's this? I generally carry it round for good luck. I've had it ages."

"Interesting!" She takes the seashell and begins to roll it gently between her palms. "You call this psychometry," she says. "Picking up vibrations. Wherever it's been, whatever it's done . . . every cell is like a hologram of its past."

That's the start of the trance or whatever it is she goes into – mainly deep breathing, in through her nose, out through her mouth, seemingly striving for a state of concentration that's putting a deep wrinkle between her closed eyes. "Right, I'm tuned in," she drones – but not talking to *me*; I don't know who she's talking to. "Yes, I hear you," she says. "What . . . a reward to come but not in this life? Wait . . . now there's pain. This person's passed over, this person . . ."

I lose track of what else she's saying. Such dreadful theatrics.

"Terri, Terri!"

I reach forward and sharply rap her clasped hands. She sits blinking like she's just woken up.

She's bloody good, I'll give her that.

"Oh, Christ," she says, "smell the wallflowers!"

I don't comment. All I can smell is the joss-stick that was spiralling its smoke when I got here.

She leans back in her chair – "Phew! I'm all of a tizzy!" – jiggling her top back and forth to force a draught down her front, and I seize the moment to reclaim my seashell. She says, "Well, wherever it comes from, it's powerful enough, I'll say that."

She then springs to her feet. She's prone to such girlish outbursts, as if maybe she thinks she's still eighteen and irresistible. "What say . . . let's have another little drink?"

"Not for me."

My reticence doesn't stop her. She downs a fresh brandy, pours another, then settles herself languidly on the settee, reaching to dim the lights via a knob on the wall. "The glare hurts my eyes," she says, then in case I'm totally stupid pats the cushions beside her.

No, thanks. Even at long range she's had a bad day. I stay as I am. She's not taking the hint, though. Like she's decided I probably need help to make my mind up, a sickly smile curdles her lips. She stands, lights another cigarette, and comes over to run a hand through my hair. "It's lovely," she says. "I get such split-ends."

I roll my head clear. "Sit down, Terri, you're drunk."

"Well, what did you expect?" She licks her lips. She's standing real close, so in the poor light the fuzz under her nose is a half-grown moustache, her make-up's worn down to real skin, and she must've been indulging fairly heavily since she arrived home from work because she reeks of stale booze and tobacco. For absolute sickeners, I can't edge my mind past her Golden Rain story.

"What d'you fancy?" she says, and I can detect her anxiety at her intentions not working out. "I know," she says, laughing, stumbling back to the middle of the carpet. "You want to see me smoke a cigarette?"

I daren't chance slapping her one – which is probably

the only way of stopping her. She works down her culottes, no pants underneath, and thrusts forward her pubis: a great mass of black pubic hair you could lose a coin in. "Denzil likes this. I can do it. Just watch me," she says.

She's got a tired, puckered belly.

"Like it?"

"Terri, I spent years at sea. You name it, I've seen it."

She needs a moment to sort out a meaning. "Bastard!" – her face distorting, and starting forwards she forgets the culottes round her ankles and so falls to her knees. "Ah, be nice to me, cherub."

I pick up the cigarette, avoiding its wet end, and rub at the singe mark. She's not one bit grateful. "Sod that, Errol! I don't give a shit for the carpet! I suppose if I were Maxine . . .?" She adopts a little girl whine that's supposed to be Maxine. " 'Terri, he hangs around me like he's just a young kid.' Good God, did you know that she thinks you're a screwball?"

She's sobbing and trying to hoist her culottes.

"If I were you, Terri, I'd get straight to bed."

I let myself out. I've come in the car so that's all right. These things happen. All the same, I can still see her face as a gargoyle of hate. So no love lost for me there – she'll be first with the hammer and nails when I get to the cross.

CHAPTER 22

At Miss Betsy's that Monday morning, the police come and go. Left by their fingerprint-man, little dustings of talcum linger here and there.

"All this story stinks to high heaven," says Maxine.

She could be right. Over the weekend, a back window's been jemmied. The alarm didn't go off, nothing of value was stolen, and not much got disturbed or interfered with, except that the intruder apparently *played* with the computer and somehow wiped clean half the files, including all back-ups.

"Surely you have to know the password to do that much damage?" says Maxine.

Did a password exist? I neither know nor care. These days, having kissed goodbye to my ready access to shop takings and stock, almost everything connected with Miss Betsy leaves me cold. It's crazily wearing me out that I should be trying to get by on the amount I get paid.

We drag through the day.

Paula, sensibly, waits for five-thirty and Maxine to leave before coming down. She's collecting contributions towards the towels we've chosen to buy from Sanjay's wedding-list. On impulse, I pull her out of sight behind the partition and give her a bear-hug, belly to belly.

She says, "Fancy this happening in auditors' week. They're still up there now, going crazy." Making an exploratory thrust back at me with her hips, she affects a playful smile. "I'll bet that's only a packet of mints you've got in there. Can I have one?"

She takes two and starts to suck. I'm still close, so use the moment to steal a hand up her blouse for a feel of soft skin and ask what else is new in her life? She says *lots*. At the weekend she was at a party where everyone took their clothes off to play forfeits and – guess what? Yes, she *won* and her prize was a tablet to swallow and she was unconscious for sixteen hours and she hopes nothing happened, there were so many good-looking fellas.

I try to smile but sigh over wondering just how dense she is.

"Anyway," she says, "see this tattoo on my hip I woke up with?"

Daisy, Daisy.

Paula's glee in unfastening and lowering her skirt has brought me a bittersweet glimpse of a child I remember.

Daisy, Daisy . . . there was a time when all you wanted was a pony.

Jesus, how that thought hurts. Because somewhere – and I wouldn't know where *exactly* – Daisy is a young woman, aged nineteen and little different to other young women, I suppose – including ones I have used and am used to. So I know how she'll be. She'll have hopes and desires, wanting the company of others, their stimulation, be deserving of love and affection.

That's the positive side. Except, alternatively, with Linda behind her, is she likely to enjoy what she needs – a Linda who without doubt will be drumming it in that the world's full of weird cunts like me?

So vindictive, so thoughtless.

"Errol Oldfield! The big man! Well, at long last you now know where you stand, and it's been a long wait for nothing is all I can say."

"Okay, go ahead, blame me." Fresh home from the solicitors' office, I still had my coat on. "For Christ's sake," I said, "I was her nephew, her next-of-kin, *like a son*! I should have been left all she had."

I knew it was madness to be handing Linda ammunition like that but, through shock, I wasn't thinking straight. Her eyes gleamed. It was her future down the drain as much as mine but she could put that aside to stick knives in.

"Oh, I'm sure you're upset and I'd say with good reason. My God, think of the umpteen good jobs you've thrown away on the strength of this moment. My God, some rich old aunt she's turned out to be! All this while you've gone on saying it was only the trust-fund's executors keeping your hands off her money ... and now what? My God, you get told your uncle left word that it's all got to pass to his side of the family? Not a penny to *you*! Huh, he saw you coming!"

"Linda, we're losing a fortune, for Christ's sake!"

"You should jump off a cliff then," she said. "Are you totally daft? It's as clear as a bell. Who sent you away to that stupid school? Who got rid of you early?"

"Is that supposed to be funny?"

"Funny? It's not me who's been taken in! Who sent you away as a sailor for years? Whose idea? Uncle Lewis? Exactly!"

What I deserved was her sympathy, support, a few kind words. But blood from a stone would've come easier. She gave no quarter when riled.

She dumped a load of towels and sheets in the old Bendix washer, switched on, and stayed in the kitchen with the noise of it.

I fetched Daisy from playing in her room. She was ten. It was raining outside. She jumped at the chance of wearing her matching yellow slicker and Wellies, which she loved, and we went for a walk in the park.

We sat on the swings.

"Won't I be getting a pony now, Errol?"

I explained that she wouldn't. More than likely I shed a few tears for us both. If I did, we'd have hugged. That's the sort Daisy was.

"Here, Errol?" I hear Paula say, jerking me back to the present, and hurrying me along by jiggling her waistband which she's pushed down past the bump of her hip. "Make your mind up. What d'you reckon? Is this sexy or what?"

"On you, Paula, *terrific* . . . a butterfly looks good."

"Well, it's only a stick-on. Still, they last you for ages. The guys said it would. Oh, by the way . . ." she's remembered some gossip, "did you hear about Karen?"

Sanjay has big brown Asian eyes. Expressionless mostly. So no use looking there for clues as to whether or not Paula's tale of intrigue might be true.

I run through it again.

The story was that Karen, on leaving Miss Betsy's employ, had been secretly approached by Sanjay who had found her an office job somewhere else at more pay. Then just last weekend – "And here's the juicy bit," Paula said – he'd invited her out for a meal at McCoy's where he fed her lobster and champagne, after which she said *thanks-a-bunch* in a lay-by. "Even in his big car, because of his massive tummy, they had such a struggle, or so Karen reckoned, and now – can you believe it? – he owns that corner-shop near her house and she says all her groceries are free when she wants."

Fact or fiction? I can't decide. Nor do I strain myself, but add it to the list of that side of Sanjay that I never get to hear about.

For sure I owe him plenty. Right now, as illustration, without being invited to share his bachelor-dinner I wouldn't be eating here at the Troutbeck. Famous food at famous prices. The ambience is such that you are supposed to imagine you're dining at someone's elegant home. Anton, the chef, personally comes out in his hat to discuss what he should cook for your pleasure. His wife helps with the serving and chats up the guests. They live on the premises and breed pedigree cats out the back.

Siamese, I think; and looking at the one staring in at me from an outside window-sill, I am amused to think that it's spotted I am wearing my new charcoal-grey. The thing was, not wanting to let Sanjay down by appearing slovenly, I figured that with the wedding being ten days away neither Uncle Mohan nor Mustapha nor Fakrou are likely to notice they've seen it before. Also, for impression's sake I am following the general example in drinking Perrier and refusing meat; though whether Mustapha and Fakrou are Hindu or Muslim or what, I have no idea.

However, thanks to whatever language or languages they are speaking, I'm no less on the periphery. Fakrou's flown in from Hamburg: nearing sixty, balding, and I'm not well-acquainted. Mustapha's come further, from Istanbul, and it's maybe the fourth or fifth time we've met, so I know him better: tall, middle-thirties, handsome, expensively groomed. He comes over not as blatantly *nouveau-riche* as the other three. I can imagine women going for him in a big way.

Whatever – I'm not enjoying this feeling of being tolerated, even if that's not what is happening. Mohan, I've noticed, uses the American method of cutting food to manageable pieces and then laying the knife to one side. As a matter of fact, I eat like that, too. What else can I say?

"Your observant eye," he replies, "does you credit. You've travelled yourself, Errol, I've no doubt. I had a home in Atlantic City for a while. Then Miami. Canada, too. Also New York. Ah, New York, New York, what a wonderful town! I still maintain a few business connections in those parts."

Thus my frame of mind is lightened considerably. Or at least if there was any ice, then it's melted, because over the next minutes what rapidly becomes obvious is that Mohan, who clearly takes pole position among the four of them, is now regarding me as someone in front of whom he can relax and speak freely.

He says, "In my younger days, I was wholesale dress trade and saw many strange things." He smiles wryly. "Too many creditors, a little tax trouble, cash not coming in as it should – all such setbacks are quickly solved by a can of petrol and a match that gets dropped accidentally . . ."

"Denzil, the cheek of him," Sanjay says. "After the break-in, he comes rushing to ask if I've got a record of everything *I* owe *him*."

"The man has airs above himself," says Fakrou, his English burdened by a harsh German accent.

"He thinks small," says Mustapha, extending it to a sneer.

Mohan airs another wise smile. "Even a midget can achieve impossible feats when pushed to the limit." He spreads his hands. "And now what can they do, these people who make lives such a misery? They have only the books that he chooses to give them."

I hide behind an appreciative laugh. Only what the fuck do I know? They're all birds of a feather. I'm just swinging through trees, catching left-over crumbs.

All the same, I congratulate myself, I could do worse. I've been vetted and cleared, as-it-were. *Mohan likes me!*

And my success on this score, I'm quick to note, becomes plainer still on the drive back to Lambton. We left Mohan, Mustapha and Fakrou drinking more mineral water in the bar; they are staying overnight at the Trout-beck: handy for the airport and wherever they're zooming off to tomorrow. Sanjay says, "I have to say I think my uncle had a good trusting feeling for you."

I act suitably humble. Do I deserve such high praise and et cetera?

And, yes, it seems I do, as Sanjay continues with telling me that Uncle Mohan doesn't normally take to people so readily, and I start to sense that the conversation has to be leading somewhere.

Another mile goes by. Sanjay's longer glance suggests he's arrived at the important part. He is wondering, he says, if over his honeymoon period I might keep an eye on his office. His tone in this is confiding, as if it's an unusual arrangement that's been cleared by Mohan. Should anything important crop up, he says, I could fax him or Mohan the details. There might be a few small bills to pay. He could leave some signed cheques in a drawer. Would that be all right, would I mind . . . if it's not too much trouble?

Sanjay, I say, and am glad of the darkness concealing my face, I'd be pleased to help out.

In the basement I need a large scotch to neutralize all the Perrier. Jesus Christ, that stuff is pure piss; give me scotch any time.

"Come on, Maxine, reward me."

And the significant word in that thought, I decide, is "reward". It's about time I had one. And my mind's clicking over because blank signed cheques, it stands to reason, must offer a golden opportunity of some sort or other.

Except – whoa! hold your horses, I tell myself. No sense in getting too excited. Yes, sir, I've lived too long within what seems a mess of blundered chances to know that nothing and no one is predictable.

Aunt Milly for instance.

Skol!

During school hols, after all those five-thirty reveilles and keep-fit runs, I wasn't one for getting up early. Saying I had earned a rest, Aunt Milly would bring me breakfast in bed: occasions when sometimes lying beside me in her nightdress she would absent-mindedly stroke my thigh while complaining of "no married life". She was still a young woman at that time.

One morning. "Into the lion's den!" I said, steering her hand. I was fully developed.

And that was the beginning, and thereafter, while I was of an age where school holidays continued, the happening became a regular occurrence, unless Uncle Lewis was home. "To make it grow big and strong," she would say, enveloping us with that and other make-believe phrases, like some slice of awful amateur dramatics.

Not that at that age I needed any such soothing to encourage my participation. More often I would wake early and lie trembling in anticipation of her arrival. I was on a good thing, I reckoned.

But then much much later I would come to learn I didn't wholly succeed in side-stepping all harm, because those early-morning frolics would turn out to be what my psychiatrist, Doctor Zissler, would call a "dark star" – one he found hiding away at the back of my mind.

He had that strange way of putting things.

"Even what may seem minor events can promote what you steer by," he said. And in my case I had drifted way off-course, he added, because an incorrect inference I'd drawn was to mistake lust for love and to believe my aunt loved me and that I was chosen. And particularly involved in that – as I came to understand him – was the snag that I had grown up believing I would end up filthy rich. So that when Aunt Milly died and all that trust-fund money went elsewhere, besides truly blaming her for letting me down, I felt disowned and rootless, my self-respect at rock-bottom.

I don't know. He might've been right, I can't say. What I recall more easily is my crumbling domestic lot, and that what Linda did was to keep rubbing in the salt. EXPECTATIONS NIL – FUTURE BLEAK, she wrote in lipstick on the bedroom mirror. And so with everything fraying at the edges like that I began bringing in a little liquid something to get me through the evening. And then come bedtimes, despite resorting to every trick in the book, I was having trouble in getting it up, and any shortcoming in that direction for Linda was like cutting off her air supply. And the only person I had to lean on and talk to through the whole of that time was young Daisy.

CHAPTER 23

Snow is forecast. Incessant chanting and crowd noise. Police horses paw the tarmac on Tubwell Row. Long queues at turnstiles. Body searches. Fans in their home-strip team shirts. Rosettes, coloured scarves, painted faces. Tribal gear: boisterous displays of group allegiance. The dazzling glare of the floodlights bathes the grass and its pristine white lines. A battlefield green upon which the knights will emerge.

Yet attending my first game in years, I detect within the atmosphere an undercurrent different to anything I remember. To make myself heard I need to press my lips into the folds of Maxine's warm little ear. She looks a million dollars in the navy-blue coat with a Highway-man's collar her mother saved up to get her. Listen, I exhort, this is true: flick-knives, hammers, hatchets, Stanley-blades taped with a matchstick between so one slash inflicts cuts too close for stitching – such weapons and happenings are commonplace at today's football matches. Therefore, hero or coward, I tell her, you've got to feel vulnerable . . . hang on to me tightly!

"Stop trying to frighten me," she says. "Here, have a black-bullet to keep out the cold."

She is terribly nervous. Superstar smiles from page two of the programme. Already we have heard his name mentioned countless times by those around us. Twenty-eight thousand in the stadium and we are here on *his* tickets. Good tip-up seats. What else can you do but feel singled out?

"I daren't look," she says. "I think his wife's back there. She's blonde."

We are four rows below what I assume is the directors' box. "There's a blonde with a boy and a girl about eight."

"That could be them." She needs a ciggy and gets one going. "By the way, what's going on between you and Terri?" she says. "She hates your guts. Your name's mud."

"I know. I think I must have upset her."

"About what?"

I shrug like it could be anything. The truth would hardly amuse her. Then I'm saved, anyhow. Frenetic activity has spread from the tunnel-mouth, the loud-speakers hiccup, then at increased volume comes what must be the club song and the crowd erupts as the City emerge, flexing, high-stepping, doing short sprints as they hit the turf. The opposition trots out more sedately like they've had a long journey.

"Where is he?"

"There," she says, and my first sighting in the flesh puts him as one of a warming-up twosome by the near touchline. Possibly he's not so tall as on TV, but he's firm. Bronzed skin, with bulging oiled thighs, a small gold medallion swinging at his neck.

The game gets under way. The play's end to end, finely balanced.

"Shoot! Corner! Our throw!"

For Maxine's sake I keep adding my shouts to those around me, but my mind is elsewhere as I verge constantly on the edge of remembering – *I had a dream* . . .

Through a haze of steam in a dressing-room cluttered with haphazardly discarded jerseys and shorts come hints of the smells of embrocation and after-shave. I can see the print-marks where someone has rubbed a window in the condensation on a mirror. The team and its handlers have gone. Only Superstar remains lolling at ease in the big sunken bath.

Enter Maxine, in black, her high heels click-clacking on the wet floor and reminiscent of her mornings of coming down the arcade. She arrives at the edge so he's looking up the full long-legged front of her. He says, "Hello, kid."

"Well done, hero," she says. "You played brilliant."

He makes ripples of nonchalance, reaching wet-handed, stroking her calf. "Come on, baby, reward me."

At which she steps back so he'll see all the better. A striptease, provocative, sensual: one remaining in keeping with her obvious good taste in underwear as she pads around the bath, dropping each item as it comes off so that on arriving back where she started she is naked but for the black stockings with elasticized tops that she much prefers to tights. Here she lights a cigarette. "Just watch me," she says – which he does. Her body of centrefold figure and posture, legs erotically parted, is as I always imagined. A gold foxtail chain swings across her boyish breasts as she takes the cigarette from herself, bends over and feeds it between his lips. He breathes in her perfume. *Bijan*, he thinks; then she slides down beside him. They kiss, writhe about. Bits of grass float in whirlpools.

Strangely, as when using a TV's remote, I appear to possess the ability to control the scene. I can also hear myself speak, giving orders: "Penetration in water's not easy. So get out."

Muscles tighten. He heaves himself from the bath, standing statuesque for a moment with an angled erection of some proportions before he reaches down to lift her upwards one-handed. He leads her child-like to a pine-looking table. Her wet stockings are gathered at her ankles like wrinkled leg-warmers. Her legs overhang the edge but she draws them up like a chicken prepared and gets her knees wide apart. Overhead is the tinny loudspeaker music and the heavy clump of feet as the last of the crowds vacate the stands. She moans, craning her head to smile her cheeky smile at me over his shoulder . . . and within my head the name "Veronica" is ringing a bell to remind me of a time I can't quite place, as he manually puts in the end, just a half inch or so –

"Did you see that?" Maxine says.

"What?"

"Hand-ball! A foul! Hand-ball!"

Time drags. A heavy ground, two tired teams. Some joker lets off a smoke-bomb. A small dog runs wild. The ref looks again at his watch. A nil-all draw is certain. Then I've a split-second in which to think that such mischance could only happen to a luckless bastard like me, as come a mindless down-wind clearance from the City's penalty area the ball soars the length of the field –

And who's there on his lonesome? Out rushes the goalie to narrow the angle. Whack! – the ball's in the net, the crowd erupts, simultaneously shrills the final whistle, and breaking free from his team's goalmouth kiss-and-cuddle Superstar comes at a hip-wriggling gallop that ends in a balletic slide on his knees right beneath us, his raised arms and clenched fists parenthesizing his wide-mouthed yell of triumph.

His gladiatorial salute could be aimed at his wife to our rear. I glance sideways at Maxine. Head back, hands to mouth, she's got tears in her eyes.

Christ, I sigh to myself, in the throes of orgasm is more what she looks like.

CHAPTER 24

Watching the chimney that next afternoon, and shivering with cold in my new charcoal suit, I've been waiting for ages and have seen a few off. The wind whips unchecked across these wide open spaces.

Finally, thank God, I spy a lone hearse. The black stretched sleekness of it reflects the light as it slowly snakes up the narrow tar-macadamed roadway between the vaults and headstones and I move clear of the bunker-like building I've been sheltering against. It has wide studded doors like a bank's, and this guy sashays out. "Holy Jesus!" he says, "what the hell are you doing?"

"'Mister Tambourine Man'," I tell him. "The tune was his favourite."

Unsympathetic, the guy's a clown and starts yanking my arm so the mouth-organ nearly knocks my front teeth out. Then we wrestle a bit, though with no real conviction, the hearse now fast approaching at snail's space. He lets me go as it stops. A trifle apprehensively, probably because of what's been on view through the windscreen, the driver alights with his helpers, all identical zombies.

No flowers; it's a cheap-looking coffin. I wait till they've eased it three-quarters out. I'm the only mourner.

"Now what?" says the same nosy bastard.

"What's it look like?"

"You can't put it there."

"I'm his friend. *Was* his friend."

"It's no place for a toy."

"It's a dog. It's called Punch. Let it lie. It's just fur. It'll burn."

"Don't be so bloody soft. Show respect. Should we send for the *police*?"

The word casts its spell. "Okay, truce." I slap a hand on the wood. It rings hollow. You hear funny stories but I figure he's in there. "So long, Sol!"

I start away. What they must do, they must do.

"Sheer bloody disgrace," I hear called behind me. "He's been on the booze."

True, too fucking true; and by early evening I'm accepting I've been all day on the ledge that's one drink below being drunk. But then that's how I am these days: I'm getting so I'm immune to the stuff.

Of course the truth, I tell myself, is that I should never have gone to the match – *kamikaze* committed.

Here in the basement, I have my faithful friend Zero keeping me company. I put down a carton, he sits in it. I lay down a paper, he lies on it. I extend a finger, he noses it. Like him, I have the ability to sit and stare introvertly for minutes on end, and after a time it's possible via having *World's Famous Paintings* wedged open on my desk to get right inside Vincent's room, where I see no gun, nor the razor or knife that he used on his ear. Still, no problem. With .38 in hand and emotively helped by the opposite page's illustration of black crows slashed on above impasto corn I can sense his distress, see the muzzle pressed against flesh, hear it fire, imagine his rearing back in amazement at the explosion of blood.

Death's stealth knows no single line of approach. Desperate situations call for desperate measures.

Heavy on my mind is that an hour ago, via my intercom network, I overheard Robert and Bernard's first-floor conversation before they left for their evening visit to poor Tina's bedside. "Bernard," I heard Robert say, "I think tonight may be the night – I think they may want to talk about switching her off."

"Rob, these things happen," came Bernard's reply. "I think you'll have to be strong . . . you'll just have to face up to letting her go."

Of course I've seen it coming. It's not been enough to know they are part-way through sharing out the best of her clothes, especially anything silky. Already I've had the mischance and proof of stumbling in on one of their trying-on sessions.

I need a shoulder to cry on. An ear that will listen. I have called Maxine's number countless times. "Come on, baby, reward me."

She *hasn't*. Her phone goes unanswered. For all I know, her house could be empty, with her mother at bingo – her mother goes every night. I start searching the desk for the keys to my car. Being way over the limit, and with everything fuzzy, I've no doubts that I shouldn't be thinking of driving, but there we are.

At Maxine's house, the house lights are on but her car's not out front. My knocking sets the dog madly barking, its claws shredding paintwork. I feel sure if there was someone at home, they would answer the door.

I stand with a lump in my throat. It all seems so unfair.

I get back in the car. Only one windscreen-wiper works. Amazingly, even beautifully perhaps, although late for the time of year, snow is falling, big white flakes cascading down through the arcs cast by street-lamps. My steering seems reasonable. All the same, I keep the speed down, bypassing the town centre to head along Tubwell Lane until I come to the high walls and security-lighting of the football stadium.

I slow down, second gear – the fan-belt's slipping and the engine sounds shit. I glide abreast of the chain-link behind which lies the club's practice ground. Whatever indoor facilities are on offer they lie within the one building. All the windows are lit.

Have I arrived here by chance? I ask of myself. Have I fuck.

"Hello!" I said earlier.

"Yes. *Hotline news-desk* – can I help?"

"Bloody right."

"Could you speak up?"

"I said *maybe*."

"You've an interesting item?"

"I could have. You've been running a story about some politician. One who got caught in a taxi."

"That was last week."

"Right. You interested in footballers, then? Star players? What they get up to?"

"Possible. Could be. Someone famous, is it? Can you say who we're talking about here? We'd need names. Are you looking for payment?"

I got no further but slammed down the phone. Which is only small consolation since I'm now surely on tape as some unknown Judas who can't make his mind up.

I pull on to the forecourt where the lines and lines of expensive cars and a BBC outside-broadcast van suggest some important function is in progress. Trust Superstar to have a personalized number-plate, but at least his Audi is easy to find, his locked driver's door presenting no obstacle to my kind of skills. I swing it wide open, inhaling the smell of newness that expensive cars somehow seem to retain and not giving a damn for the alarm going off. These days, who bothers?

Then what follows takes only seconds, and is encompassed within a hysterical giggle as I lift the swollen black balloon of the big refuse-sack from my boot and lower it on to his leather front seat, where two quick slashing strokes with a blade and the ancient mixed guts of twelve salmon spill out and honk like a decomposed whale.

Okay, I grunt, laugh that off!

I've been silly again.

Getaway completed. Now comes apprehension.

The snow's stopped. A creature of habit, parked opposite Lonnigan's disco I masturbate while watching the young girls in their short skirts and spangled boob-tubes wobbling in and out of the neon-lit doorway.

Disturbingly messy, it alleviates nothing.

I drive home. The absence of Robert's car at the kerb indicates he's not staying over. Zero gingerly feels his way down from the greenhouse roof and follows me in. I scoop some Felix into his bowl, make myself coffee, start for my room, and then in passing Bernard's open door see Bernard sitting in his underwear on the edge of his bed. Wearing no hairpiece, he is ending the day.

"Still awake?" I ask.

Dully, distastefully, he looks me up and down. I don't say more but move inside and sit next to him, the mattress creaking at my weight, and I'm immediately breathless. Because, Christ, I realize, it would be impossible to describe what a momentous step I am taking. A lack of security is a terrible thing, and unquestionably I am propelled by the terrible concern I feel for myself.

My hand trembles as I stretch to set my cup on his bedside table. On it a jam jar of water contains a spider he's drowned: a small octopus almost. "You and Robert been to see Tina?" I ask.

He thinks about it for an overlong moment. "I can't see her lasting," he says, brittle-voiced, and his eyes are fixed straight ahead, not acknowledging my closeness.

I'm aware of *him*, though. Like a Lucien Freud

painting. Not one for taking much exercise, he's got skin like white tripe and his own personal smell, not unduly strong, or unpleasant, but a little sweet; it might be his hair-piece adhesive. Cream string-singlets, too, are unflattering, exposing puckered wrinkles of fat at his joints and the long hairs he sprouts on his shoulders and back.

I put my arm round him.

He doesn't react, not a muscle – which is clever and dreadful because I am instantly speared with realizing how totally and ridiculously I have exposed myself.

Then he swivels to put our faces and eyes only inches apart. "You've left it a bit late for this, haven't you?" he says coldly. "You don't even like me."

"Bernard, that's rubbish."

"Name one thing about me you like, then?"

I don't know. I stare at my knees, and I'm *trying* . . . but it looks like he's got me. Unbelievable really, I can't think of anything.

Ten seconds maybe. The silence seems ages. I've been put in my place. No dignity left, I get up and leave – which is all I can do. In my room, five Nitrazepam tablets after drinking so much is all I dare take.

I flop out, not undressing. Zero jumps up and sprawls on my chest. He has brought his rat with him and lies licking its head. I can hear Bernard snoring full-blast already; the bastard possesses no conscience to keep him awake.

My thoughts swirl. I keep remembering the smell and the mess that I made in that car! I lie pleading with sleep, "Drag me off to your cave . . ."

Sex . . . anticipation! The words sound familiar and come from my sessions with Zissler perhaps?

"Errol, pretend you're taking part. Concentrate, concentrate. Eyes to the front. Press the button for a fresh one when you're ready."

I click the button and on screen the scene changes to one of even greater debauchery. A deviant image played out. Three men, some in masks, four women, all young, perhaps two under-age ... and beneath my smock, against all best intentions, I can feel my response measured, the ring tightening up.

"Get ready, stand by!" says Zissler – somewhere behind he is watching a meter that displays pleasure-ratings. "Right, thought-transference *now*!" he says. "Hurry, hurry, close your eyes ... concentrate, concentrate!"

Was he serious? Did he really imagine that such tricks might work? And, yes, I admit to myself, I suppose he did. But, alas, as I remember the sessions, within the heat of the moment I could never switch my mind to remembering what the agreed "aversive-fantasy" was supposed to be.

Unless –

Presenting vividly, the colours and foliage suggest high summer. It is a pleasant afternoon, the sun shining, perhaps a little too warm. An English scene, pastoral. However, it seems likely that since we are over a mile from where today's big cricket game is taking place I am most probably remembering the boyish cheers from elsewhere.

Never mind. "PLAY UP, SCHOOL!"

Watch out now. Here comes Riseman.

And, yes, I see him. My body tenses. Here he comes trotting down the Burma Road and is on course for what he believes is a secret assignation for more grumble-and-grunt in the boat-shed. But his luck is out. At this corner the reeds grow thick and tall and he is blind to what lies ahead and so has a moment to look surprised as I step out and hit him full in the face with the spade.

Crunch! His skin flies back where his nose was. There's a lot of blood. Not to worry because, intelligently, we've allowed for the spillage and gore by choosing a time when the high spring-tide will shortly seep in and bring crabs to clean up. All the same, I am momentarily transfixed by the mess of him. His limbs flay and shudder while with strange familiarity a white froth bubbles on his lips.

Thank God he is incapable of the screams I feared he might scream.

"Errol, help me!" Hugh has knelt to sit him upright and is struggling to tighten the wire he's looped round his neck. "Errol, I can't ... I can't put him out of his misery."

Hugh's grip is not what it was; he has three or four fingers that function only as claws and two that don't work at all where the tendons got cut.

"Okay, pronto, stand back," I tell Hugh, and then raise my voice, "Here, suck this, you bastard!" and let fly again with the spade, although at this same moment Riseman flops sideways and I catch him only a glancing blow in the mouth and a tooth flies out somewhere.

We crawl around till we find it. Also while on my knees, I have come on a little white seashell. I'll keep it.

"Hugh, bend him over."

Hugh does as ordered, propping Riseman to a seated position, hinging him forward, and then moving clear so I've more room to swing.

I take aim. "Come on, baby, reward me!" – and in a two-handed bacon-slicer I bring down the edge of the spade on the back of Riseman's neck, like I put my pet hamster to sleep, only harder. After that, Hugh and I take opposite ends of the length of cheese-wire I remembered to bring and our strength is doubled by knowing we have long passed the point of turning back. Thus we play tug-of-war, with Riseman's head in the middle, and his face begins to turn blue, his tongue sticking further out than I would have thought possible. But we strain and keep saying, "HEAVE!" till his heels have stopped drumming and his hairpiece falls off.

No, wait, *that's wrong* . . .

Never mind. Nothing spoiled. This is my fantasy and I can do as I like.

So skip the hairpiece. Also the watch with distinctive dials; shove it into his pocket along with his tooth.

Because as it is, we have thought of everything. We are in our boiler-suits as for fatigue-squad. We drag Riseman's limp body to where work on the road has ceased but will continue tomorrow. Treading him down, I'm surprised by how cushion-soft he feels underfoot, by how easily he sinks.

All the same, we must hurry . . . although, of course, via the wizardry of *pause* I could make the cricket match last for as long as I wished. Or, if I liked, I could hold back the tide now lapping the road, little rivulets of brine creeping over its surface. But *no*, best we make haste, and with a wheelbarrow each we scamper along to the foreshore and back, fetching gravel. See how fast we can run. See how well we have learned, protecting our hands with broad evergreen leaves snatched from bushes that border the path. We tip load after load.

Now, *fast-forward* a bit . . . I cannot stop trembling: elation and fear. *Exitus acta probat.* Our boiler-suits, scrubbed spotlessly clean, are pegged in the drying-room with hundreds of others; Hugh and me, like everyone else, are faultlessly dressed in afternoon rig of blazer and flannels. *Exitus acta probat* – "The outcome justifies the deed" – I had known we could do it.

Then, next, *play* . . . and Hugh and I are mingling as part of the cricket-match crowd. "Terrific game, what?

Did you see Hugh and I shouting our heads off for school-team to win?"

"Didn't Grossman bowl well?" some prick answers. "Still, their lot were much older."

"Hugh and I thought so, too," I reply. "Oh, well, time for tea! Come on, Hugh, race you back."

Until finally an extended *fast-forward* . . . and now police are appearing: plain-clothes and uniformed, all of whom are kind and sympathetic. Their helicopter flies overhead, but not for long. Their sniffer-dogs prove useless. Poor Riseman could only do breast-stroke, there are such powerful currents along this coast, the Argentine is too far away for his parents to travel and there is talk, anyway, of tax-evasion problems should they try . . . besides which he was one of eight children, plenty more where he came from . . . "All rise, let us sing, *For Those In Peril –* " . . . and Hugh throughout, and especially while being interviewed, or so I've noticed, has all the makings of a wonderful actor.

CHAPTER 25

Next morning comes. I have suffered bad dreams through the night when I slept, and listened to snow as it fell when I didn't.

In a turmoil I am first to the letter-box where I scan the local *Gazette*, expecting to see VANDALS ATTACK SOCCER STAR'S CAR or a similar headline. Instead, not a word.

I hear Bernard leave for work, then get up again and ring Paula at home.

"Tell Denzil I'm sick and not coming in."

"A sore throat or what?"

"Yeah, with knobs on."

After which I then, more or less, spend the next two days in bed where it seems I gradually get worse. My God, biting my nails to the quick, I am back like before. What I perceive is an arm slithering bared into black septic water – I suppose it could be my brain. I reach deep, grope, touch something firm ... and it's always a turd I'm left holding. The calmness I need, it won't come. Will I ever get better?

In all, what this means is two more days wiped from my life – two days, during which Bernard and Robert largely ignore me, hoovering outside my door, not offering meals or cups of tea.

"Snap out of it!" they say, and "Pull yourself together!" It seems so insensitive to me that human-beings should treat each other so unkindly. God knows, I fully realize I am acting ridiculously, gone-to-earth, gone-to-pieces; so is their teaching-me-a-lesson really necessary? Christ, it's bad enough that in swallowing all sorts of pills from my saved-up selection, and with sheets pulled up over my head, the sense of unrealness seems no less real.

But, for the moment, this is my life that I'm stuck with. I sleep, dream, wake, remember, sleep, dream, wake, remember . . .

We each have our means of avoiding reality. Zissler and I often talked of such matters.

"No, truthfully," I told him on one particular day. "Giving me this book on paintings was a master-stroke and I really am grateful."

"Perhaps you might like to keep it? Shall we make that your goal? On the day that you leave, you could take it with you."

"Yes, I'd like that."

"Good. One more look for today, then. Willem de Kooning . . . *Woman and Bicycle, 1953*. Look closely . . . see how it outwardly appears a total hotchpotch of shapes and blodges, all different colours mixed up and swished on in any old which-way. Worth millions of dollars, actually. *But* . . . look closely. That's an eye, do you think? And see those Hollywood teeth and a carnivore's smile? And there'll be a bike in there somewhere, I guess . . . and are those a woman's wide-open legs, could that be?"

I remember I looked at him and I thought, "Get a life!" Because he wouldn't let up: he was forever feeling me out or edging me towards saying what he wanted to hear. So I always needed to be on guard. Whatever he said it might be a ploy, a trap even.

"With these paintings, I suppose it's like looking into the coals of a fire," I said. "You see what you want. You let things happen inside you."

"Exactly!" He was so pleased he clapped. Then he lost me again, as he so often did. "Fantasies, urges, preoccupations that revolve around some imagined sexual activity – we only hit snags when the pursuit of eroticism becomes compulsive, when arousal requires something beyond the normal. Bondage, asphyxiation, paedophilia, exhibitionism, rubberware – "

"Shit! Not more dirty pictures?"

"I thought you liked dirty pictures."

"Not every day. Christ, you want to try that electric-wire thing. It's so fucking embarrassing."

"Nonsense. The counsellors are all fully trained. You need to be certain of which aversion is best to ward off what's troublesome."

"Sure. You show me some tart in the nude . . . I think of some rotting corpse. Sure, it works."

"Absolutely." He consulted his papers. "Yes, the results are quite excellent. The time it takes to kill off the deviant image show steady improvement."

"I get sick of it, though."

"A little each day. You need to stick with it. You're lucky."

"Like how?"

"Like . . ." he chuckled; he'd a weird sense of humour, "you could've grown up as a serial killer."

"Oh, yeah, fucking marvellous."

He made a tick with his pen. "Masturbation seems fine."

"Down in the ward they ask who holds the record."

He laughed harder. But I was now ill-at-ease. I stared hard at his clock. "Will that do? I've the pool-table booked."

"One more minute," he said. "Let's recap." His pen traced his notes. "There's this girl on the beach. Veronica, I think you said. She was . . . *what age* did you say?"

"I don't know. Thirteen, fourteen."

"Would that be the same age as Daisy around the time you left home?"

He sometimes did it on purpose; he just tried to upset me. "Forget that. All I know is that Veronica's mother rang the school and complained. She wanted something done, she said, but no fuss."

"Like Linda almost?"

"Linda lied."

"The police seemed to think differently."

"Yeah, well, they would." I didn't want to talk about it. "I remember that when Veronica was on the beach, she was smiling over Hugh's shoulder. She was smiling . . . *like this*."

"All right, all right, that'll do."

"Hugh – the one at my school – he's become pretty famous, an actor."

"Yes, I've got that written down." He peered at me over his glasses. "There's a lot here about your uncle. Do you look like your uncle?"

"Shit, I feel like him sometimes."

"And little Daisy . . . did she lie, too?"

I warningly narrowed my eyes, letting him see he was straying too far off limits. "You know how much that hurts me," I said. "It tears me apart. False-memory syndrome. She got fed what to say. Those things *never* happened."

He added a thin smile to his nod. "No worries. All confidential, anyway," he said, like he supposed that might help.

"There . . . is that cups?"

"Almost finished."

"I think the tea-trolley's coming."

"Errol, be patient. I know what's best."

"So you say, and your lot's so full of shit that you're leaking."

He reddened, then mimed sadness. "Errol, you carp, criticize, and try to denigrate everything, don't you?"

"That could be a fact."

"Except that throwing stones often reveals more than it injures. You know, in these little chats I sometimes get the notion you perhaps secretly see yourself as the most objectionable person you know."

"That could be another fact."

"And being continually obstructive is hardly a recommendation to get you back into the community, either."

That calmed me a lot. "Okay, okay," I said. "All I was saying was that she never objected or nothing."

"*Who*? Who are we talking of here? Is this Daisy?"

"For Christ's sake, *no!*" He was bamboozling me again with his riddles. "For Christ's sake, I'm talking about Veronica!"

He frowned. He said, "Are you sure? Think, Errol, think! Remember the tape-worm? It keeps getting bigger."

I was back feeling lost. "Aw, that's fucking stupid."

"No . . ." He smiled benevolently and wagged his head. "Not at all. But *you* calling it stupid – now that's *fucking stupid*."

Groggily surfacing into the present from the memory of Zissler's grey-walled room, I wish I could drop off again. But no Valium, Librium or Zimovane left in my stash.

"NO RASH MOVES!" I remember that said. It spared you the buckled-on crash-hat, the shock of breath bounced from your lungs as your back hit the wall of the strip-cell. "Keep active," they told us. "Busy bees, busy fingers, calm minds . . ."

I get up and get dressed. Out in the garden the unseasonal snowfall of two or three inches has mantled and taken the corners off everything. I make instant potato, add spaghetti, old bread, raisins, biscuits, a packet of muesli, then scatter the mixture and watch from the window.

First comes a robin, then a wren. Don't I know what it's like? Don't I feel for the little ones mostly – for the sparrows, the tits and the finches? Until down off the eaves swoop the oily black starlings, the greedy gestapo, their ice-pick beaks stabbing. The little ones scatter. The assertive prosper and grow ever stronger while inoffensive types eke out a meagre existence on overlooked crumbs. *Shit-and-cruelty.*

Along Welbeck Parade all the pavements but ours have been cleared. Scanning the sports page while walking back from buying the late edition at the corner-shop, I see that Superstar is doubtful for tonight's game. He is troubled by a groin strain, it says. No word on his car being trashed, though. Also Maxine can't have been told. She'd have made the connection and rung me to say so.

"Hello, Rosie!"

Rosemary from next-door, well-wrapped up against the cold and wearing her Rupert Bear trousers, is out to play beside her front wall. "No sweeties today I'm afraid," I tell her, and squat to be level. "I like your doll."

"It's Rosie, my dolly," she says, and cuddles her doll against her narrow chest. "She's two and I'm three and we're the same but my name's Rosemary and you're not to call me Rosie 'cos this is Rosie."

"I'll remember."

She is looking beyond me. "Can I see your house? We haven't got a dog. Have you got a dog?"

"No, a cat." Then in a rush of sentimentality I don't attempt to control, "I had a little girl once, and her name was Daisy."

"Is she here now?"

"She went away."

"A long long way away? Was she naughty?"

"No, she was good."

"Where's she gone, then? On a train? Past the seaside? With her mummy? Won't she come back?"

Jesus Christ, I've no answer to that.

"Don't cry, mister man. What you crying for, then? Here, kiss Rosie." She pushes forward her doll and I give it a peck. "Soon be better," she says, running off.

Then the third morning dawns. Relief comes like a toothache worn off as I realize the *Gazette* contains a small item that reveals the explanation for my vandalism going unreported has been staring me in the face all along. City are under investigation for illegal activities. Tax-avoidance, inflated transfer-fees, cash-bungs to managers, back-handers to players in motorway cafes – allegations that are almost certainly true according to Maxine. Thus it follows that the club's board will be throwing a cordon around bad publicity of any kind.

And thus the spring has returned to my step. I feel much better. Safe enough, anyway, to ring Maxine to say I'll be fit for the wedding.

"I've had three days poorly in bed," I tell her. "You might at least have telephoned. I could've been dead."

"So am I your keeper?" she says. "Besides, I know how your mind works: you'd have made bloody sure I heard about it in plenty of time."

CHAPTER 26

Ding-dong, wedding bells! Not exactly.

Up on a central dais, petal-strewn, garlanded, and hung with the photos of relatives who can't attend because they're long dead, a priest with a hand-mike is guiding Sanjay and bride-Kamala, poker-faced, through rituals involving fire, coconut shells, palm oil and so on. I estimate the guests at four hundred, all Asian but for us who've come from Miss Betsy's. Kids and adults wander as they fancy, helping themselves to gossip and soft drinks. The women's saris are fabulous; there has to be a king's ransom in gold and diamonds under this one roof. Mohan strolls like a prince holding court. Mustapha's here. Fakrou couldn't make it.

The ceremony's been going on for over four hours. None of us English was reckoning on anything lasting that long.

Then even the ending, when it comes, has a degree of uncertainty to it. Everything sort of fizzles-out. There's no blowing of trumpets, banging the gong or anything like that; just the forming of a line to offer best wishes to the happy couple.

We tag on. That's Maxine, Paula, Karen and me. We came together by long-distance bus. Terri and Denzil motored down, then on arrival found seats on the opposite side of the hall. We haven't spoken and I've been getting the evil-eye from Terri each time I've glanced over there.

"Congratulations!" I warble at our turn. "Enjoy your honeymoon."

Sanjay slaps my shoulder like a brother and slips me the office keys. No one's kissing the bride, I observe. It's perhaps not allowed. A pity, I think. This Kamala is some lush fruit. This applies even if her strong Midlands accent seems oddly out-of-sorts with how ceremoniously she's garbed. She is looking forward to nights out with Sanjay and me: badminton and ten-pin bowling in particular, she says.

I tell her I look forward to it. Still, with Sanjay being so overweight, I reckon she can pass on the sports. I've never seen him run once.

So is she going to feel wasted?

An hour later, I have this thought in mind and a hell of a hard-on to soap up and play with. All paid for by Sanjay I could live like this always, no bother, particularly these needle-point showers. The hotel booked for Terri and Denzil, as far as I know, is not so luxurious, but what perhaps counts for more is that it's where Mohan is staying. They've declined to be part of our night on the town. It tends to suggest there's some deal going down. *Money-money.*

Eight o'clock. The girls are dressed to kill. We first eat Chinese. I don't catch the restaurant's name going in, but it's noisy and smart, the food's good; we have a table with a revolving middle so we can pick as we fancy.

In other words, a good start, I say to myself. Since Mustapha is handling the tab on Sanjay's behalf, I'm only mildly annoyed that with his money, looks, and the intrigue of being foreign, the girls are sucking up to him. It doesn't bother me, either, that away from his own he loves Crispy-Duck and his tipple is vodka.

He's a nightbird, too, it turns out. Or at any rate, Drury's Barn is a club where he's known. He signs us in. Earsplitting music accompanies film from the 14–18 war being jerkily screened on video-banks in the walls. Waitresses dressed like Edith Cavell nurses have their tits hanging out. Lights shoot like tracers. Shells and whizzbangs keep going off. Karen's quickly on song with Mustapha, offering herself up like some willing bedtime-sacrifice. So that's him taken care of, leaving the new major opposition as a muscular black guy who, seemingly modelled to some Robert Mapplethorpe image, keeps dragging either Paula or Maxine away into no-man's land.

At one point, Paula returns wild-eyed from prancing with him to say, "Errol, see him in the leather, his backside cut away? Can you credit his cheek? Says will I wank him off round the back?"

I dance with Maxine. "Just be careful in here," I tell her.

"I can look after myself. I'm not some daft stupid schoolgirl, you know," she yells back.

When we get past midnight, the time for Mustapha's return flight to Istanbul has come and gone; so he's signed up with Karen, that's obvious.

We taxi back to our hotel where one bar remains open for nightcaps. The girls are giggly and tousled.

One drink later. "Surprise, follow me," Mustapha says, leaning clear of some bloke he's had whispering to him.

We pile into the lift. Watching the little green lights, I'm apprehensive enough to decide I'm not letting Maxine out of my sight. Fourth floor. Knock-knock, a door opens a crack to permit mumbling, a fistful of notes changes hands, and we're inside a room filled by thirty people or so. "You get drinks included," says someone. It tastes like white wine.

"Is it all right all us being here?" Maxine says. I shrug a don't-know. I've lost track of the others.

"Ladies and gentlemen . . ." around us a mild outbreak of coughing breaks out, "no photographs, please."

The girl's aged about twenty, the two guys are older. I glance at Maxine, thinking if she wants to leave, but see she's on tip-toe so as not to miss anything.

All three get naked. The men have tight excited balls. The girl looks more like the proverbial one from next-door than some tart with a habit. I suppose she could be a student or something, it's all about cash, and to her it's just nightwork. "Oh, baby, the size of your cock . . ." With deadpan face, she's used to it, though, and never mind that every moan is feigned and the script is rubbish – couples around us are visibly getting worked up about each other. I take Maxine's arm. "No, I'm all right," she whispers, misreading my squeeze – which was meant to convey that I'm flesh and blood, too.

Whatever – despite that I'm watching with a certain dreary fascination, my excitement's no less. As a trio, they go down on each other, and indulge in various other acrobatics. Then the guys get her perched so they've both got a hole, and start pumping her up. As for Maxine, I figure the eroticism, and therefore the thrill, must be greater for her. She can't out-guess the moves like I can. I know the tart will end up fingering herself, flat on her back – which she does. That leaves the guys, who've pulled out, to drop to their knees to shoot semen from close range at her face and breasts. It's to convey all's for real, no refunds given. She licks at what she can reach. End of show. Slight applause.

Carried in the first wave drifting out into the cool of the corridor, I keep tight hold of Maxine.

"Eighty-one, eighty-two," she says. "Yes, we're on the right floor."

One in every five women on trips away from home has some kind of sexual, physical adventure. That's a known fact I'm carrying. Our rooms are adjacent. In watching her unlock her door I'm breathing steam over her dishevelled hair and smudged eye-shadow.

"Night-night, see you tomorrow," she says, and is gone. Jesus Christ!

I spill into my room. I strip off, feel provoked, stalk up and down. See it swings in the mirror. I begin to jack off at the basin. A knock comes on the wall. My prayer answered. I make a grab for some covering and get myself in there.

Cold-creaming her face is as far as she's got in putting herself to bed. The amber glow from the bedside-lamp accords a sun-tan effect to where she is lying naked outside the covers. I hurriedly yank off the towel I've thrown on, then bustle across her and between her legs.

After which, if in slobberingly humping and clawing, she's totally drunk, and perhaps not clear where she is, and maybe not even sure that it's *me* . . .? So all right, but so what? I mightn't like that it's Superstar's name that she groans in my ear. But I'm not getting off. I've been saving this up. It's in pints. "Come on, baby, reward me."

Being Sunday, all the train timetables are slashed. I'm required to change at Grantham. The further north, the greyer the sky. A few miles short of York it starts to snow. Snow on snow.

I didn't want to face Maxine at breakfast or travel home with her. Vacating my room, I lingered outside her door . . . to say *what*?

What was there to say? Staring out the carriage window, I can think about nothing else. But too late now for second thoughts. No regrets, anyway. Ignore the circumstances. Mine eyes have seen the glory, as-it-were, and maybe that's enough.

"Zero's gone missing."

I was figuring Bernard would have some crack ready for when I got home, something to spoil whatever good time he thinks I may have had, but he's caught me flat-footed.

"What d'you mean, he's *gone missing*?" Zero sleeps indoors at night and detests all bad weather. "Bernard, it's snowing like crazy outside, don't you know?"

He cups a hand to his ear like he's trying not to miss whatever TV programme they're watching. "What d'you expect?" he throws at me. "If you will go off gallivanting . . .?"

"We've not seen hide nor hair since you left," Robert offers.

Bastards. Silently I curse the pair of them and head for my room where I change to boots and long coat. Then in setting out to check the gutters of the surrounding streets I feel sick about what I hope not to find. Honestly speaking, I could cry. With pets you get to think they rely on you when really it's the other way round.

I plod the three nearest fields and cover the first length of river. The sun dips, the snow forms a crust, my calves protest. Nearly dark. A lost cause. But I cling to faint hope and along the last bit of Welbeck Parade am whistling Zero's whistle.

A man's at his gate. "Lost your dog?"

"No, my cat."

He stalks off, slinging back, "Long-haired sod."

I arrive in to find Bernard and Robert playing back-gammon. Cans of beer and peanuts are on the coffee-table between them. They've had their main meal without me and cleared away.

"Is he back?"

"A five and a six," Bernard says, then inspects me scornfully. "You should see yourself sometimes. You're a laughing stock round here the way you run after that cat."

No comment. I slink away and get myself to bed. I've set the alarm in case I can sleep but I can't. I keep straining to hear plaintive miaows.

The wild geese go over, an unmistakable sound. Not such big numbers now. Which is sad. Every day they get fewer.

CHAPTER 27

We are in the Casablanca Cafe, seated at a table beside its sign-written window. Outside, more snow is falling. "You sure you don't mind here?"

"No, this is fine," Maxine says.

She hasn't unbuttoned her warm Highwayman's coat, a strong hint that she's intent on not staying for long, "I rang Miss Betsy," I tell her. "Paula said you were poorly."

"Only sort of," she says. "So what's *your* excuse for not working?"

"I got home, Zero was missing. I've spent the last two days searching."

"Oh, no . . . Well, don't worry. He'll be fine."

"No, he won't. They set snares in the fields where I am."

She sighs wearily. "That's typically you. You always look on the black side."

"I've seen rabbits that've pulled their own heads off in trying to get free."

"Errol . . . God, I don't want to know things like that!"

Well, she should. *Shit-and-cruelty.*

"So how poorly are you?" I ask.

"Not much. I think it was something I ate. That Chinese meal. Then the long bus-ride home was awful."

"I came back by train. That's why I left early."

"Yes . . . some ungodly hour."

We're not fooling each other. Having set down my cup, I am stuck with not knowing what to do with my hands. She's got her cigarette to hang on to and she's wearing her spectacles. They suit her but she hates their appearance. She's sheltering behind them.

She says, "You said on the phone it was something important."

"Did I? I just wanted a chat. You know, the other night . . .?"

She says nothing, not taking me up on it, then starts gazing around. The lunchtime clientele is mostly male middle-management enjoying lasagne, a glass of chilled house wine, portable phones on display. Successful people. The adult thing, I fancy, would be to let matters lie.

I try again. "The other night . . . we were pretty drunk." I'm offering her room to manoeuvre. "I'll bet you don't remember a thing. Christ, I was so pissed my lips were numb."

She considers a reply. "No, I've a very good memory," she says, and now her forceful expression suggests she's ready to quarrel if I want to make anything out of what we've now apparently acknowledged.

I wait a few seconds more. "You don't need me, do you?"

"What?" She was expecting different.

"You don't need me."

"What d'you mean *need you*?" she says. "We're friends, aren't we?"

"That's not what I said. Say it was the early hours of the morning, say I was in distress, say I needed someone . . . You wouldn't be there for me, would you?"

"I don't know!" She's liking the subject even less. "How am I supposed to know a thing like that? I *might*."

"It's okay. Forget it." I slide the velvet-covered box across the table-top and towards her.

"Oh, no!" She's reluctant but pleased – she lifts the lid.

I watch her slide on the bracelet. Solid gold. She twizzles her hand to enjoy how it catches the light. It's odd,

I remind myself, that she's never once asked how it is that I've always got money.

"A talisman of good hope for you," I tell her.

"Meaning . . .? You're not going to do anything silly?"

I smile thinly. I could explain that the bracelet has cost every cent I possessed; that the emptying of my bank account was deliberate and somehow symbolic. That there's a different tired hand round my heart. That a terrible calm is upon me.

I tell her, "For one thing, I'm not coming back to Miss Betsy's. I figure Terri plans to sack me the first chance she gets, anyway."

She hesitates for an overlong moment. "I'm not coming back, either."

I don't know why I'm not surprised or why I feel neither of us needs to explain our intentions further. Possibly I even detect an understanding between us that didn't exist before. Perhaps an acknowledgement of truth. What was there always for her and me, anyway, but nothing?

She says, "I ought to be going. I've got things to do."

"Important things?"

"Do I ever?"

I pay the bill. Out on the pavement, probably intending to forestall any speech I might have rehearsed, she stretches on tiptoe to plant a kiss on my cheek.

"*Eternity* by Calvin Klein?"

"Not wrong," she says.

I start left, she goes right. If she turns and looks back, then I'll wave . . . but she doesn't.

The arcade's where I'm heading; I need to check Sanjay's office.

A minute, perhaps two, is all I have on my own once I get beyond Sanjay's closed door. Not enough time to do anything, anyway.

"Any keys?" says one of the two.

"Here, this bunch looks right," says the other, picking the keys off the desk where I laid them.

Sitting limply in the chair where they've pushed me, I'm struggling to come to terms with what's going on. To avoid the Miss Betsy's office, I used the back stairs. But these two spotted my arrival, nonetheless. In other words, like in the movies, they must've had the building staked out, *and* with a purpose, because along with opening their brief-cases they've waved what they say is some kind of court-order under my nose.

"Errol – it is Errol?" The tubby one seems the friendlier. "Don't look so worried. You've turned up here today for what reason?"

"Nothing really. I got asked to. To see the place was safe. To empty the mail-box."

"There is none. It's been intercepted. We've got it."

"So you think your friend's *where*? You think Bangkok?"

"On honeymoon," I answer. "He went three days ago. He's due back."

"Yeah? And so's Jesus Christ and look how long we've been waiting. No, siree. A few weeks' growth of beard and your mate will be will-o'-the-wisp, that's for sure!"

"Mohan," I start, "that's the name of his uncle – "

"He's another gone missing . . . *no trace.*"

Questions, questions. There's none I feel I can answer.

When they switch on the computer, the screen comes up blank.

They use the keys to open cabinets and drawers. All are empty. No paperwork. No letters. No invoices. Not a sign of the signed blank cheques I was hoping to find. Probably no fingerprints, either.

"Should I ring his home number?" I say.

"Just his old mum down there."

"He owned a few corner-shops."

"No, he didn't. They're self-owned by cousins. He's got *cousins* all over."

"Know the parlance for all this kind of scam, do you, Errol? A 'long firm', for instance? That kind of thing mean anything to you at all?"

This time I can genuinely look vacant because I haven't a clue.

"A good number," says tubby. "They set somewhere up on the cheap, then order small. They pay for just enough to get the right credit. After that, they then order big – they order as much as they can over three or four weeks and then bugger off with the lot, without paying nothing. Little things. Done nationally in enough different places – internationally even – it soon mounts up. You're talking big loads of dosh. No VAT, either."

"Oh," I say, non-committal.

"So . . . you ever meet any more of these foreigners, Errol?"

"Were you down at this wedding?"

"You've been driving that Peugeot, we know that."

"That Mercedes he owned – d'you know where that went?"

"There's a lock-up garage he's got across town." I figure they'll already know.

"Empty."

"Oh."

So it continues, with me nodding or shaking my head, choosing whichever seems applicable to whatever they ask; and, although frightened, I know I've undergone worse. To survive, you simply shut off you brain and let your senses go limp. Better still, if you can, is to act a bit simple.

"Are you market research?"

They're amused. "Fucking hell! Are we *what*?"

"Immigration perhaps?"

"Immigration? Fuck off!"

I sit with head hung.

"All right, Errol, we'll be stuck here all day. You get home to your tea. We know where we can find you."

I act humbly grateful – which is what they expect. It takes little effort because that's how I feel.

Once outside, though, my mind starts to fizzle. A High Street call-box is the nearest. A selection of phonecards pilfered from Miss Betsy's to sell cheaply round the pubs was always an earner for me, and using one from a wad in my pocket I dial the number and wonder what time it is in Istanbul.

"Hello, Mustapha, this is – " He hangs up at once.

I try Hamburg. Fakrou isn't known there.

That still leaves others to ring on the list Sanjay gave me. Relatives to judge by their names. But *amazing* – nobody can speak English any more!

I catch the next bus. Zero's back on my mind as what's more important.

"Bernard, promise me you've not seen him."

He was scared; he could see there were knives lying handy. He said, "Errol, I mightn't always have shown it but I swear on my honour I thought the world of that cat."

I know he sets store by his honour, fuck knows why. However, had he been a true friend he would have helped me with searching. And Robert the same. Whereas neither has offered.

But I'm not beaten yet. *Exitus acta probat*.

I refuse to give in. As the bus enters Lambton Spa, I peer through mud-spattered windows to a flooded chocolate river meandering through countryside deep in snow. An inhospitable landscape for all warm-blooded creatures. I ring the bell and get off at the Otter & Trout. Not to drink – I have finished drinking *forever* – but the longer walk home will allow me more yardage for happening on cat-tracks.

Mink, domestic dog, an abundance of bird-shit, the pugs of a fox. Hungry foxes around here in bad weather will come knocking on doors: during last winter's chills a chihuahua went missing.

I name what I see as I travel, until some extra sense sparks a fear and tells me *look back*.

Which I do. A road deserted except I can see two young men forty yards to my rear. I stop and shield my eyes to peer harder, an automatic reaction to being so cautious these days, and the fact that's it's *two* seems particularly significant. I can't say I like how they're staring towards me while earnestly stepping into footprints I've left.

I feel anxiety grab me. I turn to my front and step up the pace – which wearing Wellington boots in this snow isn't easy. My hand sneaks inside my coat to test the weight of my priest. I count twenty-five strides, glance astern, and they've gone.

They have sprinted ahead.

The shock doesn't come until I'm passing the Methodist Church and they step out together. I go limp, caught unawares, no point in resisting as firmly gripped in a head-lock, heels dragging, I'm heaved into the alley and slammed against brickwork.

"Jesus, leave off me," I gasp. "What's all this for?"

My mind's swirled in panic. Was it the salmon, the badgers, Sanjay, the mess in Superstar's car . . . maybe even the high-jinks with Davina Forbes-Tyson?

"Slime-ball. You've been monkeying about with our little Rosie."

"What?"

"Yeah, *you*. She's our niece. You've drove her mother

frantic. Giving her sweets? Said you had a dog she could look at inside."

"No, I never! I've not got a dog."

"You kissed her as well."

"I did not! She just lives next-door. She showed me her doll. I don't go for that stuff."

"Yeah? Up in the village, we heard different from that."

"You're well known as a beast – you've been at this before."

"Like that puftah you live with."

"Yeah, you fuckers are spreading. Degenerates."

I spot the neck movement but the head-butt's too fast. All goes black for an instant until I realize I'm dropped like I'm abattoir-felled. I spit blood along with my bridge of four front-teeth. Seen from ground level, the tall one stamps it flat while the short one's swinging the boot. I take a kick in the ear, drag myself up his legs, lash out and start running. I don't care which way and don't slow till I reach the main road's black ribbon and knee-high banks of slush.

I look back; they've not followed. Taking deep breaths, I prompt myself to stay calm. Hanky pressed to my mouth. My face throbs as I scurry. Alongside the school's wire-netting fencing is the quickest route home. Stripped of their nets the hockey-posts look stark and plundered. A few crows awkwardly goose-step where snow has melted.

Then at first I'm not sure. A stride later I am. The girl in the lorry's front seat at the kerb is the blonde from form four, her face pressed to the windscreen.

I see the driver in overalls jumping down.

"Hey you," he shouts, "*you!*"

I stop and point to myself. I suppose he's her father.

"YES," he shouts louder. "YOU . . . I want *YOU!*"

Panic grabs and controls me. Escape's all I know. A

woodyard's fence blocks my way. I climb over. At the first shed I come to, I glance back. The man is a gesticulating figure against the overcast sky. I run harder, am coursed, braking left and right up the alleyways formed by stacked timber, gaining cover where I can. A five-foot wall appears in my path. Whip-and-spur ridden, I'm up and across it to fall and lie winded in somebody's garden. A cold-frame pressed to my face might have broken my back. I gulp air like a fish out of water. My saliva's thickened to cream. My eyes pop.

Hark! – I urge myself to stay quiet. Is that boots?

I thought that was the end but it wasn't and isn't.

In my teenage years, I fell over the side of a ship and was dead but got rescued.

I heard the boots go thumping by.

So again I was saved – and the chance to confront one's own ending more than once has to be privileged, I suppose.

"Come on, baby, reward me."

Calling Maxine's number, I have spoken to her mother who has promised to urge her to ring me the moment she sees her, though where she can be she can't think. It's just I feel so alone, and the basement, perhaps, is where I'd feel safer, although darkness has entered the living-room to extend a sanctuary of sorts.

Whisky, too, is a solace. I have misplaced the glass but not the bottle.

The phone warbles in my lap and makes me jump.

"Yes! Hello!"

"Bloody hell," Paula says. "Your line's been engaged ages. I've had to stay working late. There's murder on here."

"There's murder all over."

"What? Are you all right? You sound funny." She

giggles. "You're drunk again, that's what you are. You're a devil. Hang on, I'll transfer this through. It's Terri who wants you. She's screaming."

I'm left with music-on-hold until, "Errol? Well, fine fucking friends you've got."

In the background I can hear Denzil shouting: "TERRI, TELL THAT SWINE HE'S – "

"My God . . ." she again drowns him out, "we go all the way to that poxy wedding, we even bought him a cut-glass decanter, and he now pisses off owing thousands."

" . . . A SECOND BIG LOAN WE TOOK OUT TO JOIN UP WITH THEM WHEN THAT BLACK BASTARD PROMISED US HE'D – "

I yank the telephone plug from the wall. Anger fills my head as a snarl. You play with snakes, you deserve to get bitten. Besides, fuck you all. Maxine's not going to ring, either.

Then the key sounds in the door. Whisky spills down my front as I grab a last swig before hiding the bottle under a cushion.

Robert comes walking through. "He's in here," he says over his shoulder; and to me, "In the dark, are you? No TV either?"

"Does he want fish and chips?" Bernard calls from the kitchen.

I shake my head, full of dread at what has to be.

"He says *no*," Robert calls, and I'm shading my eyes with my hand as he clicks on the light. "Christ Almighty!" he says.

I squint to combat the glare. His expression is lodged between incredulity and wondering how amused he should be.

"Christ Almighty!" he repeats, and is clearly even more shocked than I feared. "Errol, that is *you*, right? Christ Almighty, where's the beard . . . what's brought this on?

Have I seen you clean-shaven before? I don't think I have."

"I fancied a change."

"Bloody hell! You've not had your front teeth out as well?"

"I lost them." I sound odd with a lisp.

"Good God! And your hair!" He takes a step backward, all part of continuing to air amazement and attempting to collect himself. "Your hair's fucking awful! Like alopecia. It's just lumps off and scalped. You've not hoovered up, either. Here, Bernard, hurry . . ." he stoops to pick up the big kitchen scissors and a handful of hair, "come and see what he's done."

"I'm just warming these through," Bernard calls.

It's no good: to remain seated and readily available as a side-show is asking too much of me. I stand up, swaying. The floor as I walk to the window seems a deck in motion.

"Aren't you going to ask how Tina is?" I hear Robert say.

"How's Tina?"

"The same, just the same." He comes up behind me and squeezes my shoulder. "Hey, it's okay, old son," he says, and I can see him reflected: a gentle compassion. "You've not been yourself lately. All the drinking and that . . . And now *this*."

In response to his kindness, he expects . . . *what*?

I stare ahead, engrossed, bewitched, hypnotized even. Vega, Capella, Aldebaran, Polaris, Arcturus, Altair. Mirror-mirror of the starry night in which I can see hands touching the face superimposed against the sky. Skin so smooth. It neither looks like me, nor feels like me.

Until I see the mouth smile. Shapes beyond the glass are assuming identity, including Zero up on the roof of the greenhouse in the sphinx-pose he does.

I can't think where he's been. Probably stalking some queen, spreading genes. *Little sod.*

"Robert, if anyone wants me," I say, turning round, "I'll be down in the basement."